DEATH OF A HIGH FLYER

D.P. Hart-Davis

Merlin Unwin Books

First published by Merlin Unwin Books, 2018
Text © D.P. Hart–Davis, 2018

Merlin Unwin Books Limited
Palmers' House, 7 Corve Street,
Ludlow, Shropshire, SY8 1DB
www.merlinunwin.co.uk

A CIP record of this book is available from the British Library.

Printed and bound by Jellyfish Print Solutions

ISBN 978-1-910723-81-4

To Karen McCall
who gave the High Flyer her best shot!

Contents

PRINCIPAL CHARACTERS

Dunmorse Hall estate
Hans Hartzog, financier, 42, owner
Tobias Hagley, 53, head gamekeeper
Cecil Barley, 60, underkeeper
Luz Fernandez, 25, housekeeper

Castle Farm
Marcus Bellton, 62, cattle breeder
Pauly Bellton, 32, his son

Grange Farm
Marina Oak, 36, owner
Jericho Oak, 34, Farm Shop entrepreneur, her husband
Max Vereker, 8, her son, his stepson
Tomasz, 50, farm shop manager
Pavel, 9, his son
Anita Carew, 32, manager of Grange Farm Small Businesses
Duncan, 72, head gamekeeper
Sally Robb, 20, apprentice gamekeeper

Eastmarsh Country Sports
Locksley Maude, 35, proprietor

Others
Julius Lombard, 47, primary schoolteacher
Detective Chief Inspector Martin Robb, 53
Detective Sergeant James Winter, 28

CHAPTER ONE

The Draw

Supporting his paunch on the edge of the central table, and using both hands to heave his eighteen stone upright, Arthur Longwood OBE, Chairman of the Gamebird Preservation Trust, rose ponderously from his seat and surveyed the crowded room. He clinked sharply with his knife on a water-glass, waiting for the clatter and chatter to die away as all faces turned to him.

He cleared his throat. 'Now we come to the moment you have all been waiting for,' he announced in his deep, gravelly bass. 'The moment which – dare I say it? – may well be the reason we are enjoying your company here tonight.

'Ladies and gentlemen, I have the great pleasure of asking Mr Hans Hartzog to draw the winning ticket for the Starcliffe Highflyers' raffle, which he has so generously organised to raise funds for this very good cause, entitling the winner and his team to a day's shooting over the five best drives in the glorious Starcliffe valley next December.' He raised a beckoning hand. 'Hansi: over to you.'

Hans Hartzog, tall, thickset, and heavily handsome, rose from Table No 1 and swaggered to the dais with the

1

assurance of one whose financial wizardry had made him a millionaire in his teens and a billionaire before he was forty. His smoothly-tanned face seemed set in a permanent smile as he acknowledged the scattered round of applause: it was no secret that his nickname 'Mr Merger' had been earned at the expense of many small businesses which Hartzog Holdings had gobbled up in the past decade, and though widely respected he was not greatly loved.

He clasped the chairman's hand in both his own before turning his attention to the open game-bag filled with coloured raffle-tickets that had been placed on a baize-topped card table.

'Take a look at those!' he exclaimed. 'Better make sure they're well mixed. We don't want the ones on top to have an advantage.' Only the faintest flattening of vowels proclaimed his South African origins, but it was enough to grate on the ears of Jericho Oak, sitting stony-faced at Table 2. Look at them all, he thought disgustedly, glancing round the room. Eating out of that shyster's hand because he's set up this silly stunt, and bulldozed me into taking part in it.

'Now, are you ready? Here goes...' Hartzog stirred the papers vigorously, then fastened on a single ticket.

In expectant silence, he unfolded and read it. 'The winner is...' – long pause for effect – 'number 467, blue. Can anyone here produce the counterfoil to ticket number 467, blue?'

There was a rustle and stir at the far end of the room, where a party of City boys were scrutinising their tickets, then they began laughing, shouting, and pushing one of their friends to his feet. 'Go on, Rods! It's yours. You've won! Go and show him.'

Propelled towards the dais, ticket in hand, young Rodney Owen appeared completely overwhelmed. His face was scarlet and his throat moved convulsively as he tried to speak. 'It's... This is ...'

He thrust the counterfoil at Hartzog, who looked at it carefully and nodded. 'This is indeed it,' he announced. 'Well done and congratulations. And your name is?'

Rodney's response was drowned by the cheers and hoots from his table and an outburst of clapping from the rest of the room. Above the hubbub, the chairman tapped his glass again.

'Ladies and gentlemen: we have a winner. Mr Rodney Owen from Berkhamstead – a very worthy winner. Now, Mr Owen – '

'Rodney, please,' mumbled the boy.

'Very well. Rodney, let me tell you exactly what you have won and who has donated each of these drives as a contribution to a very special day. First and foremost, let's show our appreciation to Mr Hans Hartzog, owner of Dunmorse Estate, whose world-famous Stubbles will be your first drive.'

'World-famous! What rot,' muttered Jericho.

'And whose very testing drive known as Skyscraper – for obvious reasons – will sort the men from the boys after lunch.'

A ripple of laughter.

'Your second drive has been given by Messrs Marcus and Paul Bellton, of Castle Farm, known to many of us as prizewinning breeders of the noble Devon Red cattle. Marcus, do you have a name for this drive of yours?'

With his rubicund face glowing beneath a thick grey thatch of hair and side-whiskers, beefy Marcus Bellton lurched to his feet, grinning broadly. 'Can't say as we do,' he rumbled.

'Call it The Splash, dad,' shouted his copper-haired son from across the room. 'That's 'cos half the birds we shoot fall in the river.'

'Very good,' the chairman beamed. 'That gives you an idea what to expect, Mr Owen – er – Rodney. And your third drive, kindly donated by Mr and Mrs Jericho Oak of Grange Farm – where are you, Jericho?'

'Stand up,' hissed Marina to her husband. 'Try to look as if you're enjoying yourself.'

But I'm not, he thought, rising reluctantly and forcing a smile that was more of a grimace. I'm not a performing monkey and I never wanted to take part in this wretched circus of Hartzog's, damn his eyes.

'Ah, there you are,' exclaimed the chairman heartily. 'Good to see you and Marina here tonight. As I was saying, your very challenging Maiden's Leap will be the last drive before lunch, which Mr Hartzog has kindly offered to provide in the Dunmorse Barn; with Skyscraper to follow and then, as a final treat, Mr Locksley Maude of Eastmarsh Country Sports has offered to wrap up an outstanding day with an evening flight over his oxbow lakes. Thank you, Locksley. That should provide a memorable finale.'

And put your fledgling shooting-school on the map. Just what the doctor ordered, thought Jericho, watching Maude bowing and saluting towards the dais, an excited flush on his high-cheekbones and tanned face beneath a thatch of strongly-waved dark hair. He's a first-class instructor, thought Jericho, watching him, even if he was lucky to keep his licence after that trouble in Afghanistan. Only escaped prison by a whisker. Oh, God, here comes Hansi to make my day...

But Hartzog was heading for Marina, bending to whisper in her ear in his damned proprietorial way. Rage bubbled up in Jericho as he watched. With her fair hair drawn smoothly back and coiled in a classic chignon, emphasising the lovely line of her neck, and her gentle enigmatic smile, she was by far the most beautiful woman in the room, and to see Hartzog placing one of his pudgy paws on her bare shoulder made her husband feel sick.

What was he asking her? What delightful cultural treat had he planned – something that he knew would bore Jericho to tears but draw Marina into Hansi's company, if not into his bed? A first night at Covent Garden with supper in his box? A recitation of works by post-War German poets? A quick flip to Bayreuth for the new production of *Parsifal*? Anything that would reinforce the perception that the brilliant and beautiful pianist Marina, who had played in many of Europe's greatest concert halls, would have been better suited by marriage to Renaissance Man Hansi Hartzog, rich, sport-loving, clever and cultured, than that lumpen proletariat hick with earth beneath his fingernails, Jeremy Richard Oak.

Then she shook her head, making her emerald drop earrings flash green fire, and Jericho, who had been unconsciously holding his breath, let it out with a sigh. Whatever it was, she had turned it down, and all was well with the world.

He sat down and picked up his wineglass, but now Hansi was edging round the table, pushing between the chairbacks with smiling apologies, in order to give him a politician's greeting, left hand clasping forearm while right did the shaking, pulling Jericho forward into such uncomfortable proximity that he feared a man-hug might follow.

'Jerry, old boy!' Jericho winced, and then cursed himself for wincing. How could Hartzog know that 'Jerry' was his pet hate? The loud, harsh-edged voice boomed on: 'Great that you could make it tonight. Well, we've got our winner: Owen seems a nice lad, even if he is still wet behind the ears. His uncle gave him the ticket as a birthday present — which is just the sort of story the press will love — and he's going to pick a team of friends and let me have their names asap. Couldn't be better. A Highflyers' Day will be a real treat for them rather than having the prize go to some old blimp who shoots three days a week all winter.'

Jericho said stiffly, 'You must let us help with the costs, Hartzog. Fair do's. We'll all kick in — be glad to.'

'Balls, old boy. My idea – I'll pay for it. Can't have Maude and old Bellton feeling they have to fork out their hard-earned cash for something I dreamed up. They're doing their bit as it is by letting us shoot over their ground, and so are you.'

Across the table, Marina was listening. Hartzog glanced at her and said, 'On quite another tack, I've been trying to persuade your lovely wife to come to a Benefit Concert at the O2 next Thursday. It's being given by an old friend of mine, Klaus Leprovitch, and it should be pretty special. I know he'd love to meet her and they'd find a lot of friends in common. Won't you try to talk her into it?'

'Too kind of you, Hansi,' said Marina smoothly, flicking a glance at her husband, 'but it's one of our Open Days, and we've got a lot of schoolchildren coming. I really can't let them down.'

First I've heard of it, thought Jericho, but her eyes were pleading with him not to contradict her. 'Ah, yes, of course. Hang on a tick.' He fiddled with his smartphone and nodded. 'You're right. Thursday the sixth. Open Day. Good job you remembered, darling.'

Hartzog's smile vanished. 'Surely one of your staff could take them round the farm?'

'Wouldn't be the same,' said Jericho firmly, cursing both Hartzog and Marina for forcing him into a corner. Now he'd have to make it true by organising an extra Open Day, or the word would surely get out. Not for the first time he wished that the Dunmorse Estate had been bought by anyone other than Hans Hartzog.

All too clearly, he remembered the morning when this whole charade had begun.

CHAPTER TWO

Setting Up

On that bright morning last year, Jericho and Marina had been finishing breakfast in companionable silence, sipping and sorting the mail: letters, junk, charity appeals, catalogues, while the March sun streamed through the east-facing window and in the farmyard the regular scrunch of tyres on gravel signalled that the small business units in the Rickyard were opening for the day.

Abruptly the peace was shattered by Jericho's exasperated growl. 'He's at it again. Unbelievable!'

'Who's at what?' The long thick envelope in slightly too bright a blue provided Marina with an unwelcome clue.

'Hartzog. Who else?' Slapping down the letter he was holding, her husband looked at her with such an expression of outrage that she nearly laughed. She was well aware that his views on their most recent neighbour were unlikely to be charitable.

'Take a look.'

He flicked the sheet across to her and waited, glowering, as she read.

'Bloody cheek, if you ask me,' he muttered. 'First he tries to buy our woods, and when that doesn't work he comes up with a cock-eyed proposal like this. Look at that garbage about 'joint endeavour' and 'good of the community' – pure hot air. What he's after is publicity for his Shoot and that bloody great barracks he's probably run out of money to pay for. No wonder his wife can't stand it.'

Third wife Kelly-Louise Hartzog had made it clear from the start that she had no interest in shooting and meant to spend very little of her time in the big old Victorian house.

'Not a country girl,' added Jericho. 'Happier on the cat-walk, I imagine.'

'More like the front row of the Collections. Still, Hansi can afford it. Everyone knows he's made of money.'

'Ah, but how was that money made?'

She shrugged. 'Dot-com start-ups? I think that's what he said when I sat next to him at the Macleans'.'

'Putting small companies out of business and their employees on the dole,' he corrected, recalling with renewed annoyance how she had listened, apparently enthralled, as Hartzog droned on.

'Who says that?'

'No one you'd know. You're not interested in business, remember?'

'Oh, darling! You know perfectly well I was joking.'

Nevertheless, he brooded, remembering her laughing explanation as they drove home. 'Honestly, darling, I never take in a word when men tell me about business. I can't even pretend to work up any interest. I just say Yes and No and Super when they pause for breath, and they love it. Gives me time to enjoy the food.' She had smiled, shaking her head gently. 'I think the message did trickle through eventually, but it took some time.'

Jericho wasn't ready to let her off the hook yet. 'Well, at

least you'll agree that the way he treated Tommy and old Nan was a disgrace. Even the Maltese developers behaved better than that.'

This was hard to deny. Old Nan had been nurserymaid to Marina's father, and come out of retirement to look after Marina herself. Over eighty and still in full possession of her wits, she had eventually gone to live in the Dunmorse gatehouse with her ancient husband Tommy, who acted as caretaker and handyman during the interregnum, and neighbours had been shocked when Hartzog gave the old couple notice to quit barely two months after buying the estate.

'Turfed out without a word of warning,' said Jericho, rubbing it in. 'All I can say is, it was lucky we had the cowman's cottage empty to give them a roof over their heads. And they weren't the only ones, not by a long chalk. Typical Hartzog. Out with the old and in with the new. Grab what you want and never mind who gets trampled. I bet he was the kind of boy who likes pulling wings off flies.'

'That's a horrible thing to say.'

Jericho fingered the envelope, seeking something else to complain about. 'Bloody man. Pops up everywhere, changing things, interfering in matters that are none of his business. Must have a hide like a rhino. Look at this! Should have been addressed to you, not me.'

'It's a natural enough mistake, I suppose, because you've always run the Shoot.'

'So what about it?' he nagged, as she sat holding the letter, apparently lost in thought. 'Thumbs down, I take it?'

'Hang on.' Marina's fair head nodded gently as she turned the page, then re-read the letter from the beginning. 'It's not such a bad idea, you know.'

'It's a terrible idea. And who the hell asked Fancy Hansi to butt in anyway? He's only been here five minutes – '

'Five years, darling, and just look what he's done in that time. Rebuilt Dunmorse from scratch. Well, from worse than scratch, really. The house was in a terrible state. And that was only the beginning. He's re-fenced the whole estate, built walls, restored the farm buildings, re-roofed all the cottages. Ploughed money into every charity, every fund-raising effort in the county.'

'That's what gets me. Thinks he can wave a cheque book at anything. Well, I for one am not prepared to roll over and agree to let him take our best drive bang in the middle of the season so that he can invite a lot of over-fed, under-bred, Eurotrash millionaires to shoot our birds for the benefit of the Gamebird Preservation Trust or anyone else.'

She said gently, 'Come on, love, get off your high horse and read his letter properly and you'll see that's not what he's proposing at all. It's not his millionaire friends who'd be shooting our birds, but whoever wins the raffle.'

'You mean it's a raffle? For a day's shooting here? Fellow must be off his rocker. You need thousands of acres and probably a title as well to run one of those.'

'I don't see why not. It's just a question of scale. Two hundred tickets which anyone can buy for £80 each, and everyone has the same chance. So for less than the price of a meal out, the winner and his friends – or she and her friends, come to that – get a day's shooting over – what does he call it – 'five world-famous drives,' one of which would just happens to be – ahem – generously donated by Mr and Mrs Oak of Grange Farm, i.e. us.'

'Let's have another look...' he took back the letter and scanned it with more attention. '"World-famous" is a bit rich,' he mused, 'Dunmorse has only got one halfway decent drive – the one they call Skyscraper because you only get head-high birds anywhere else. And what about the rest of it? I see he's copied this to old Marcus Bellton and that chap who's started a shooting school up at Eastmarsh, what's his name?'

'Maude. Locksley Maude.'

'That's right. So he must have his eye on the best drive each of them can produce, and presumably he'll offer Skyscraper plus one other. Well –' He sat back, unwilling to give up his objection entirely. 'The thing is, darling, it may look all right on paper, but I just don't see it working.'

'Because?'

'You know as well as I do that the Bellton Syndicate and the shooting school outfit are at daggers drawn. Why the silly buggers don't merge into one decent shoot rather than fart about on two pocket-handkerchiefs beats me, but they won't.'

'That's why I feel this might be the chance to kick-start some kind of co-operation.'

'In your dreams!' Jericho stamped over to the windowsill and blasted himself another shot of Nespresso. He said reflectively, 'Sometimes I honestly believe they all enjoy needling one another, Dunmorse included. Pinching one another's beaters. Enticing birds across the boundary. Playing Tom Tiddler's Ground in no man's land. It all adds spice – a bit of drama. A bit of fun.'

Marina's nose wrinkled. 'Not so funny when people get hurt.' As Chair of the Parish Council she took a dim view of petty law-breaking, and the recent theft of a quad bike which had led to a vehicle wrapped round a tree and two teenagers in intensive care had seriously blotted the village's crime record. 'Or when it gets racial. Haven't you noticed the Poles Go Home graffiti down at the car-park? The supermarket manager says every time he gets it scrubbed off it's back again next day.'

'Low grade stuff,' said Jericho dismissively.

'You may say that, but I've noticed it's getting worse every year. Using different pubs. Dividing the village. Where guns are involved there's always the chance that some idiot will lose his rag and do something...well, idiotic. And don't forget both those other shoots are commercial to some degree. We may run ours for family and friends and absorb all the costs ourselves, but they're out to make money. The Belltons call themselves a syndicate, but the members have to pay for every bird they shoot; and as for Locksley Maude's lot – haven't you seen his ads? They're plastered all over the sporting press, both here and on the Continent. On the internet, too, for all I know. Improve Your Score. Take on the Highest Birds. Success Guaranteed. that kind of thing.'

Jericho laughed. 'Talk about hype.' He spread Marmite out to the very edges of his second slice of toast. 'Anyway, that's their problem, not ours, and that's why I think you'd be well advised to turn this ridiculous proposal of Hartzog's down as flat as a pancake.'

'I'll think about it,' Marina had tucked the letter back into its envelope, and given him a long, considering look. 'Tell me honestly, darling: why have you got such a down on him? It's not like you at all.'

For a moment he met her eyes, then looked down at his toast again. 'Wrong sniff,' he said shortly.

'Be serious. Right from the first time we met him, you've disliked him, haven't you? Why?'

Because he's too good to be true. A dozen reasons chased through Jericho's mind as he envisaged Hansi Hartzog. Too rich, too smooth, too confident, too... entitled, and a damned crook as well, according to his City friends. The rumour that "Mr Merger" was eyeing up their company would send a chill through the boardroom of many an under-capitalised business. 'Don't let him get a foot in the door,' his old mate Archie Swindon had advised after Trading Standards had forced his once-thriving brewery to close. 'I know Hartzog was behind the campaign to choke off our suppliers, but there was no way I could prove it.'

The damned thing was that all these reasons to dislike him sounded so petty. Almost as if he was jealous. Was he jealous? Jealous of Fancy Hansi's effect on people. On women. On his own wife?

All right, let her laugh at him if she wanted. At least it would be out in the open. He said, 'It sounds ridiculous, but when he smiles at you, I feel a great urge to punch his nose.'

'Darling!' But she looked as if she knew this already.

'Call it personal chemistry,' he blundered on. 'Natural antipathy. And when you smile at him, I want to pick up a club and beat out his bloody brains.'

'Why, Dad?'

Neither of them had heard the boys come in. How long had they been standing by the door?

'Why what?'

'Why do you want to beat Mr Hartzog's brains out?' Max took a good view of anyone who offered boys rides in his helicopter.

'Your father was only joking,' said Marina repressively. 'Now hurry up, or you'll be late for school.'

'Stepfather.' Max grinned, circling the table, seeking something to devour. He was a solid, square-built eight-year-old, curly-headed and fresh-complexioned, a compact rubber ball of a boy, while Pavel, son of Tomasz the foreman, an inch taller although only six months older, was pale and rangy, his melancholy dark eyes almost obscured by a floppy, over-long fringe.

Max stuffed an apple into an already bulging pocket, then grabbed the one remaining bread roll and menaced Pavel, who stepped back nervously. 'Look out, you snivelling Slav, I'm going to beat your bloody brains out.'

'Max!'

'Joking. Just like you.' He threw the roll back on the table. 'Come on, slavering Snivel, or we'll miss the bus.'

'Ghastly child!' Marina rolled her eyes as the door slammed behind them.

'Feeling his oats,' said Jericho, grinning. 'Time he went to boarding school.'

'Oh, darling, you couldn't! You know what ghastly things happen there. The redtops are full of it, day after day.'

Jericho pulled a face. 'Besides, think how much I'd miss him,' she added, 'and Pavel would be bereft.'

'Shouldn't be too difficult to replace him,' he teased, and she gave him a darkling look.

'I don't think I heard that... All the same, he'd better watch his language at school. Miss Montague is mustard on Race Relations.'

'Don't worry: they're best mates, and anyway, Pavel gives as good as he gets. It's a mercy that Miss Montague doesn't understand Polish.'

'But you do.'

He grinned. 'Well, the odd word, and those are enough to make Miss Montague's hair stand on end. God, look at the time! I must be off to the Rickyard. Anita says that reams of paperwork await me, dammit.'

Which super-efficient Anita will have in perfect order long before you get there, thought Marina, who knew how many little detours and chats he usually had before running out of excuses to avoid his desk. Though the Rickyard was no more than a couple of hundred yards from the main house, Jericho could effortlessly spin out his approach for half an hour.

He said guilelessly, knowing she liked to be consulted on farming matters, 'Will you look into the Rickyard later, darling? Haldane has delivered a consignment of seed potatoes

I don't think much of. You'd better give them the once-over: see if they're fit to plant. Oh, and –' he hesitated, nodding at Hartzog's letter – 'what shall we do about this?'

'Leave it to me.' She had swept the bright-blue envelope off the table and added it to her bulging folder. 'Old Marcus Bellton's bound to sit in on the Planning Committee hearing this afternoon, so I'll sound him out about it then. My guess is that he won't want anything to do with it. He's pretty sore about this application for a vast dairy unit that Hansi's put in – says it would swamp his whole business.'

Let's hope you're right, thought Jericho, making for the door.

This was how their farming partnership was structured, and on the whole it worked well, though he could never forget that it was not what she had trained and strained for at the Royal College of Music, and then on the concert circuit. The trouble, as she had reluctantly recognised at last, was there were too many super-star accompanists for the merely talented to flourish. She had married a velvet-voiced American tenor specialising in Lieder, and for several years they had toured European concert halls, but when he ran away with a pupil half his age, Marina – pregnant with Max – had returned to her family home to lick her wounds.

There she found Jericho, trained in Land Management and full of new ideas, helping her father turn his loss-making mixed farm into a small business park combined with an organic farm shop; and two years before her father died, she and Jericho were married.

A match made in heaven, said friends and neighbours with determined optimism overlaying their doubts. She's a couple of years older than him, and their interests are worlds apart: in fact they're as different as chalk and cheese, but they need one another – and so it proved. She made the strategic decisions; he carried out her plans. She handled the money; he bought and maintained the machinery, and together they hired and fired labour and decided who should occupy the various cottages and redundant buildings unsuitable for modern farming methods.

Jericho's claim to understand the odd word of Polish was an understatement. During his years at Agricultural College, he had spent every vacation ferrying farm machinery from his uncle's factory in Leeds to Eastern Europe, where newly-liberated barley barons were hectically mechanising former collective farms. Week-long stays in villages up and down the country while each consignment was distributed had led to many friendships, and these had been followed by sporting invitations – shooting wild boar in Hungary, partridges and pheasants in Poland – and inevitably plenty of requests for help with visas, work permits, and job offers for family members.

'Father's a pal of Jericho's,' people would say. 'Used to shoot with his family near Krakow,' and this was usually recommendation enough. However poor their English when they arrived, these smiling, hardworking sons and daughters of "Pals of Jericho's" slotted into English country life very easily. They were delighted with the minimum wage, and much in demand locally as gardeners and grooms, happy to clip and weed, cook and clean, ride work and muck out in a way that most digitally-savvy products of the British education system were not prepared to.

'They're more like we were when we were young,' people would say. 'Before we had all these labour-saving machines, and forgot how to do things by hand.' Indeed, their understanding of farm work and how to handle animals, both wild and domesticated, was something their English contemporaries were in a fair way to losing completely.

Nobody's perfect, of course, and at times these rural skills that came so naturally were put to illicit use. Many a pheasant poult, struck senseless by a stick flung horizontally, end over end, found its way into a Polish oven weeks before the shooting season opened; and who would not prefer a handsome rainbow trout from the well-stocked lakes owned by Locksley Maude to a pack of frozen fish fingers?

Pub landlords, too, quickly learned to identify the most heroic drinkers among their new customers as well as the ones who liked to conclude a convivial evening with a punch-up in the car park; while keen-nosed housewives lamented their otherwise perfect cleaners' and home-helps' addiction to tobacco. However, these were mere pinpricks. Over the past ten years, attendance at the Catholic church had doubled, and there had been a number of Anglo Polish marriages.

It had been Jericho's cousin, big, blonde, bouncy Anita Carew, whose mother's family once owned Dunmorse Hall, who suggested that he and Marina should turn their redundant rickyard into self-contained units for small specialised rural crafts and businesses – blackmiths, makers of wicker furniture, saddlers and wood-carvers – as well as Anita's own party-catering enterprise, and these had flourished, attracting so many customers that they were thinking of expanding into the old cart-shed and stable as well.

Anita herself had moved into a converted loft belonging to her cousin. This overlooked the Rickyard, and where once half a dozen stable-boys had eaten and slept, she installed huge freezers, an office and a well-equipped kitchen to supply pubs, restaurants, and private clients with upmarket, locally-sourced food.

While Grange Farm had flourished, Dunmorse Hall and its estate had declined steadily in the ten years since the death of its last owner. When childless and choleric Sir Philip Dunmorse had chosen, in a misguided attempt at fairness, to bequeath the big early-Victorian house to his elder niece, a psychologist, and the furniture to her sister, a struggling housewife, while the land was left to his glass-engraver nephew, the three heirs were left with no option but to sell up.

Since then the Dunmorse Hall estate had passed through several more or less savoury hands before being acquired from a Maltese property development consortium by Hans Hartzog, and while anxious locals held their breath waiting to see what he would do with it, he set about restoring it to its former glory, no expense spared. He even made a point of asking Anita to shoot.

'What was it like?' Jericho had asked with assumed indifference, waylaying her as she arrived at her smart little office in the Rickyard.

Anita had shaken back her blonde mane and sighed. 'Oh, amazing. Everything completely perfect. Well, a bit too perfect, really. OTT.'

'Then why the sigh?'

'Well, I suppose I'm not used to such splendour, particularly at Dunmorse. You know what a shambles my uncle made of a Shoot. Order, counter-order, disorder. Gamekeeper shouting at beaters, dogs running wild. Uncle Phil purple in the face and roaring at everyone. You know.'

'It could be a bit chaotic,' he agreed. 'Not always,' he added, and she laughed.

'Don't try to be diplomatic. You know it was frightful. Always. Mum simply hated it, particularly after that poor beater was peppered. That took a bit of hushing up, I can tell you.'

'So what was your day like?' Jericho had asked again, adding, 'Actually, I'm surprised you could bear to see it under the new management. It would have stuck in my throat to have someone like Hartzog lording it over my family home.'

Anita grinned. 'Ah, but I'm not a romantic like you. Of course I went. Sheer nosiness. I couldn't wait to see what he'd done to the old place, and as I said — it's amazing. But —' she hesitated.

'But what?'

'Well, OK, some of the Guns were slightly strange.' She saw his sharpened interest and added quickly, 'I don't mean dangerous, nothing like that. If anything they were too correct — as if they'd read books about shooting etiquette but never done it themselves. Dotting the i's and crossing the t's, you know.'

'Anyone you knew?'

'Oh, no — but they were very friendly. I think they were surprised to see me there, even though I shot like a drain, alas. Out of practice: I should have booked a lesson at Locksley's shooting-school to bring me up to speed.' She sighed histrionically. 'Ah, gone are the days! Since starting my business I've rather taken my eye off the shooting scene. Got to earn a crust these days.'

'Pull the other one, Anny!' He knew very well that in his cousin's order of priorities, business would always come a very poor second to pleasure. Anita was a party girl with an impressive range of friends and acquaintances. Lovers and ex-lovers he knew about included dukes and water-bailiffs, policemen and nightclub managers, diving instructors and professional polo players, who had darted in and out of her life like a shoal of minnows ever since she left Cheltenham Ladies' College, and it stood to reason that there must be a good many more of whom he had no knowledge at all. No matter how hectic she claimed to be, the many little "trip-ettes" and sporting breaks she managed to fit into her working schedule was a source of wonder to her clientele.

'Did you get the Guns' names? Maybe I know some of them.'

'Somehow I doubt it.' Her eyes had laughed at him,

knowing he was longing for a damning verdict to confirm his own prejudices but unwilling to provide the ammunition he wanted. Hansi was certainly noisy and brash, either unaware or dismissive of country people's sensitivities, but she was sure he would tone things down by degrees. Until she had proof of the stories about his ruthless business methods, why not give him the benefit of the doubt? Besides, she had scented a commercial possibility at Dunmorse: Hartzog had hinted he wasn't satisfied with his present arrangements for shooting lunches and was looking for a new caterer.

'Oh, you know I'm hopeless with names,' she said vaguely. 'Some were foreign –'

'Mafia thugs? Russian oligarchs?'

'Lord, no! Business friends, I gathered, and judging by their cars, all of them absolutely rolling. Very competitive, too. Keen on their numbers.'

'How many did they shoot? Two hundred? Two-fifty?'

The corners of her mouth turned down and she wrinkled her nose. 'Something like that. I don't really like wholesale slaughter, especially so early in the season, but that was obviously what the Guns were expecting. '

'Were they surprised to see a woman shooting?'

'A bit. But Hansi explained that my family used to live at the Hall.'

So bloody Hartzog had added Anita to his collection of scalps, thought Jericho mournfully. He gave up his interrogation and started the quad to move out of her way. 'Well, I mustn't keep you. Business won't wait while we stand here gassing, will it? Glad you had a good day, anyway.'

Sitting on the long verandah of the Canadian log cabin he had erected overlooking the larger of his oxbow lakes, Locksley Maude pinched out the stub of his roll-up as he watched the tail lights of the day's last angler bump away towards the main road. Then he gathered up the day's takings to dump on the scarred table in the cubbyhole of an office at the back of his workshop, and sat for a minute staring at it.

Three catch-and-release fees, and those of the two fishermen who had opted to take their catch home to eat: £70 all told. Slim pickings, which were all he would have to rely on from now until the clay-pigeon shooting season got underway, with novices booking private lessons for him to tell them where they were going wrong. Then the money would start trickling in again but meantime the bills arrived in torrents. Timber for building his towers. Clay pigeon launchers. Hire of diggers, hire of labour, hedge-cutting and mowing the rides between the traps. Tree thinning. Even though he did most of the work himself it all totted up to a hell of a lot going out when little or nothing was coming in. The continual worry of how he was ever going to pay back the bank loan he'd needed for the clubhouse, let alone hiring heavy plant for digging the lakes and landscaping... and on top of it all, of course, there was the bloody maintenance. The kids didn't get any cheaper when they left primary school, or Marlene's demands any less outrageous.

Seventy pounds for a day's work! Maude switched on the table-lamp and twiddled the combination lock of his safe until the door swung open. A far cry from the heady days of the winter months when his continental clients flew in with money to burn. Say what you liked about their manners and their notions of gun safety, Continentals expected to pay for their sport, and tipped lavishly. If a group booked the whole weekend for lessons and unlimited use of the traps, he could be looking at thousands, rather than miserable small change.

If only he had room to expand! If only Hansi Hartzog, damn his eyes, was not so infernally territorial, and if only Tobias Hagley, his head keeper, had the sense to point out to his boss that the fifty acres of Waterstone Wood were stuck out in a corner of the Dunmorse estate too far from their release pens to hold anything but a few wild birds. No use to them, but potentially extremely useful to Eastmarsh Country Sports.

Stealthily, before the sale to Hartzog went through, Maude had encroached on Waterstone Wood until he had come to think he had the right to shoot there; a notion that was swiftly terminated by a sharply-worded letter from Hartzog's solicitor, accompanied by a large-scale map with their respective boundaries highlighted in yellow. It didn't do to mess with anyone who reached for his lawyer so readily: you'd think neighbours would be ready for a bit of give and take in the interests of good relations, but with Hartzog it was all take and no give. He certainly wasn't slow to ask favours himself, whether cut-price shooting lessons for his City bigwigs, most of whom couldn't hit a barn door at fifty paces, or fishing for their WAGs, and there was always the veiled threat within the request: don't forget that I could close you down if I wanted, so don't make me want to.

The worst of it was that this was true. If only I'd had a proper search done before I went ahead and bulldozed out the lakes, thought Maude. If only I hadn't listened to old Simon Jackson who said no one but fly-tippers ever used that lane because it didn't lead anywhere. Jackson had been keen to sell his land and move to his daughter's bungalow on the outskirts of town: Maude had been keen to buy.

With money from the sale of his garden machinery business burning a hole in his pocket, and an equally burning wish to put distance between himself and Marlene, he had snapped up the old quarry and four marshy fields where nothing would grow except reeds and willow, and excavated two lakes, one above the other, connected by sluices and fed by the Arne brook, which continued its downhill course to join the Starcliffe river at the bottom of the valley.

Only when he had landscaped the banks into attractive bays and promontories, and planted shrubs for windbreaks, nesting sites and year-round colour, did a chance remark from big bluff Marcus Bellton, neighbouring beef farmer, who had watched the creation of the lakes with interest tinged with suspicion, alert Locksley Maude to the possibility that his access to them might be challenged.

'Nice job you've made of them ponds,' he had rumbled, leaning on a metal gate with barbed wire wound round the top bar to stop bullocks rubbing against it. 'Might take a day's fishing off you meself, if I ever get the time.' A pause, then the killer question: 'Suppose you got an agreement with Dunmorse's lawyer to use that lane?'

'It's a public right of way,' said Maude, with a chill touching his stomach.

'That it ain't.' Bellton's certainty carried complete conviction. 'It's Dunmorse land, that is. Old Sir Hugh bulldozed out the lane when they were quarrying stone for the Orangery, couple of generations back. Nothing to do with a PROW.'

Maude said nothing more, but a hurried search of the Land Registry showed that Bellton was right. In order to approach the Shooting School, vehicles had to cross eighty yards of Dunmorse's back drive before turning on to Eastmarsh, and unless he was prepared to cut down about twenty trees, there was no other feasible spot for an entrance. While Dunmorse Estate remained on the market, its infrastructure slowly crumbling, Maude felt safe enough; but Hartzog's arrival altered matters and sure enough the new owner lost no time in pointing out that he could cut off access to the lakes any time he wished.

Not only did he refuse to consider establishing a permissive path for Maude's clients, he declined to allow him to pay a rent. 'Look here, I've bought this estate in its entirety, and I've no intention of chopping off bits here and there to accommodate businesses like yours. I'm sorry, but that's final.'

Sorry! thought Maude bitterly. But it was no use. He'd just have to keep well in with Hartzog and make the best of things. As a former weapons instructor, he was used to making the best of things, never complain, never explain, bend with the wind, take the rough with the smooth – great mantras which kept him steadily climbing the ladders and dodging the snakes until the shockingly unexpected day when his career's upward trajectory was halted by the discovery of two unexplainable Heckler and Koch semi-automatic pistols in his mate Bill Creedy's kitbag after their second tour in Afghanistan.

Pressed to divulge their provenance, Bill had attempted to implicate Maude, and although the court martial exonerated him, and his service record remained unblemished, the episode effectively stifled any hope of promotion, and when his service commitment ran out, he was glad to leave the Army and accept his brother Geoff's offer of a partnership in his garden machinery business.

The change from the military to civvy street had not been an easy one, particularly for his wife. She missed the social side of regimental life and resented having him at home so much. To his horror his fluffy, giggly, cuddly Marlene transformed almost overnight into a shrill, nagging duplicate of her mother – just as his brother Geoff had warned she might. Geoff had always been a cautious bird where women were concerned, with the result that he had never married; whereas he, Locksley, could hardly see an attractive girl without wanting to have her in his bed. This had been a cause of friction with Marlene right from the start.

An acrimonious divorce followed. If it hadn't been for Geoff making him a partner in his garden-machinery business, things would have gone badly for Locksley Maude.

'Mind you keep your nose clean now, Locky, and I'll see you right,' Geoff had said with the fruity chortle that seemed to come from the depths of his big belly; and Maude had sworn on their mother's head to go straight as a die from then on. He meant it, too. Super-sized Geoff was one person he would never let down. The coronary thrombosis that killed poor Geoff in the last few minutes of a Premier League match five years later was not only a tragedy for Locksley but removed the constant support he had relied on since childhood. Thereafter, he knew, he would be on his own.

'Play to your strengths,' Geoff used to advise when they were boys, with Gramma and Grandy bringing them up in their cottage backing on the woods, while Mam worked for a fruit importer in Cardiff. 'You're not very big, but you're quick – quick-moving and quick to learn. You'd make a good scrum-half.'

Geoff was always positive, no matter how unpromising the situation. Even when his younger brother left the Army under a cloud, he refused to see it as a disaster.

'Cheer up, Locky. This may be the best thing ever happened to you. Join me in the business and we'll make a go of it together. We'll be a team, see? You've got the looks and I've got the business brain. You get on with people, especially the ladies. Don't deny it – you've had girls after you ever since you were fifteen. Plus, you've got a good eye. And you understand machinery in a way I don't. That alone should be enough to give you a start.'

As usual, he was right, and their partnership had flourished, with Locksley attending to the repairs and management while Geoff did front-of-shop sales. But after his brother's death all the fun went out of the business, and he was not sorry to sell up.

With money in the bank for the first time in his life, he was determined to follow his dream of creating a sporting enterprise which would pay for itself, with well-stocked lakes to attract fishermen all year round, plus a shooting school geared to the tastes of aspiring continental sportsmen. A crazy dream? He had tried to assess it through Geoff's eyes. After all, you only live once, he told the ghostly echo of his brother's voice, urging caution. If I can find the right place, I reckon I can make it work.

A weary hunt he had had for the right place. Yorkshire – too expensive. Ditto Norfolk. Northumberland – too remote for those all-important Continentals. Kent – too tame. Devon, Shropshire, Somerset – now you're talking... His lucky break came at last when he chanced on old smallholder Simon Jackson advertising Land for Sale in the Starcliffe Gazette, and snapped it up before anyone else could.

Everything he had been looking for: swampy ground in a natural hollow below the double-ridged escarpment, whose thickly wooded slopes ran down to Grange Farm on one side and the stableyard of Dunmorse Hall on the other. The existing pond could, with very little difficulty, be enlarged and landscaped to form a good-sized lake, and with a couple of hired diggers a smaller oxbow could be joined to it by a short stretch of running water crossed by a humped wooden bridge. He had no doubt that the waterfowl now commuting between the pond and the river below would quickly adopt the new lakes as their home; and if he positioned his butts and launch tower on the steep wooded slope behind Jackson's decrepit stone byre, the sound of gunfire would not disturb them.

Everything he needed was here – or had been, before Hans Hartzog moved in. Surely he would see sense in time, and agree to sell him a right of access from the lane?

The winter sun was underlighting gunmetal clouds in a

final spectacular blaze as Maude locked up the wooden cabin and sat for a moment on the steps of the verandah watching circles on the dark, glassy water showing where the rainbow trout were feeding. Lifting his gaze to the horizon, he surveyed the great sweep of escarpment to the north-west, then focused his binoculars on the patchwork of fields in the V-shaped valley. He loved this view; all he had slaved to create with his lakes and winding paths, glades and thickets in the foreground, and below it the valley wreathed in tendrils of evening mist rising from the river.

I made this, he thought. Created it out of a patch of useless neglected swamp that no one wanted and no one thought worth trying to improve. It's mine now, whatever bloody Hartzog's solicitor may say, and no one's going to take it away from me.

Rush-hour in Starcliffe, he reflected with an ironic grin, as familiar vehicles moved about the lanes in their habitual evening pattern. The big blue tractor towing a load of bales would be Pauly Bellton feeding his father's youngstock; if he looked hard enough he might be able to make out the dogs that went everywhere with him, a sheepdog perched on the ledge at the back of the cab, no doubt, and a couple of labradors crouching between the black bales. Dogs loved Pauly, and he had quite a reputation locally among owners who had let their pets get out of control. 'Six sessions with Pauly or a lethal jab – it's your choice,' Locksley had heard a furious husband exclaim when his wife's Yorkie savaged the vicar once too often.

There was the red postvan, too, stopping to open the mailbox on the junction of Fiddler's Lane and the main entrance to Dunmorse Hall; and now Locksley could see the smart new Yamaha quad bike issued to Tobias Hagley, headkeeper for Hans Hartzog and scourge of vermin up and down the valley.

Here at the summit the land might be useless to a farmer, but as an OP it was without parallel: without moving from this seat Locksley could monitor most of his neighbours' movements and activities. Dunmorse Hall's immaculate gravel sweep and row of neat cottages behind the house made a striking contrast to the Belltons' chaotic farmyard cluttered with machinery, stacks of polywrapped round bales, and turnip clamps. Two large covered yards housed the mahogany-coated Ruby Reds which were Marcus Bellton's pride and joy. Their heads could just be seen as they jostled against the crush barriers which kept them from trampling their feed. On this still evening steam rose in a column from the huge sprawling muckheap.

Swivelling in his seat, Locksley could also look down on the shining greenhouses and polytunnels of Grange Farm, and the space-age floating roof of the new Farm Shop, which had been such a game-changer for Oak finances. He had heard that Jericho borrowed a million and three quarters to get it up and running, but now it was paying for itself hand over fist. Unlike Eastmarsh Country Sports, he thought grimly.

The temperature was dropping fast, and in the cubbyhole of an office two days' mail awaited his attention. Bills and more bills, he diagnosed, riffling through the heap. A bright blue envelope looked more promising: he ripped it open, and after reading it sat for a while deep in thought, wondering how best he could turn this proposal of Hartzog's to his own advantage.

Marina Oak was right: Marcus Bellton's initial reaction to Hartzog's letter was a torrent of four-letter words and obscene suggestions as to what Hartzog could do with his Starcliffe Highflyers.

'Easy, now, dad,' said Pauly, in much the tone he might have used to soothe a fractious bullock refusing to load. 'Your blowing a gasket won't help none, will it? We've got to play this one long. Let Hartzog think he's got his thousand-cow unit all tied up, then put the boot in with our environmental assessment. Believe me, the Planning Committee isn't going to like his siting those settling tanks so close to the river one little bit.'

Marcus regarded his son with a degree of admiration that was usually lacking in their relationship. Nobody could call Pauly a hard worker, but in his easy, laid-back fashion he sometimes came up with a way of solving problems that would not have occurred to his father.

'Got it all worked out, eh? Why don't he put them farther away then?'

'Cos that would mean having the seepage run uphill,' said Pauly with a grin. 'Natural law known as gravity.'

'Tcha!' said Marcus. 'So sharp you'll cut yourself one day, my lad.' He blew out his cheeks and smiled. 'So what d'you want me to do with this here shooting match of Hartzog's?'

'Give over, let's have a butcher's.' He twitched the blue envelope from his father's hand and scanned the contents. 'OK. Easy. You get Ma to type him a nice little note saying great idea, we'll be happy to donate a drive in support of your Highflyers' Day, and look forward to hearing further details. See? Not a word about the dairy unit or effluent or anything like that. Put the ball in his court. Let him think he's got us eating out of his hand.' Pauly laughed, showing all his teeth, and for a moment his bronzed, good-humoured face looked truly malevolent. 'He'll find out his mistake soon enough. And so will his murdering bastards of 'keepers.'

Pauly was not the only Starcliffe resident incensed by the strict regime of vermin control imposed on the Dunmorse estate since Hartzog moved in. Nature abhors a vacuum and during the quiet years since Sir Philip's death, the neglected woods and overgrown fields had witnessed an explosion of growth, both animal and vegetable. Birds had flourished. Hanging curtains of wild clematis obscured many woodland rides, and undug ditches flooded into hollows to create unofficial ponds. Stoats and weasels, foxes and badgers, roe deer and muntjac made themselves homes and bred prolifically. The rabbit population ballooned, collapsed, and ballooned again with each passing year.

Nor was the human population backward in taking advantage of the interregnum. Walkers – with and without dogs – twitchers, and wildlife photographers made use of the woods with increasing confidence. Mountain bikers wove narrow paths through the trees, and cantering horses churned once-manicured grass into deep muddy tracks. For all these opportunistic users of the Dunmorse woods it was a nasty shock to find their activities curtailed by the dour bearded Yorkshireman Tobias Hagley, and his stout local sidekick, Cecil Barley. Anyone who strayed from a public footpath was curtly ordered to return to it. Dogs were forbidden to run loose through the coverts, and hunting cats were shot without compunction.

Worst of all in the eyes of wildlife lovers was the relentless persecution of any creature that might compete with or pose a threat to pheasants. Around the woods there were half a dozen grim gibbets festooned with the shrivelled corpses of stoats, weasels, foxes, carrion crows and magpies, displayed like macabre trophies.

'Boss's orders,' Hagley would grunt if anyone questioned the need for such carnage.

Neither of the keepers was popular in the village, but few cared to tackle them directly. One who did, however, was forthright Liz Cunningham, who kept alpacas and volunteered at the Community Shop.

'Well, I call it barbaric. Medieval. In this day and age it

shouldn't be allowed,' she told him roundly. 'You hardly ever see a fox hereabouts nowadays, and my neighbour says that sidekick of yours chased her Siamese cat right back to her own garden gate. If she hadn't shouted out he'd have run her down, for sure.'

'Shouldn't let her hunt in the woods, then,' countered Hagley. 'Cats is every bit as bad as foxes for killing pheasant poults. Keep her shut in at night and she'll live out all her nine lives.'

'Never heard of the balance of Nature,' put in her colleague Pam from the Post Office counter, 'nor the survival of the fittest. Other people shoot in this valley, you know, and they don't kill every living creature. Take Pauly Bellton. He's more likely to make a pet of a stoat than peg its hide on a gibbet like you do. Same goes for Grange Farm.'

Hagley lowered his head and shook it like a bullock bothered by horseflies. 'Can't hardly say they run a shoot properly, neither,' he countered belligerently. 'How many birds do they put down at the Grange? Five hundred, a thousand? We're talking about fifteen thousand poults a year, give or take a few – '

'Those poults of yours!' said Liz scornfully. 'Stupid birds – not got a bit of sense, and why d'you need so many? Huddling together all over the road so you can hardly drive through them.'

'And the waste!' said Pam heatedly. 'That's what gets me. Those birds are so stuffed with corn they can hardly fly. You could feed the Horn of Africa with half the tailings you dump in the lanes.'

Hagley glowered at them and turned away without answering, but both women had the uncomfortable feeling that they would have to keep their own dogs under very strict supervision from now on if they were not to meet with some unaccountable accident.

31

CHAPTER THREE

The Watcher

For as long as she could remember, Sally Robb's ambition to be a gamekeeper had caused friction with her parents.

'Not a job for a woman,' said her father firmly. Detective Chief Inspector Martin Robb had seen quite enough of the seamy side of life to know what he was talking about, and his wife Meriel agreed wholeheartedly. Sally was no fool, and they wanted her to follow her elder sister to university, then establish a career that made use of her brain and entrepreneurial drive. The thought of their middle daughter skulking about the woods at night trapping vermin and chasing off poachers was repellent to them; whereas for Sally it seemed to represent everything she had ever wanted: excitement, freedom, work in the open air and closeness to the natural world.

After years at school punctuated by tersely-worded complaints that the small animals, snakes, and insects so often concealed in her clothes had unleashed chaos in the classroom, a compromise was reached. Sally applied for and was accepted by Downland Agricultural College for a three year course in Woodland and Wildlife Management, and after her second year, thanks to a little judicious arm-twisting by her Head of Department, Jericho and Marina Oak had been persuaded to offer her a year's practical experience as a trainee 'keeper on their Grange Farm shoot.

'She's a nice kid. Keen as mustard even if she is only knee-high to a grasshopper,' Professor Carless had said to Jericho after the Annual College dinner. 'I'd be grateful if you'd take her on trial. Look after her a bit. Father's a copper who did me a good turn some years back, so I feel I owe him one.'

'We're hardly a high-powered shoot –' Jericho had begun to protest, but was waved to silence.

'Doesn't matter. Basics are the same, aren't they? Rearing, feeding, hygiene, vermin control, all the usual? She's a bright lass and keen to learn. Gets on well with all ranks. Trust me, you won't regret it.'

'Hmm. Well, I suppose we could put her in one of the cottages, and she could give Duncan a hand. He's not as young as he was.'

Indeed, Grange Farm's old keeper Duncan had welcomed Sally warmly, allowed her to shadow him on his daily rounds, and went out of his way to teach her skills the college course had not covered. He was a wizened gnome of a man, seventy-two and looking every day of it, his big-knuckled hands were crooked with arthritis but still powerful, while the roseate pits and corrugations on his large weather-beaten nose might, at first sight, have been taken for evidence of hard drinking. One look into his kind, twinkling brown eyes banished any such thought, and his slow, gently burred speech was instantly reassuring.

Sally had never been squeamish, and she found his hands-on demonstrations of how to kill and when to kill more interesting than repulsive.

'Think of it as doing 'em a favour,' he advised. 'No more hunger or fighting. Just one little click – ' Deftly he dislocated the winged pheasant's neck, severing the spinal cord –'And it's done. There. Give it a try. See? Easy if you do it right.'

She learned to handle, feed, and rear gamebirds and helped him build pens. He taught her diplomatic ways to protect their coverts without antagonising the public, and how to maintain the ancient quad bike which Jericho had allotted her with a warning to be wary of its tendency to skid. She learned to use the dry-plucker and dress game-birds, to set traps and snares, to track deer, and — under Duncan's tutelage — to shoot and gralloch them.

'Farmers round here will stand a few deer in their corn, no problem,' he explained, 'but when they find twenty settled on a field of spring barley, all eating their heads off, they get a mite stroppy and small wonder. That's when they call me in to break up the party. Me or Pauly Bellton.'

Tall, curly-headed Pauly, with his open face and engaging smile, was a local favourite, welcome wherever he went. Despite warnings from Duncan about the string of illegitimate children he had scattered throughout nearby villages, Sally soon fell under his spell.

'Keeps an eye on 'em all, and stays friends with their Mums, I will say that for him,' said Duncan with a kind of reluctant admiration. 'Just can't seem able to stick to one woman for long. You be careful, young Sal, and don't go losing your heart to him or he'll love you and leave you, sure as eggs. Same goes for that scallywag up at Eastmarsh. Him with the lakes. Thinks hisself God's gift to women, but he'll find out his mistake one day. They say the husbands are always the last to know.'

'Don't worry, I'm not planning to lose my heart to anyone,' she assured him, though her mind flashed back to the morning soon after she arrived at Grange Farm. Pauly had driven up to her cottage, asking where to put a load of corn for Duncan, who was late back from an appointment at the surgery. While waiting for him, she had offered a cup of tea, and Pauly followed her into the small, cosy kitchen.

'Real nice, you've made it,' he'd said, looking round approvingly. 'All you need now is a young dog to keep you company, and cheer that fellow up.' He nodded at Pilot, stretched out close to the woodburning stove, nose on paws, who responded with a languid wave of his tail, then rose slowly and padded over to sniff Pauly's hand.

'Pilot's all right,' said Sally shortly.

'Bit down in the mouth, eh? Doesn't find life a load of laughs?' Gently Pauly scratched behind the Alsatian's ears.

'He misses my mum.' Suddenly, shockingly, Sally found her eyes full of tears, and with one swift step Pauly was beside her, his arm round her shoulders.

'Easy, gal, easy. I'm sorry. I didn't mean to upset you. I didn't know.'

'How could you?' she gulped, fighting her absurd desire to lean against him and howl like a wolf. 'I – I try not to think about it, but sometimes it just – just catches me all over again.'

She sniffed determinedly and moved out of his sheltering arm. 'Look, here's your tea. Lucky I didn't spill it. Sugar?'

'Want to tell me about it?' he asked, ladling in spoonfuls. 'Might help a bit.'

And to her surprise, out it all poured: the crash, Mum's death, and with it the instant destruction of their happy family unit. How with her father in a coma in hospital she and her sisters had to arrange Mum's funeral, and decide what was to be done with their house and animals until he was fit to return, all this with the background of Helen due to give birth in six weeks' time and Claire's imminent return to school.

'Didn't you have aunts and uncles to help?'

'Oh yes, they were so kind, but one lives in Scotland and another in France. And our neighbours were wonderful...' Her voice trailed away but he could guess the rest. Outsiders – even family members – can only do so much, precisely because there is so much they don't know, can't understand and besides, they have lives and responsibilities of their own.

She said more steadily, 'So I rang Mrs Oak – Marina – and asked if I could come two months earlier than planned, and she said of course. She was really helpful. And I brought Pilot with me, because my elder sister was about to have a baby, and the younger one is still at school. He was always very much Mum's dog, and that's why he's moping.'

A car door slammed: Duncan was back. Pauly slurped down his tea, patted Pilot's head and gave Sally's hand a reassuring squeeze.

'Poor little 'un. You've had a rough time, all right, and so have your sisters. Thanks for telling me – I'll know not to put my big feet in it in future. Cheer up, gal. Things will get better from now on.'

Little 'un! she thought indignantly, as the door banged behind him, but from Pauly's 6ft 3 viewpoint no doubt it was fair comment, and she couldn't deny that spilling the beans had made her feel better.

The door inched open again. 'How about a tabby kitten, then?' he asked, and withdrew grinning when she shooed him away.

'Pauly's not a bad lad,' ruminated Duncan, 'though his Ma reckons he likes animals more than people, and she could be right, at that. Do anything for a sick animal, he will. 'Taint right, by my reckoning. You've got to let Nature deal with its own. What I say is, don't never let no wild creature suffer. That's my bottom line. If it's injured, put it out of its pain and don't go taking it home to try to cure it. That's where Pauly and I part company.' He pushed back his cap, showing a line of startling white just below the brim. 'You think you're doing the right thing, but you're just prolonging the suffering. It'll never survive in the wild. I've had a man turn up here, and there in his car-boot was a fallow doe he'd found in the road. Beautiful creature. "I couldn't leave it," he said. "It's only shocked. There's not a mark on it." Thought he'd keep it as a pet for his kids. Wouldn't believe there was nothing I could do but wait till he'd gone and then take a hammer to its head. Any wild creature as lets you pick it up is a goner, believe you me.'

The hard frost in early November that greeted Jericho Oak's first formal shoot of the season signalled a change of tempo for the Grange Farm staff. Blessed with keen recruits eager to escape the monotony of work in the polytunnels and glasshouses, Jericho's gamekeeper had no need to tour the pubs in search of beaters, nor did this multi-lingual private army have to forfeit a day's wages.

On the contrary, each of them pocketed an extra £40 in cash, and when pheasants were distributed to the guests in the stable-yard at the end of the last drive, Tomasz the farm shop manager, a jovial, red-bearded giant with a booming laugh and fists like sledgehammers, brought out crates of home-produced fruit and vegetables and encouraged the beaters to help themselves.

'Come on, pitch in!' said Jericho genially. 'There's plenty for all of you.'

Laughing and cracking loud jokes in Polish and Romanian, the beaters swarmed round the crates.

Jericho grinned and moved to the yard tap. 'All right, Mariusz, got enough for supper?' he said, hosing down his clay-clogged boots; and the skinny boy who was swagging away two loaded shopping bags looked momentarily guilty, as if afraid that he had taken more than his fair share.

'Is too much?'

'No, no. Not a bit. You take all you want. No sense in anything going to waste.'

'Talk about spoiling your beaters,' said Hartzog with forced jocularity, as he awaited his turn at the tap. 'Causes no end of resentment among the locals. It's hardly surprising my keepers complain they find it difficult to recruit a team.' Marina had insisted in the teeth of her husband's opposition that Hartzog must be invited – 'I know he annoys you, but Daddy's rule was a chop for a chop, and heaven knows how many times Hansi has asked us to things.'

Bloody man, thought Jericho. Grudging my beaters a share of the stuff they've grown and picked themselves – how mean can you get? Aloud he said blandly, 'They've had quite a tough day going through the thick stuff on those banks, while we took it easy at the bottom. God knows how far those boys have walked, so I reckon they deserve it – don't you agree?'

'Of course! First time through is always hard work. They did an excellent job,' said Hartzog, 'and I think you made a good investment in your new little 'keeper. Good to see you contributing to gender equality, old man! Pretty little thing, too. What's her name – Val? Sal?'

'Sally,' said Jericho through clenched teeth. And you'll keep your lecherous hands off her if you know what's good for you, he added silently.

He was pleased he had taken on Sally, particularly since, as the Professor had promised, she was a tiger for work and since her arrival good old Duncan seemed to have taken on a new lease of life, using his voice to save his legs like an ageing sheepdog. Still, he wouldn't call her exactly pretty. Elfin, perhaps? Gamine? A bit like an outdoors version of Audrey Hepburn before she cut her hair in that Roman film? No matter. She was a worthwhile addition to the farm staff.

'How are your plans for the Highflyers' Day going?' he asked with careful civility as they followed the rest of the Guns back to the house.

Once, twice, three times the spine-tingling scream echoed through the woods, dying away with a gasp as if breath had suddenly been choked off. Raped teenager? Mating vixen? Impossible to tell, thought the watcher, and equally impossible to do anything about. That was not why he was here. He settled his shoulders more comfortably into the fork of the wide-branching beech whose span conveniently overlooked a fork in the track. He might have a longish wait.

A fitful moon, just past the full, cast intermittent patches of light through the wind-blown branches, and from time to time the night's silence would be broken by the startled cocking-up of pheasants disturbed by a sudden gust. Not that a wood at night was ever truly silent: small squeaks and scuffles in the dry leaves told of nocturnal mammals astir, and a pair of owls hunting along the edge of the trees signalled to one another with distinct short shrieks, but the watcher zoned them out, his attention wholly focused on sounds from the steep and muddy lane, a hundred yards to his left.

Beneath his perch, one arm of the woodland track — well-used and well-marked — led directly to the back entrance of Starcliffe Golf Club. The other, narrower, path ended at a locked farm gate on which was displayed a notice warning there was no public right of way and stray dogs would be shot. Ever since the herd of alpacas that grazed the field had been harassed by a pair of village mongrels and two pregnant females had aborted, their owner had taken a tough line on interlopers, whether two-legged or four, and good luck to her, thought the watcher. Liz Cunningham, who rented a cottage and a couple of fields from Jericho Oak, was a busy lady, running her smallholding and knitwear business as well as working shifts at the Community Stores.

Of course the locked gate didn't make her popular with ramblers who saw the alpacas' field as a handy shortcut between Shearwell Lane and the footpath along the stream, but ramblers – in the watcher's opinion – were altogether too keen on putting their own convenience before the right of landowners to protect their livestock. Alpacas were timid, flighty creatures, and a pregnant female was worth four figures. Rumours that Liz Cunningham kept a 12-bore to hand beside the kitchen door sent a strong signal for dog-owners to keep their distance.

In the angle between gate and track, the steep bank was honeycombed with holes and an extensive network of tunnels stretching deep into the hill which, as droppings round the entrances indicated, were much used by rabbits and foxes as well as the badgers who had excavated them.

The unearthly, tearing scream came again, sounding much closer, but in this funnel-shaped valley sound played tricks. What seemed to come from behind might well have originated somewhere else, bouncing from one tree-clad face to another so that both direction and distance became distorted. Certainly plenty of drink-fuelled teenagers were whooping it up tonight in the annexe to The Bell. It was doubtful any of them knew why or what they were celebrating on 6th January, but any excuse was good for a party, and most of them would be keenly aware that the long midwinter break had run out and tomorrow they'd be back at work.

If one of those buxom semi-clad nymphets was the source of the screams, she probably deserved all that was coming to her, he thought; if, on the other hand, it was a vixen calling her love he'd better make sure his elderly neighbours' hens were shut up before the pair launched an attack in tomorrow's gloaming. It was all very well for Mabel and Peggy to claim they liked having foxes around and had too many cockerels from the last hatch anyway, but the trouble was that gender meant nothing to foxes, and they never knew when to stop.

Close to his tree four sharp staccato barks, twice repeated, settled the question. He strained his eyes for movement on the track immediately below, picked out a patch of darker shadow, and stealthily raised his night-goggles. A dog fox glided into view, moving purposefully towards the screams, which increased in volume and then abruptly ceased, while yelps, growls and scuffling noises indicated that the happy pair were achieving their objective just beyond his field of vision.

Get on with it, then, he thought impatiently. And don't trigger any of my traps while you're at it. It had taken more than an hour to set up his movement-sensitive cameras, and he had a hunch they might be needed tonight.

Away in the lane to his right, the gruff beat of a diesel engine muttered, came nearer, and was stilled. He listened intently as muffled clunks told of doors opened and quietly closed. Now what? It would be just his luck if randy teenagers as well as foxes had decided to conduct their courtship under his tree, but although there was something indefinably furtive about the indistinct murmurs, it didn't sound as if courtship was part of their agenda.

He waited tensely for a few minutes until he could make out several pairs of feet crackling and crunching the dry leaves shed by overhanging hollies – heavy-booted feet trying to move quietly – plus the muted shuffle of dogs. Now he could see a pinprick of light advancing along the track at head-height, followed by a beam held low to the ground. As they passed beneath his tree, one of the dogs paused and whimpered but was roughly jerked on. Moonlight gleamed on the barrels of a shotgun, carried upright over the shoulder of the leading figure, while the shorter, thicker outline of the second man was deformed by a large box or crate, slung by straps across his back. A spade-carrier brought up the rear.

Were there terriers in that box? It was important to establish beyond doubt the purpose of this nocturnal foray before trying to disrupt it. Bovine TB was rife in this part of the country, and for the past three years, DEFRA-licensed teams of marksmen had been trapping and shooting badgers perfectly legally, but such was the unpopularity of the cull that these official teams preferred to carry out their work in as much secrecy as possible.

Digging out live badgers for the purpose of baiting them with fighting dogs in vans or backyards and gambling on the result was, on the other hand, strictly illegal, punishable with fines and confiscation of equipment, though even that barely reflected the horror and cruelty of the crime. He had seen mutilated corpses of badgers, some of which had had their jaws broken and teeth pulled out before death, after which the carcass had been deliberately run over to make it look like a traffic casualty.

In fact, the tip-off for this night's operation had come from a disgusted bin-man whose round included the Upper Starcliffe woods, but before the watcher could make any accusation that led to prosecution he needed hard evidence – hence the camera traps. His editor would not be amused if he landed the paper with a libel suit, or disrupted a legitimate Ministry-approved badger-cull.

The heavy boots chose the lesser track and pushed through overhanging brambles towards a big oak whose spreading roots were undermined by diggings, then halted a few yards short of the locked gate to the alpacas' field. Though it was too far away to distinguish words, he heard what sounded like curt orders, and sundry shuffles and bumps as if they were shedding clothes and arranging equipment, together with random flashes as torches surveyed the ground. The whining of dogs became suddenly louder and more urgent.

What were they doing? He needed to get closer, but fear that those dogs would wind him if he descended to ground level kept him immobile in the fork of the tree. He would have to rely on imagination and experience to supplement the hidden cameras silently recording the scene. All but one of the openings to the sett would be blocked with nets, firmly pegged to trap a fleeing animal. Next one or two sharp terriers – quivering with excitement – would be unboxed and fitted with locator collars before being shoved head-first down the mouth of the single remaining tunnel.

Silence fell: a taut, listening silence. The watcher guessed that one man at least was lying with his ear to the ground, while another moved the locator to and fro, tracking the dog's movements.

'Gone in deep. Going on...deeper...' The growled words were low but audible. 'Found summat...'

A long, listening pause, then sharply: 'Ere, look out! Catch 'im quick!'

A yelp, a curse, and a sudden flurry of thumps, whacks, and bumps were followed by a pain–filled, terrified yowling, unmistakably juvenile in pitch. All three men were struggling with whatever they had captured, while the tethered dogs whined and strained at their leashes.

'Shove 'im in,' gasped the growler. 'Garn... Get on – use the noose. Oh, you would, would you? Now! That's right.' Abruptly the yowls were cut off as the lid of the carrying-box slammed shut.

'Bit me, the little sod,' The speaker had abandoned any

attempt at silence. 'Here, take a look at that. Hell of a nip. Wouldn't believe it, that size cub.' A pause, suggesting the wound was being inspected. 'Well, that's two on 'em. Now for the old un. Where's those dogs got to?'

'Over here. Deep down, from the signal. Right under the tree.' The second voice was slower, with a little hesitation between words, not quite a foreign accent, thought the watcher, but not local either.

'Are they moving?'

A long pause; then the slow voice said, 'Not moving, no. I think they have met together. That, or one dog is caught. Listen, you can hear... See, my bitch is coming out. Here, Meg. Here! Sit!'

'Where's t'other then? What's going on? Something's up...'

'I think there is trouble. Listen.'

All three flung themselves to the ground. Even from a distance the watcher could hear mayhem beneath the surface. Muffled growls and yelps, snapping and snarling came to his ears, and the leashed dogs danced and jerked at their tethers.

'Badger's got 'im cornered,' decided the growler. 'Come on, get digging. Damn these roots, they're right in the way. Where's that axe, Smiler?'

Forget about the dogs, thought the watcher. He would never get a better chance than this to take a look at the car. As heavy blows of spade and axe began to thud into the earth, he slid cautiously from the forked branch, hung for a moment by his hands, and landed softly on all fours. Without waiting to hear if he had been detected, he ran towards the lane, trying to avoid crackling twigs and overhanging branches as the sound of digging faded behind him.

He would have to be quick. Out to the road, plant a tracker, and get back to his hiding place before the diggers could extract whatever the dog had cornered. Not much doubt of what that would be: either a sow badger, bloody and embattled, backed up at the end of a tunnel, or perhaps the clan's senior boar with his grim teeth embedded in a terrier's throat.

The hidden cameras would have recorded the digging, but he also needed a clear shot of them carrying away their prey: hard evidence that would stand up in a magistrate's court.

A few yards short of the lane he halted to catch his breath, then went forward cautiously. Yes, there was a vehicle parked in a drift of leaves close up against the bank, a scarred, mud-spattered Trooper, once-black but now grey over-all, number plates unreadable in the moonlight. Even with his night-goggles it was difficult to be sure there was no one inside, but time was short and after a moment's careful scrutiny he decided to take the risk, bending low as he emerged from the shelter of trees and slid quietly down the bank on the passenger side. Shielded from the lane by the car itself, he felt underneath the axle, prising off handfuls of mud until his fingers encountered a metal ledge on which to clamp the tracker's magnet.

Job done. Now to see what progress the diggers were making. With long silent strides he climbed the bank out of the lane and hurried back through the wood. In the ten minutes or so that he had been away, the diggers had certainly made progress, but evidently their efforts had not been rewarded. From the fork in the track, the watcher made out a triangular pyramid of spoil from the sett heaped against the base of the big oak, and a man standing knee-deep in a hole, flinging up spadefuls of earth, while another attacked the bank above the trees. Both were breathing hard.

'Another bloody root,' gasped the man in the hole. 'Where's that axe?'

'Shoulda brought a chainsaw.'

'Aye, and fetched out the old woman with 'er twelve-bore? Thanks, mate.' He heaved himself out of the hole. ''Ere, you take over. I'm bushed.'

Handing over the spade, he shone his head-torch on the faintly bleeping tracker. 'Bloody useless thing! Can't hardly hear nothing.'

'That's 'cos there ain't nothing to hear. Listen, now.' Without the steady thud of the spades, the silence was profound.

'What's up? They've gotta be down there. Let's 'ave that axe again.'

Where was the third man? Hidden by the tree trunk, most likely, keeping quiet, waiting for an animal to bolt into one of the nets. Uneasily the watcher scanned the bushes and brambles that surrounded the digging area. Though the moon was high, flying clouds scudded across the paler arc of sky between the tall bare-topped beeches, its light was fitful, the shadows merging from grey to black, and sudden gusts of wind rustled leaves in an illusion of human movement.

He was standing on the edge of the narrow path, and the alien whiff of tobacco plus the sudden awareness of a presence right behind made him step sharply aside, so that the blow aimed at his head struck him on the shoulder instead. He whirled like a dancer, the edge of one hand chopping karate-style at his attacker's throat, but beard and scarf softened the impact and the attacker followed up with a tremendous kick to the groin. Swiftly the watcher stooped to seize the leg, throwing Beardie off balance. Together they fell off the path, grappling as they rolled down the slope, each trying to pin the other down while using fists and elbows to pound head and face. Grunting and thrashing, evenly matched for size and weight, they struggled grimly, slipping on half-frozen mud and entangled in brambles, unable to break clear.

Moonlight flashed on metal, a wicked stub of blade aimed at the watcher's heart. With a sudden desperate twist, he seized the hand holding it, forcing it to deflect. Instead it pierced his bicep with a sting like a venomous insect, stabbing through the kammo jacket and layers of wool and loosening his grip on his attacker's knife-hand. In an instant Beardie was scrambling to his feet, knife held low, ready to rip the watcher's belly.

But before he could strike, all four men were startled by the roar of a diesel engine – a quad bike, driven fast. A roof-mounted spotlight scythed across the paddock, dazzlingly bright, and stopped by the gate, pinning the diggers in its beam. For a moment the watcher saw the whole scene in brilliant detail – men and dogs, frozen in shock, surrounded by nets, sacks, cages and spades – the very image he most needed. Shakily he groped for his camera, dabbing his right eye which had blood running into it. Then the frozen scene dissolved into chaos.

'Go, go, go!'

Shoving and bumping each other to avoid that searchlight beam, the gang snatched up their equipment, clothes, spades and dogs.

'Stop or I'll shoot!' called a high, clear voice edged with nerves. Not Mrs Cunningham, thought the watcher muzzily. His head was ringing from meeting a stone or a fist, and he could feel blood filling his sleeve. Female, certainly; young, with a note of recklessness or fear, and oddly familiar: where had he heard it before? Did she mean it? Would she really shoot?

Certainly the badger-diggers were not going to hang about to see if the threat was real. Quitting the track, ducking away from that searching, searing beam, they stumbled uphill to disappear in the dark wood, crashing through brambles and snapping branches.

'Stop!'

A spurt of flame followed by the echoing report of the twelve-bore sped them on their way.

Half-deafened, the watcher found himself alone, caught

in the searchlight's beam beside the vandalised sett with the axe, the spade, and a gently-moving sack. He put up a hand to shield his eyes and began to back away. He thought the girl had fired into the air, but there was no way to be sure she would do the same with the second barrel.

'You, too. Don't move. Stop right where you are,' she ordered, her voice high and edgy, tantalisingly familiar.

For another long moment he froze in the glare, feeling both vulnerable and ridiculous, unable to summon words to explain that he was not one of the gang, but had been trying to stop them.

'Put that gun down, for Chrissake. You've got it all wrong,' he began hoarsely, but she cut him short with a startled exclamation.

'Mr. Lombard! Just what the hell d'you think you're doing?'

CHAPTER FOUR

The Sister

From: Sally Robb salvolatile@nixmail.com
To: Helen McFarlane hellzapoppin@aircloud.com
Subject: Should I tell Dad?
Message: *Hi sis, Advice, please, on a slightly tricky subject.*
I was woken up last night by the alpacas in the field behind my
cottage making distress noises, and when I went to see what was
up I found Mr Lombard, who teaches at the local primary school,
fighting a bunch of thugs who were trying to dig badgers out of
a big sett in the wood. Three against one with Mr L getting the
worst of it. They had netted two young badgers and lost a terrier.
Mr L had tried to photograph them, and got attacked. One of them
stabbed him in the arm and his face was a mess.

Sally paused, resting her fingers on the keyboard. Should she
mention putting a shot over their heads? Helen was five years
older and as a solicitor she could be quite uptight: she decided
not to.

I shouted and scared them off and we let one of the badgers go,
but the other was injured so Mr Lombard said he'd take it to a

vet who runs the Brock-Aid Protection scheme. I helped him dig out the terrier, but it was dead so he took that too. He wouldn't let me ring the police – said it would muck up an article he was writing, and anyway there was nothing the police could do. He tried to rope me in to this Brock-Aid outfit but I said no way. Half the farms round here are under bovine TB Standstills, and no one likes badgers. There are far too many of them.

He got very shirty and pushed off. My question is, should I tell Dad? He sounds bored stiff with docs and physios, and rural crime is rather up his street. He might able to talk some sense into Mr Lombard.

Again she paused, thinking over last night in the farmhouse kitchen, after she had washed off enough mud and blood to assess the damage. Nothing too serious: one eye half-closed – how would he explain that shiner to the children? – and the knife wound in his upper arm was more of a rip than a stab, easily patched with gauze and strapping.

Persuading him that he was wrong about badgers had been far more difficult. In vain she had tried to convince him that far from needing protection by people like him, badgers were much too numerous and a perfect pest to cattle breeders because they spread bovine tuberculosis wherever they went. They were top of the food chain and had no natural predators, and farmers, who were forbidden to disturb or kill them, were at their mercy. Of course she thought badger–diggers were criminals and lowest of the low, but she wholeheartedly supported the Ministry cull and deplored the activities of animal rights protesters who tried to disrupt it.

That revelation had gone down like a lead balloon. To Julius Lombard, wild creatures were precious and cattle wholly expendable. He had looked at her with genuine surprise as she argued, hazel eyes intent and words tumbling over each other.

'I thought you'd be bound to want to help me save them,' he said.

'Badgers don't need me to save them. Nor people like you,' she said shortly. 'They're an absolute menace.'

'But since the cows are going to be killed and eaten anyway what does it matter if they're slaughtered a few months earlier?'

'Spoken like a true townie,' she said scornfully. 'You're missing the point, Mr Lombard. Cattle infected with bovine TB can't be eaten. They're not allowed to enter the food chain. Reactors to the test are sent for slaughter and after that it's incineration. Landfill. Total waste. Don't you see – they're a farmer's livelihood. He could have spent generations building up a herd, rearing the best animals he can, and then bang! Everything he's worked for gone for nothing.'

'He gets compensation.'

'Less than market value. How would you feel if the cows you'd spent your whole life rearing, feeding, and looking after were sent for slaughter because badgers had infected them with bovine tuberculosis?' but before she'd even finished the question he was bristling.

'You couldn't know it was badgers. There are other transmission routes.'

'Of course there are, but if you'd lived here all your life as Mrs Cunningham has, you'd know jolly well that the problem's been steadily getting worse ever since badgers became protected by law. It's really bad now round here, and that's because the badger population has exploded. Farmers used to be able to control their numbers, keep them at a reasonable level. If there were too many around, they'd trap or shoot them – but they can't do that now.'

'Then they should keep their cattle away from them,' he had snapped, and she gave an exasperated sigh.

'And just how would you do that? Have you any idea how badgers climb walls, slide under fences, dig their way into turnip clamps? A gap seven inches high is all they need. Seven inches! Think about it. Do you know that an infected badger urinates continuously as it hunts, contaminating the grass wherever it goes? It's impossible to keep them out of farm buildings at night. A friend who lives near here has CCTV covering his cattle-yard. He showed me film of a whole family of badgers running over the troughs where his cows were feeding, and there was nothing he could do to stop them.'

He wasn't listening. 'Don't you even want to get those thugs prosecuted? Do you know how they torture the badgers they catch? Pulling out their teeth. Making them fight dogs in the back of vans.'

She grimaced. 'That's sick.'

'Not only sick, but criminal.' He had pressed his advantage. 'If you'd make a statement to the police about what happened here tonight, we might be able to nail that gang, at least. I put a tracker on their car, so it should be simple enough to find out where they come from and who they are.'

'And that's perfectly legal, is it? Planting trackers on cars?' She shook her head. 'No, I'm sorry, but you're on your own here. There's no way I'm getting involved with any badger protection outfit. As far as farmers with livestock round here are concerned, badgers are Public Enemy No 1. Not only do they transmit bovine TB to cattle, but Mrs Cunningham's alpacas are susceptible too. Probably even more susceptible than cattle, because being non-native they haven't had time to build up much immunity to English diseases.'

The animation left his face. 'Then I suppose there's no more to be said. I'd better be on my way.'

'Don't forget your evidence.'

A feed-sack containing dead animals was the last thing

she wanted left in her kitchen. Lombard picked it up and made for the door. 'Thanks for patching me up.'

'Hang on a tick. Where's your car? I'll give you a lift.'

'No need. I came on a bike,' he said, and had disappeared into the darkness before she could protest.

Obstinate as a mule, she thought, but animal rights protesters always were. Obstinate and wrong-headed. What on earth was he teaching the children in Nature Study classes? It hardly bore thinking about. She sighed and returned to her email.

Hope you're OK now and my godson has learnt to Sleep Through or soon will. Have you tried opium on the fingernail? Ayah used to swear by it. (Joke.)
Love, Sal

CHAPTER FIVE

The Cop

Detective Chief Inspector Robb raised his right leg, planted the foot on the carpeted step, and cautiously brought the left foot up to join it before reversing the process and standing on the lower level again.

'Forty-eight,' he said aloud, and breathed out heavily. Only two to go and then he would pack it in for the day. His new knee still hurt like hell when he bent it, but that was because the painkillers he had taken with his cup of tea were wearing off. He didn't want to become dependent on them, or at least any more dependent than he had been for years, but limiting himself to six doses in twenty-four hours was a struggle. It was just sod's law that the stolen van which had forced the operation had chosen to collide with his good right knee rather than the dodgy one where damage dated back to his rugger-playing days.

It had shattered his knee-cap, shin bone, and ribs, and shattered his family as well. Bitter black rage rose in his throat and he gritted his teeth, breathing in deeply and out again, forcing it down. 'Give it time,' the shrink had said. 'It's natural. I'm afraid there's no shortcut: you've got to go through it.

Concentrate on the things you can change, and keep at bay the ones you can't. One day you'll be able to deal with them, but not now. Not right away. The first thing is to get that leg sorted. There's a brilliant chap who was my best mate in medical school, and I'll put you in touch. Most of his patients have stepped on IEDs, so he's used to dealing with real messes.'

A real mess just about summed it up. Even three months after the last operation Robb could hardly bring himself to look at his lower leg, though he had to acknowledge that Mr Knowsley had done an astonishingly skilful job with what he had to work on. But worse by far than physical pain was the torture of knowing that it should have been him, not Meriel, who took the force of the collision as it would have been if, after Sunday lunch with friends, he had allowed her to take the wheel of the new Ford Fiesta which she had bought after passing on her own ten-year-old 2CV to her elder daughters.

'I'll drive,' he had said, opening the driver's door.

'Oh, no. Let me. You know you hate having so little leg-room.'

'It's only a few miles; I'll be all right. Hop in, darling. Tim and Serena will freeze if we keep them standing about any longer.'

So she had hopped inside in her neat, birdlike way, and leaned back with a sigh, saying, 'That was fun. We must get them to come over to us at Easter, when the girls will be at home,' and those were almost the last words she spoke to him before the pizza delivery van driven by a teenage Albanian hurtled round a curve so far on the wrong side of the road that he hit Robb's car on the passenger side, spun it around like a top, then mounted the nearside kerb, turned over and burst into flames.

For a terrifying moment Robb had fought to control Meriel's car as it skidded towards a low wall, rammed through it and plunged into the canal. His last memory was the shriek of tearing metal just before water flooded in through the gap where the passenger door had been, and his own fingers searching desperately for the release catch on her seat-belt; but as the doctors told him days later, she must have been dead already.

Bit by bit he had pieced together the story: the stolen van and its uninsured driver, newly arrived from the Calais migrant camp via the slit awning of a transcontinental truck. The Lewisham squat shared with a dozen fellow illegals, begging at tourist hotspots, the opportunistic theft of the pizza-van's keys as the driver made a hurried delivery.

Water under the bridge. No good would come of rehashing all that, or asking What if...? though awake or asleep it revolved maddeningly in his mind. For someone who'd thought himself reasonably capable and self-sufficient, it was lowering to realise how helpless he was in domestic matters without Meriel; though the girls had done their best to fill the gap, they had busy lives of their own, and it seemed inevitable that the moment they went back to them, he would run out of something, or need the use of some unfamiliar appliance. Strangely enough since he had never been much of a dog-lover, he very much missed Pilot's silent presence, though at the same time he was glad that Sally had him as company in her isolated cottage.

He hadn't actually seen the cottage, but he could imagine it: tucked away in the woods at the end of a track, with a leaky roof and bathroom only recently installed. The kind of primitive two-up, two downer which Beatrix Potter might have chosen to draw as a dwelling for Mr Tod or Mrs Tiggywinkle, pretty short of mod cons, but Sally was so delighted when offered the job by Mr and Mrs Oak that she would have pounced on any accommodation rather than turn it down.

And now here was Sal inviting him to stay and sort out a spot of bother for her – wonders would never cease. When had she ever asked or taken his advice before? It had been a standing joke between him and Meriel that their middle daughter's middle name was Independence and she would never accept anyone else's plan of action until she had tried out her own and found it didn't work.

'Pig-headed,' Robb called it.

'Unsuggestible.' Meriel flashed him a challenging look from beneath her lashes. 'And where does she get that from, I wonder?'

Oh, how he missed her! Since the accident everyone he spoke to treated him so kindly, so gently, as if his mind was as fragile as his battered body, giving in to his whims, agreeing with everything he said until he felt like screaming. He missed his colleagues, he missed his work, and most of all he missed the buzz of getting to grips with a case and the exciting unpredictability of criminal behaviour. Sometimes wicked, sometimes unlucky, sometimes merely foolish or overtaken by events they could not control, but always interesting. Not that he would have put it like that, but he was clear in his own mind that early retirement held no attractions. Deep down, he was also firmly convinced that given time and the right treatment he could regain his physical strength: it was simply a question of willpower. And time.

'Take your time,' the Super had said in his downright way. 'Don't worry if it takes a year, eighteen months, whatever. The budget will stand it. We don't want you coming back until you're 100%. Understand? One hundred per cent, OK?' His rat-trap mouth had widened in a rare smile. 'As you ought to know, we're not in the business of looking after invalids.'

Take your time. Before the accident, time had been precious. Something he never had enough of, but now it had become the enemy. Time to think, to brood, to worry.

What I need, he reflected, is a reason to get off my arse and use these new joints and bones for something more fulfilling than these damned repetitive exercises. Something to stop me thinking about myself and whether I feel better or worse than I did yesterday.

He looked again at Sally's message and picked up the telephone.

'Hi, Jim. Are you still on for Wednesday?' he said when James Winter answered.

In his careful, ultra-correct way, his Sergeant had been Robb's bridge between hospital and the real world for the past ten months, and he had been both touched and grateful for his tact and loyalty. You'd think that with his batty old mother being shuffled from one care home to the next as staff at each rebelled at dealing with her, plus working for his – Robb's – replacement who was not, by all accounts, the easiest of bosses to admire, Jim Winter would have quite enough on his plate already; but no: not a week had gone by since the accident without him making contact, filling in the gaps, fetching and carrying and keeping Robb in touch with reality in a way that his daughters, with the best will in the world, could not.

'Wednesday's fine by me, boss. What's up?' said Winter.

'Up?'

'You sound – well – different.' He didn't elaborate on the difference, nor did Robb much want to hear about it.

He said, 'I've had a change of plan. Wondered if instead of spending the day here, you'd be prepared to drive me down to Starcliffe, just on the Devon-Somerset border?'

'Where Sally's working? Sure, I know it, and sure, I'll drive you over. No problem. It would be great to see Sal again. How's she getting on with the job?' he said guardedly, knowing that this particular father–daughter relationship was often prickly and could erupt in painful rows, with groundings, accusations of parental tyranny, insults and tears. Without Meriel to mediate, he didn't fancy the role of piggy-in-the-middle

'Well, OK on the whole, as far as I know; but apparently she's come up against something a bit awkward, and wants my advice. She's asked me to stay with her for a few days.'

Advice! Stay with her! Winter was careful to keep the surprise out of his voice. 'Sounds a good plan. Make a nice change of scene for you,' he said neutrally. 'Then when you've sorted whatever it is, let me know so I can pop down and bring you back.'

'Very good of you, Jim. Sure it's not too much trouble? Right, then. Shall we say ten o'clock?'

Whatever Robb had been expecting, it was not the charming gabled cottage in a sunny, sheltered glade, with beech woods behind and a high-fenced field dotted with grazing alpacas in front. Every window-frame was freshly painted, a blaze of red-berried cotoneaster trained in a fan against the nearest wall, and low-growing hummocks of evergreen *Sarcococcus confusa* starred with white blossom flanking the steps leading to the front door, where the sight of old Pilot lying at his ease in a patch of sunlight brought an unexpected lump to Robb's throat.

'Looks a nice place,' said Winter, parking neatly parallel to the wall.

Robb grunted and began the laborious business of extracting his stiff leg from the passenger seat. Push door wide. Grab stick and pivot until both feet can reach the ground. Clutch dashboard and lever –

'Slide the seat back, Dad,' advised Sally, appearing from nowhere. 'Give yourself more room.'

Robb tried not to bristle. 'I'll do it my own way, thanks.'

She bit her lip, started to say something, thought better of it, and transferred her attention to Winter, darting round the car to give him an uninhibited hug. 'Hi, Jim! Good of you to bring Dad all this way. It's great to see you. How's your mamma? Still laying waste the Care Homes of south Oxfordshire?'

'Pretty much.' Winter grimaced, taken aback as usual by the way Sally's habit of saying whatever came into her head never seemed to give offence – not to him, at any rate. Other people, even Robb, treated the vexed subject of his mother's disruptive behaviour with careful diplomacy, and he found it refreshing that Sally saw no reason to.

Robb had completed his struggle to rise and now stood propping himself between his stick and the roof of the car. 'Well done, Dad,' said Sally. 'Is it safe to kiss you?'

They exchanged cautious pecks on the cheek. Pilot had recognised his master and pressed against his leg, ears flat back, plumed tail waving gently.

Robb said, 'I'm all right, really. It's sitting in the car makes me seize up. Takes a while to get everything moving again.'

'Come in and have some tea. We can sort out your luggage later.' She was ushering them towards the door, steeling herself not to interfere with Robb's system for managing the two steps, when a muddy Land Rover swung into the little front drive, and a tall, curly-headed young man in none-too-clean stockman's overalls jumped out.

'Got a present for you, Sal,' he announced, beaming, holding out a cardboard box.

'Oh, God, Pauly! You do pick your moments. Can't you see I'm busy?' she said with a distinct lack of enthusiasm. 'This is my Dad, who's come to stay for a few days, and this is my great friend James Winter, who was kind enough to drive him here. Dad, this is Pauly Bellton, who farms just across the valley.'

You could, thought Winter, almost see the wheels of thought revolving in Pauly's mind. 'My Dad – ' no problem there; but 'my great friend James Winter – ' well, that was another matter. That could be a big, big problem. His well-disciplined heart gave a tiny, unauthorised skip before being sternly called to heel.

Pauly's wide grin faded; his manner cooled several degrees. 'Glad to meet you,' he said formally. 'Nice for Sal to have some company. It gets lonely up here at times, eh, Sal?'

'I don't get lonely.' Her level gaze challenged him to contradict her. 'Listen: if that's a kitten in the box, I've told you before: I don't want it.'

Sal turning down the offer of an animal? Unheard-of, thought Robb. He watched in fascination as Pauly reacted to the rebuff, shaking his head gently, easing open the lid of the box.

'No, no. T'ain't no kitten. You told me your dog wouldn't accept it. These are just two poor little ducklings whose ma got swept away in the storm a few nights back. Four of the brood went with her, but these little fellows got left behind. I thought they'd settle well on that pond of yourn out the back. It's got an island, and I can let you have a coop to shut them in at night.'

Sally glanced at her father, who was shifting uncomfortably as he leaned on the stick. 'All right, Pauly, leave them here on the step. I'll do what I can for them later, but right now I've got to give tea to my visitors, so if you don't mind...'

'Right, I'm off.' Though clearly he was disappointed that she didn't ask him to join them, Pauly jumped back into the Land Rover. 'I'll pop round in a couple of days and see how they're doing,' he called, and roared off.

Sally rolled her eyes at Winter. 'Typical!' She turned to Robb. 'Come on in. You must be longing for a cuppa after the drive, and it's all ready.'

Again his expectations were confounded. Sally had no domestic skills, as he knew very well, so the kitchen table loaded with scones and biscuits, jam sandwiches with the crusts cut off and a good-looking chocolate cake was unlikely to be her own work.

'Who made all this? You could feed an army with this lot,' he said, staring; not altogether pleased that his arrival had evidently been well advertised.

'Fallout from a christening my friend Anita was catering,' Sally admitted with a touch of embarrassment. 'She said it was a shame to waste them, and I thought you'd be hungry.'

'Spot on.' Winter was always hungry. At Sally's urging he demolished two jam–and–cream filled scones and a slice of chocolate cake while Robb sipped tea and nibbled a sandwich. The painkillers took away his appetite.

'Well, what's all this about scaring off a badger-digging gang?' he asked without much enthusiasm. 'Sounds just the sort of thing your mother and I were afraid you'd get into in this job.'

Sally flushed at the criticism, and said heatedly, 'I could hardly leave them to it, could I? It's cruel and illegal. Besides, they were frightening the alpacas, who'll be unpacking in a couple of days.'

'Unpacking?' Robb had visions of Louis Vuitton suitcases.

'Giving birth. They were getting so upset they could have miscarried.' She flashed him a defiant look which reminded him piercingly of her mother. 'I wouldn't even have mentioned it to you if Mr Lombard hadn't been involved.'

'Who's he?' Winter pricked up his ears and took another sandwich.

'He teaches at the local primary school. Fancies himself as a naturalist, but he's got some weird ideas.'

As Winter absent-mindedly demolished the rest of the

scones, she outlined her encounter with Lombard and the unsatisfactory conversation that had followed.

'Sounds a thorough-going anti,' commented Robb with finality. 'Sort of chap you'd better steer well clear of.'

It wasn't the advice she wanted. 'Yeah-yeah-yeah,' she said impatiently, 'but shouldn't he be stopped? Skulking about the woods at night dressed like a para...'

'No law against that, as far as I know.'

'Planting trackers on other people's cars?'

'Have you any evidence of that?'

'Well, he said he had.'

'Not good enough, I'm afraid,' said Robb. 'Look, Sal, you're new here. There are a lot of things you don't know or understand about what goes on. You can't go meddling in other people's business just because you don't like the look of them. Leave it to the local coppers to deal with. They know the background, and it's likely they're well aware who these diggers are and what they're up to. They certainly won't thank you for sticking your nose in. Understand?'

Sally was silent.

'I asked if you understood,' said Robb with a familiar edge to his voice, and her shoulders drooped a little.

'Yes, Dad,' she muttered, then burst out, 'I thought you'd be pleased.'

'Pleased that you deliberately put yourself in danger? What sort of father do you think I am? Well, I'd better spell it out: I daresay you meant well, but in my opinion you behaved in a way that was both stupid and reckless. Why didn't you ask for back-up? Where was this woman who owns the alpacas? It was her business to protect them, not yours. Why didn't you call the police? Or someone else who works here –'

'Dad – there wasn't time! I had to do something at once. Mrs Cunningham was visiting her sister in hospital, and it would have taken Duncan twenty minutes to get here.'

'What about this chap Pauly?' put in Winter. 'Sounds as if he's always dropping in.'

'Well, yes, but –' she hesitated, then said in a rush – 'that's a bit tricky, too. Mr Lombard thinks he was one of the gang.'

'Does he, indeed,' said Robb. 'What makes him think that?'

'He heard one called 'Smiler.'

'Is Pauly known as 'Smiler?'

'Sometimes.' She bit her lip. 'Oh, God! Those ducklings. I'd better do something...' She dashed to the door, peered outside, then came back looking relieved. 'They've gone. He must have come back and picked them up. So – what were you saying?'

'I asked why Lombard thought Pauly was part of the badger-digging gang? It doesn't quite square with all these kittens and ducks and so on he keeps pressing on you.'

'I know, but he hates badgers and makes no secret of it. The Belltons' farm has been shut down twice because of bovine TB, and the second time their show heifer was one of the reactors. That was a frightful blow for them. They've spent a fortune on bio-security, trying to make all their feed stores and cattle sheds badger-proof, but when the cattle are out at grass there's no way of preventing an infected badger wandering across their fields, spreading disease as it goes. It's a real problem.'

'And no doubt this outfit that Lombard's involved with – what did you call it? Brock-Aid? – no doubt that will be doing everything in its power to disrupt the DEFRA cull?'

Sally nodded. 'My own guess is that Pauly may be one of the Ministry's marksmen, but if he is, he keeps pretty quiet about it, and I can see why. People get so steamed up at the smallest hint of killing badgers, even when they haven't a clue what's involved.'

'Right. Well, that explains why you didn't call him in to help, but really, Sal, you should have had more sense than to rush off and tackle the trouble on your own,' said Robb more moderately. 'Promise me you won't do it again.'

'With any luck it won't happen again.' Sensing that she was off the hook, Sally was rapidly regaining her natural bounce.

'I want your promise.'

'O.K.'

'Good. Now I'd like to know more about the people you're working with here,' said Robb, and Sally sighed, but to Winter's relief she didn't bristle up again.

'Oh, yes. OK. Well, you've talked to Jericho — that's Mr Oak — already, haven't you?'

'Only on the telephone.'

'He's the boss, and had the idea for the Farm Shop and polytunnels and so on, and now Grange Farm makes real money and has been given a terrific facelift, according to Duncan — did you notice all the fresh paint around? — but actually everything belongs to Mrs Oak — Marina. It's her family home. She's very beautiful, and I like her a lot, but she doesn't exactly get her hands dirty because she's a brilliant pianist. Her first husband was an American tenor, and they gave concerts all over Europe. Then he ran off with someone else, and she came home with her baby and married Jericho. So Max, who's about eight or nine, I suppose, is actually Jericho's stepson, though he looks incredibly like him.' She grinned. 'Max is quite a handful and they talk about sending him to boarding school, but I don't think they will because he's best mates with the Polish manager's son, and they both go to the local primary.'

'Where this man Lombard is a teacher?'

'That's right. That's what makes it so awkward. In fact that's why I didn't tell anyone else about the fight in the wood.'

'Hmm. What else do you know about Lombard?'

She thought for a moment, then said with her usual rapidity, 'He has a house in the village, just opposite the pub, which he used to rent out when he was posted abroad.'

'Married?'

'Not now.' She hesitated, then added, 'People say that he's been a bit — well — odd ever since he was invalided out of the Army. His patrol was ambushed on his second tour in Helmand, and two of them were killed. Afterwards he was sent home with PTSD... Post whatever-it-is.'

'Post Traumatic Stress Disorder,' supplied Winter.

'That's it. Not mad, but not himself either. He's a terrific walker, even though he hasn't got a dog, and Jericho sort of looks out for him because they were in the same regiment. I think he may have pulled strings to get him the teaching job. The kids think he's great because he was in the Army. I didn't want to mess things up for him, but all the same...' Her voice trailed away.

'Yes. I can see that,' said Robb. 'As you say, tricky. Go on about your work.'

The two men listened carefully as she rattled away, describing her mentor, Duncan Pegler, with his lop-sided gait and arthritic hands.

'He calls me his new legs because his old ones are worn out. He wanted to retire this year, but when I came he changed his mind — for the moment, anyway. He's lived in this valley his entire life, and what he doesn't know about it isn't worth knowing. His dad was a gardener and handyman up at Dunmorse, for old Sir Philip's parents, so that goes back a fair way, but after the war lots of the farm buildings were knocked down, because there wasn't the labour to maintain them, and they weren't suitable for modern machinery.'

'Same old story.' Robb nodded. 'So Duncan took a job here instead — when?'

They all heard shuffling steps approaching the door, followed by a resounding knock. Sally wiped her sticky hands down her thighs in the well-remembered gesture that used to irritate her mother, and sprang up. 'Here he is; you can ask him yourself. I forgot to say he was coming round to tell me what he wants me to do tomorrow. Come in, Duncan, and meet my father. We were just talking about you.'

'Glad to meet you, sir,' rumbled Duncan, shaking hands and accepting a cup of tea. He glanced at Robb's crutch propped against the table and said simply, 'I'm right sorry to hear of your wife's death, and all your trouble.'

'Thank you,' said Robb, grateful for sympathy expressed so straightforwardly. Most people avoided this particular elephant in the room for as long as they could, which made it hard for either him or them to behave naturally.

'And this is our friend James Winter, who's been kind enough to drive Dad here.'

Our friend, this time, Winter noted. 'My friend' had clearly been a signal to Pauly to keep his distance.

As the men settled back in their chairs and Sally skated an extra plate across to Duncan, he said, 'I expect Sal's been telling you about this Highflyers' shoot Mr Hartzog's organised next week? Means a deal of extra bother for us, and I'm main glad to have your daughter's help. She's a hard worker and taken to the job like a duck to water. You should be proud of her.'

The colour rose in Sally's cheeks, but if she expected praise from her father she was disappointed. 'I'm sure she's a lot to learn before she's much use,' he said grudgingly, cutting across Duncan's protest to add, 'What is a Highflyers' shoot, anyway?'

A lot of nonsense, according to Duncan, settling down to an enjoyable description of how the Dunmorse shoot differed so much from the infinitely superior sporting operation here at Grange Farm.

'We do things the traditional way, sir. No fads and fancies. Most of our birds are wild, and we don't pump them full of antibiotics, either, because they don't need it. Give 'em plenty of room and keep down the vermin, and they look after themselves, near enough. Now take Dunmorse and you're looking at a different kettle of fish. Oh, yes! With them it's all numbers – how many birds shot against how many they put down – ratio of shots to birds picked up – clickers going nonstop – every Gun counting his score...' He cackled with laughter. 'Chalk and cheese, sir. Chalk and cheese! Anyone doing that in Mr Jericho's hearing wouldn't be asked back.'

Winter listened attentively as he rambled on. Nice old boy, he thought; well-meaning but physically well past it. Duncan would certainly not be his back-up of choice in a poaching affray. Admittedly Sally's solo intervention had been reckless, but he could quite see why she had chosen not to involve the old keeper.

After tea, when he had seen Robb installed in the small parlour converted into a temporary bedroom, Winter made his excuses and prepared to leave. In somewhat subdued mood, Sally accompanied him down the steps. 'Thanks for bringing him down, Jim, but I just don't think this is going to work.'

'Come on, Sal!' he said briskly. 'Don't give up before you've even tried to make it work. Your Dad's had a rough time and he's not himself yet. Not by any means. You'll just have to be patient.'

'I am.' Her suppressed irritation gave the lie to the words. 'But he's been out of hospital for months now, and it's nearly a year since the accident. I thought at least he'd be interested in hearing about Mr Lombard, but all he wants to do is scold me.'

She sounded so childish in her disappointment that Winter had to suppress a smile. 'Try putting yourself in his shoes, Sal. Ten months isn't long when you've got to reboot your entire life. I think he's doing pretty well, all things considered, but there's a long way to go yet before he's back to his old self.'

'If he ever is.'

'Of course he will be. Just on the way here, he said something about having had enough of being helpless. Well, that's progress, at least.'

'But what will he do here all day? I'm out most of the time. He'll be climbing the walls.'

'Don't you believe it. He and Pilot will get on very comfortably while you're doing whatever it is you do, and you may even find he's made supper when you get home. How about that for a reversal of roles?'

'Dad can't cook,' she said scornfully.

'You might be surprised. That friend of your Mum's – Lorna Greenfield, isn't it? – she's been giving him lessons. Taught him all the basics, meat and veg, that kind of thing. And besides – ' His eyes lighted on the muddy quad bike parked along the wall – 'that yours? Well, the boss may not be allowed to drive a car yet, but I guess he could manage that. It'd give him a bit of freedom.'

As she still looked doubtful, he said on sudden impulse, 'Tell you what, Sal. I've got a bit of leave due and I'd like to tackle some of these hills around here before the Harriers' season starts. I could drop in from time to time and see how you're getting on. How would that be?'

He would have liked her muted 'OK' to have sounded more enthusiastic, but one couldn't have everything. As he drove off he glanced in the mirror, hoping for a wave, but Sally had already gone back into the cottage.

CHAPTER SIX

The Highflyers

The big day, 20th January, dawned clear and cold, with a nipping north-east wind and the threat of rain later. Quite how much later was unclear. As the party assembled in the handsome old courtyard behind Dunmorse Hall, many a glance was directed up at the sky, and there were murmurings of, 'Nice enough now. Let's hope it stays that way,' from those who had consulted the local forecast.

Marcus Bellton's naturally florid complexion was tinged an alarming shade of purple and his body language expressed barely contained rage as he swung his legs out of his Land Rover and stomped across the wet cobbles to where Jericho stood with his team: Duncan in old-fashioned baggy plus-fours and tweed jacket with bulging pockets; Sally slim and neat in matching tweed breeks and jacket, with her thick dark hair pulled back in a pony-tail under an over-sized butcher-boy cap; and Tomasz in his usual faded jeans and windbreaker, keeping a wary eye on the boys. Max and Pavel had pleaded to be allowed to accept Hartzog's proposal that they should pick up spent cartridges at the end of each drive, and although Jericho was not keen on their restless presence, he gave way to pressure from his wife.

'Having a job will make them feel involved,' she argued. 'Teach them how to behave.' Marina herself had agreed to join the party for lunch in the revamped barn of which Hartzog was so proud.

On the other side of the courtyard, as if to emphasise their sense of ownership, was grouped the Dunmorse home team. Black-browed, craggy-featured Hagley, the head keeper, had the physique and self-confidence to carry off his dark-brown corduroy suit and high-cut waistcoat with assurance, though his deputy Cecil Barley looked awkward and uncomfortable, his dumpy figure constrained in all the wrong places. Behind them stood an untidy shifting crowd of beaters with sticks; and on the periphery small groups of weather-beaten men and assertive women chatted idly while keeping working spaniels and labradors under close control.

Welcome to Sandringham, circa 1907, thought Robb, watching with amusement from his perch on Sally's quad bike. It was pretty well his quad now. Winter's suggestion that it might give him much-needed freedom of movement had proved outstandingly successful, and a week in the country had improved his mental state as much as his physical one. Winter had phoned twice, as promised, but the summons to come and fetch the boss back home had not materialised. Just a few more days, he had been told on each occasion; and though Robb had not actually admitted that he was enjoying himself, reading between the lines Winter concluded that the therapy was working.

Today Robb had volunteered to drive the game-cart, a light trailer with a superstructure of parallel rails on which to hang the bag, hitched behind the quad bike – a role that assured him an over-all view of proceedings with few physical demands.

Locksley Maude leaned on his bonnet. 'All present and

correct, but where's the Big Cheese?' he said quietly.

Anita laughed as she joined them. 'Luz told me he went off in his chopper yesterday to buy a polo team, or a football club. As one does.'

'Get away!' said Locksley disbelievingly. He glanced at his watch. 'He's cutting it pretty fine. The lads should be here any minute. What's up with old Bellton, any road?'

Across the yard, Marcus was haranguing Jericho, while Pauly tried unavailingly to calm him.

'Where's that bloody double-dealing snake?' he exploded. 'Opened my mail this morning, and there it was in black and white. A thousand cows on zero grazing, milked three times a day. Forage harvesters and tankers up and down our lane twenty-four seven. Just what the Planning Committee turned down flat and Hartzog swore he'd accept their decision. I could murder him.'

'Take it easy, Dad.' Pauly patted his sleeve, but angrily Bellton shook off his hand.

Jericho sighed. 'So he's appealed?'

'You knew?' Bellton's furious face swung round on him.

'Marina thought he might.'

'And she'd know, of course!' sneered Bellton. 'She's thick as thieves with that lying con-man, always has been.'

Jericho counted ten before he said in a tightly controlled voice, 'As Chair of the Parish Council she's sent advance warning of all challenges to planning decisions. I know you're upset, Marcus, and you've good reason to be, but I can't listen to you blackguard my wife, who has absolutely nothing to do with Hartzog's machinations. Is that understood?'

'Sorry,' muttered Bellton; then burst out again, 'but it's iniquitous! It'll put us out of business. I tell you, he swore he wouldn't go against the committee's decision. We talked about it only a couple of weeks back when he was all sweetness and light – "so glad you've agreed to support my fund-raising shoot, blah-blah," and now the bloody man goes to Appeal! I've a good mind to withdraw from this shoot here and now. If he won't keep his word, neither will I.'

'Easy, Dad, easy,' murmured Pauly again. 'You can't disappoint these boys who've been looking forward to their big day for months. 'Tain't fair on them and it's not their fault. Look, here they come.'

In his anxiety that none of his team should be late or get lost on Starcliffe's network of lanes, Rodney Owen had hired a luxurious grey minibus with tinted windows and uniformed driver. As this vehicle swung round the corner and under the stable arch, Robb's ears caught the whump-whump of rotors and glanced up to see a metallic blue helicopter heading straight for the house.

'Behold the deus ex machina, bang on cue,' murmured an ironic voice behind him, as the chopper touched down on the helipad like a cumbersome insect, and the deafening scream subsided.

'A very good morning and welcome to you all,' called Hans Hartzog, immaculately dressed in a collarless green loden jacket and breeks, standing in the open cabin door. He clumped down the steps and went to greet his guests, now piling out of their minibus and collecting guns and cartridge bags.

Certainly knows how to make an entrance, thought Robb, glancing round to gauge others' reaction: Bellton and his son with closed, granite-like expressions; Jericho smiling with a hint of contempt at this deliberately dramatic appearance; the Dunmorse keepers carefully impassive, and Team Owen openly admiring. This, said their expressions, was Something Like!

Sally turned her demure face towards him, raised her eyebrows, and gave him a conspiratorial wink; unexpectedly his heart rose. At least his daughter had her head too well screwed on to be impressed by such posturing.

Hartzog strode over to greet the newcomers. 'Rodney – delighted to see you. Well done getting here in good order. Now please present me to your team. I've got your list of names, but now I'd like to match them to the faces.'

The young men – boys, really, thought Robb – lined up to shake hands. Just the mix you would expect: Rodney's schoolfriends, work colleagues, cousins, and identical twins Basil and Barnaby Foster, who lived next door to Rodney's parents. The only mould-breaker was heavily built and in his sixties, Uncle Thomas Owen, who had given Rodney the winning raffle-ticket. He, too, was the only visitor to bring a dog: a rangy, ribby, gingery bitch, with a wild look in her eye and a plumy tail clamped between her hindlegs.

'Meet Mitzi. Part-Vizsla, part-Red Setter. Hunts, points, and retrieves as well,' said Uncle Thomas expansively, dragging her behind him as he was introduced to Jericho and the Belltons.

Pauly's quick eye noted the upside-down choke-chain collar and, while fondling Mitzi's silky ears, quietly refitted it the right way round.

'Now I'd like to say a few words about ground rules,' said Hartzog, gesturing to gather Team Owen around him. 'I'm sure you're all well aware of basic shooting safety, but there's no harm in spelling it out. So... no shooting through the line. No ground game, hares, rabbits, muntjac – '

'Foxes?' asked Uncle Thomas.

'Not even foxes. A horn to start and end each drive. Move up two places each drive, and please leave your cartridges, which these boys will pick up.' He pointed out Max and Pavel, armed with magnetic sticks and glowing with pride. 'You may not see them, but the pickers-up and their dogs will be right behind you, ready to deal with any wounded birds, and I shall act as backstop.'

He looked round the circle. 'And I think that about covers it. Any questions? No? Most of all I want you to enjoy yourselves, so remember the rules, have a good time, and the best of luck to you all.' From his pocket he produced a small leather folder containing slim ivory sticks. 'Now we'll draw for places. You first, Rodney.'

Beaters and gamekeepers had already dispersed before these formalities, piling into 4WD vehicles and heading for the gently undulating fields known as The Stubbles, where overnight rain had left mist hanging in hollows and turnip leaves glinting with a million diamond drops.

This was what it was all about, thought Robb. Forget the game, forget the killing, the ritual, the marshalling of a virtual army to pursue and shoot beautiful, harmless, expensively-reared birds. What gave shooting its addictive charm was the chance to spend a day in glorious country owned by other people, and feel – however briefly – that you belonged to it, and it to you.

Rough shooting had been part of Robb's childhood, walking with his father and their old spaniel Jessie around the gorsey margins of his uncle's Shropshire farm, potting the odd rabbit with the .410 his cousin Freddy let him borrow, and marvelling at his father's ability to bring down high pigeons.

Gun safety and shooting etiquette had been drilled into him at an early age, and though this lark of Hartzog's could hardly be more different from those far-off Shropshire memories, the basics were the same. He could easily understand the half-nervous, half-proud feelings of Team Owen as they followed their host, who had fallen into step with Uncle Thomas, out of the courtyard and down a rutted lane to a gate, where Hagley was waiting to show them to their pegs along the far edge of the turnip field.

Heaven alone knew what this day was costing Hartzog,

thought Robb, but he seemed in his element, ordering people here and there, needling Jericho about Marina's non-appearance, ('Not an early riser, I imagine? I'll just have to hope she makes it in time for lunch,') and hassling Hagley about the placing of the Guns.

When at last all was ordered to his satisfaction he positioned himself a little behind the line, while Jericho, Marcus Bellton and Pauly – mere observers for this first drive – stood together by the gate. Hagley spoke into his radio, some of the young men nervously worked their shoulders to loosen them and practised swings while others stood rigidly expectant, and faintly in the distance sounded the horn.

A classic country scene, thought Robb, almost absurd in its Englishness. Shades of green and brown: the lush viridian of stubble-turnip leaves and dull grey-green of winter pasture; the reddish-umber of the untrimmed hedge and dark, stark branches of beeches, all overlaid with twinkling frost; mist rising now from the fields in front of them as a confused far-off mumbling resolved itself into the shouts of still-invisible beaters.

Immediately in front of him, Uncle Thomas was fiddling with his ear-defenders, which refused to clamp neatly over his flat cap, while Mitzi lay quietly, tethered to his shooting-stick.

'Damned thing,' he growled and, stepping backwards, he trod on the dog's tail. With a startled yelp she yanked the lead loose and was off, bounding fifty yards straight forward into the thickly planted ranks of turnips with the choke-chain dangling behind her, sending an explosion of partridges into the air.

'Stop that dog!' roared Hagley, lumbering forward at his best pace.

Mitzi swung abruptly left, and began to range back and forth along the line of guns, quartering the ground like a pointer, now disappearing in the foliage, now pronking stiff-legged as a springbok, with her tail straight out behind and ears flapping, deaf to Uncle Thomas's furious roars. Wherever she passed, partridges took to the air, flying straight back towards the beaters.

Hunt, point, retrieve ...hmm, thought Robb, watching in fascination.

'Stop her!' gasped Hagley, still in hot pursuit.

Pauly put two fingers in his mouth and whistled piercingly, and the dog froze in mid-pronk, head turned enquiringly and then, as if remembering something long forgotten, came racing back — not to her owner, but to Pauly. Quickly he put a foot on her lead and stroked her head.

'Good dog. Good little lady.'

'That bloody dog!' Uncle Thomas was shaking with anger and humiliation.

'Don't take on, sir. She's done no harm,' soothed Pauly, handing over the lead. 'Stirred the birds up a bit, but that's all to the good. There's plenty more where they came from. Just look at them! Best get back to your peg, sir.'

Indeed, it was quickly clear that Uncle Thomas had the hot spot; birds were already streaming overhead, but by the time he was loaded and ready for them, the first flush was over. To his left and right the twins, Bas and Barn, were downing birds with their matching twenty-bores, quick and efficient, while behind the line Hartzog himself was mopping up any they missed.

The rest of Team Owen had been taken by surprise by the number and speed of the birds, but canny old Hagley was a pastmaster at 'trickling' — halting the line of beaters from time to time to regulate the flush — and by the time the second wave of partridges flew over, the young Guns were ready, shooting accurately and safely, as Robb noted with relief, taking them mostly in front and scrupulously avoiding any swinging through the line. A steady thump-thump of fallen birds testified to their efforts, while the cameraman from the *Starcliffe News* clicked away industriously.

'Well, those lads can deal all right with driven birds,' admitted Marcus Bellton grudgingly, 'we'll see in a bit how they cope with the thick stuff in our —'

He was interrupted by a full-throated bellow from Hagley: ''Ware deer!' and all the observers saw a fat, glossy roe doe and her half-grown fawn leaping through the turnips towards them on a diagonal path which brought them within easy shot of Uncle Thomas. Either he was slightly deaf, or had not been paying attention to Hartzog's preliminary orders, but to general dismay he raised his gun and fired both barrels at the leader.

In the nick of time, both animals jinked, and continued through the line of guns, though the fawn appeared to limp for a few strides before recovering momentum. They disappeared into the brambles beyond the hedge, and a moment later the horn signalled the end of the drive.

'Pity,' commented Uncle Thomas, strolling over towards the game-cart. 'That would have made an interesting addition to the bag.'

Robb could see that Hartzog was torn between the desire to lambast the old man and conscious of his duty as a host, but Rodney Owen was not so restrained.

'No ground game!' he hissed, putting his face close to his uncle's. 'What d'you think those were? Flying saucers? Just be thankful that you missed.'

'Sorry, Roddy. Couldn't resist.'

'It's Mr Hartzog you should say sorry to, not me. For God's sake switch on and stick to the rules, or you'll ruin the day for all of us.'

Scarlet with embarrassment at this public dressing-down, Uncle Thomas turned his back and stumped away, dragging

Mitzi with him. Pauly gave a little wince and shook his head.

Ever since the horn sounded, the band of pickers-up, whose retrievers had been collecting every bird they had marked during the drive, approached the game-cart with their spoils, and Robb climbed carefully off his perch to tally the bag, tie them in braces, and suspend them along the trailer's rails.

Max and Pavel, armed with their magnetic sticks and sacks like mini-gladiators, and wild with excitement, dashed from peg to peg collecting spent cartridges. Though Max had pulled a face when told to travel between drives in the back of Locksley Maude's battered pick-up instead of his father's comfortable Range Rover, the boys knew they were there on sufferance: Jericho had not wanted them at the shoot and any bad behaviour might get them sent home.

'What's the score?' asked Hartzog eagerly.

'Eleven pheasants, 43 partridges, 4 pigeons, with one or two still to be picked, by the looks of it,' said Robb, pointing to where three women were directing their dogs to search an area some fifteen yards in from the field's margin.

'That's the worst of stubble turnips. Play havoc with scent. It's hellish difficult for the dogs to work in them.' Hartzog turned away to greet the driver of an old-fashioned tub-cart that was just negotiating the field gate. Freshly painted pea-green, and drawn by a fat, snow-white pony with shining brass fittings on his well-polished harness, it clinked and rattled enticingly as it bumped across the turf. On the bench-seats either side of the tub sat blonde Anita and raven-haired Luz, waving and smiling.

Odette and Odile, thought Robb. This was his first glimpse of the exotic beauty whom, in the absence of his wife, Hartzog had installed at Dunmorse some fifteen months ago. Hostess? Bed-warmer? Secretary? From all reports she seemed adept at filling any of these roles.

'Good timing, Jonas. Bring it over here, and we'll give

the troops a stiffener before the next drive,' ordered Hartzog, lowering the tailboard to form a table. The girls jumped out and began unloading hampers and wicker bottle-carriers from the cart. Rapidly they set out glasses and a wide-mouthed thermos full of hot sausages, and began to cut up an immense dark fruit-cake. Elevenses at half-past ten! Whatever next? thought Robb, torn between amusement and disapproval.

'Come on, all of you,' Hartzog called to Team Owen, whose rising voices now showed no trace of their earlier nervous tension. 'Time for bullshots.'

Since several of the young men had skipped breakfast for fear of missing Rodney's bus, they needed no urging, and whatever his personal grudges, Marcus Bellton was not one to turn down a free drink. He accepted a silver beaker full of King's Ginger and a large hunk of fruitcake before any of the Guns reached the pony-cart and, like a grumpy old dog swagging away a bone, retired to a distance to down his spoils.

'Come on, Pauly. Knock it back. You're in the hot seat next,' teased Anita, filling his beaker with sloe gin.

'Right you are,' he grinned, taking a hefty swig. 'The lads have had the Rolls-Royce treatment, and now we'll have to show them how the other half lives.'

True enough, thought Robb half an hour later, as he drove into the Belltons' decrepit yard at Castle Farm and parked alongside the Dutch barn, from whose deeply-manured interior a jostling herd of rich-reddish brown cattle peered curiously at the newcomers. A sprawling muckheap oozing greenish effluent filled one corner of the yard, and erratically-piled round bales of silage threatened to topple if even one of their number was removed. Cats, ducks, a one-eyed sheepdog, and a variety of chickens hurried away to private refuges as the procession of vehicles swung through the double metal gates, whose bent bars bore witness to many a bovine charge.

In a muddy second yard, glimpsed through a cattle-barrier, farm vehicles old and new were parked randomly: smart new trailers alongside rusty wifflers and ploughs ripe for donation to an agricultural museum; a well-used forage harvester hitched to a state-of-the-art John Deere; and, half-hidden by nettles, an elegant old milk float missing one wheel, and a chain-harrow so entangled with wire and weeds that it would take a morning to unroll it.

Round the perimeter were individual sheds and stables, their doors chewed into scallops by generations of teeth and, judging by the banging and lowing that came from them, mostly occupied. In a corner of the barn was a wire-fronted cage housing ferrets.

It was a mystery how such a chaotic set-up would pass even the most cursory DEFRA inspection, but if Pauly and his father were embarrassed by the contrast it made with Dunmorse's manicured perfection, they gave no sign of it.

'Welcome! Welcome to you all!' shouted Pauly, as Team Owen, seated on haybales on a low-loader, stared about them in bemusement. 'No, don't get off yet – just let me get these gates open – and we'll take you to where we start the drive. We'll have Numbers One, Three, Five, and Seven walking, and the rest on the far side of the river. Is that clear? One, Three, Five and Seven to walk. Which are you, sir?'

A pause for mental arithmetic, then Uncle Thomas said, 'Four. I was Two last drive, which makes me Four now. Right?'

'Perfect. We'll put you and your dog beside the water. Swims a bit, does she? Great! OK, everyone? Then off we go.'

How the other half shot – let alone lived – was immediately apparent when the trailer, having ground its way up a steep track to a flat field at the top of the hill, stopped beside a bramble thicket and the passengers jumped off.

'Line out along the edge of the wood, one Gun between

each two beaters, and when you hear the horn start walking forward. Don't worry, it's not as thick as it looks from here, and Dad will mop up any birds that go back. Keep the line straight, and make sure you can see who's next to you. OK, lads? Off you go, and the rest come with me.'

He swung the tractor down a steep track that ran diagonally between high banks through the hanging wood, and emerged on a long flattish ribbon of pasture bisected by a narrow fast-flowing stream fringed with willows. Pauly drove cautiously across a bridge that barely looked strong enough to support the vehicle, and parked against the hedge on the far side.

'Now we'll have some fun,' he said, jumping out and taking Uncle Thomas's gun from its sleeve. 'You and your dog come with me, sir; and the rest of you space yourselves along the near bank. This is what we call The Splash. Your mates will be driving the birds off the ridge, so you want to shoot them in front, not to lose too many birds in the water, OK?'

The Guns scrambled off the trailer and hurried to line the nearside bank, while Pauly, Thomas Owen and the dog positioned themselves at a bend on the far side.

Leaning against a gate, Hagley and Cecil Barley watched with barely concealed contempt. 'Call this shooting? More like a bloody shambles to me,' said Hagley, loud enough for Robb to hear. 'Look! They haven't even bothered to put out pegs.'

It was true that the Guns were by no means evenly spaced, and even before the horn sounded a number of canny birds had run out of the corner of the wood, or flown low over the wire fence and scuttled into the brambles.

'There's the horn. Better stop that corner,' said Barley. 'What they need is a line of sewelling...' He moved forward, but Hagley caught his sleeve.

'You stay where you are and let the Belltons sort it their

own way. That Pauly's too big for his boots and needs to be taught a lesson. That covert's got precious few pheasants in it and a mort of foxes and stoats. Does nothing about vermin control, but that's him all over: thinks he knows it all and won't listen to a word of advice.'

For a tense ten minutes nothing flew out of the wood at more than elbow height, but the steady stream of running birds continued, and the Guns fidgeted, longing to loose off but afraid of breaking rules. Nearer and nearer came the tapping of sticks on trees, and the incoherent growls and chirrups of the beaters. High on the bank above, there sounded a random scatter of shots, and cries of 'Mark!'

'Mark!' Bang!

'Mark over!' Multiple bang-bangs!

The riverside Guns looked at each other and shrugged. Too bad. It looked as if they weren't going to get any shooting at all on this drive.

A solitary pigeon flew out of the trees, well out of shot, Robb would have thought, but Barn and Bas fired simultaneously, and it dropped with a thump.

As if a spell had been broken, a dark cloud of pheasants erupted from the wood with a clatter of wings and loud cockling cries, to be greeted with a barrage of shots. Up and down the line of guns the noise was so deafening for the next five minutes that it was difficult to distinguish where the action was hottest. Firing, ejecting, re-loading as fast as they could, Team Owen had never known such exciting sport, and though they missed many more birds than they shot, the steady thumps on turf and splashes as bodies hit the water proved that Hagley's pessimistic estimate of the covert's capacity was well short of the truth.

Silence – and then a second wave of birds burst from the wood as the beating line reached the limit of the trees. Again Team Owen fired until their barrels were hot; and when the horn sounded they broke into excited chatter, laughing and boasting as they collected their own birds and compared notes on where others had fallen.

With half a dozen pheasants to his credit and Mitzi plunging enthusiastically in and out of the river as she retrieved them in copybook style, Uncle Thomas was in his element.

Pauly collected them on the bank. 'Six of yourn, and five came down in the current. We'd have lost the lot without your good bitch, sir,' he said, and the old man glowed with pleasure.

They made their way towards the game-cart, where Hartzog had joined the observers. 'Perfect demonstration of how not to drive a covert,' he was grumbling. 'One big bang and it's all over. Never mind. It's no good expecting chaps who shoot for the pot to understand the science behind a decent show of birds.'

Robb nodded non-committally. Forget about the science, he thought; the young Guns had certainly enjoyed their big blast-off. Flushed and excited, the reunited Team Owen compared notes. 'I'll never forget that as long as I live,' declared Rodney to No 3 gun, who had walked with the beaters. 'From where you were, you couldn't have seen it, but I promise you, down here at one point the sky was absolutely black with birds. Never seen anything like it.'

'Well, well,' said Hartzog tolerantly though his smile had a hint of contempt. 'Don't let's forget the object of the exercise. We've got two more drives for you before lunch, so we'd better crack on. This is where Mr Oak of Grange Farm takes command, but first let me tell you what you're about to take on. As those of you who have done their homework will know – Maiden's Leap is the most famous drive in this part of the country. Crowned heads have shot there, I forget which –'

'Alfonso Xlll of Spain,' came a shrill shout. '*King* Alfonso.'

'Thank you, Max. And he said – '

'It was really, really difficult,' supplied Max, scarlet faced as everyone turned to him.

'So there you have it. Quite a challenge, but I'm sure you're up for it.' He paused, then added, 'As you know, we're going to shoot through. No stopping for lunch, but if I know Marina — that's the lovely Mrs Oak — I'm sure she will have arranged a little something to keep the wolf from the door. Right, Jericho, over to you.'

CHAPTER SEVEN

ACCIDENT

Back in the spring, when Jericho was persuaded – strong-armed – steamrollered – into donating his best drive to the Highflyers' day, he had not thought twice about nominating Maiden's Leap as his contribution. It seemed to tick all the boxes: spectacular, famous, challenging, and something participants could boast about subsequently, even if they personally had not connected with a single bird.

Hartzog – damn him – had pounced on the offer, and made sure it featured heavily in pre-raffle advertising. As the months passed, however, and the background of the raffle-winner became known, second thoughts and even third ones questioning the wisdom of letting inexperienced Guns shoot in this steep and craggy gorge had begun to trouble Jericho's sleep. To withdraw the offer now was impossible: all he could do was make sure that Team Owen's members were adequately supervised and placed where they were least likely to lose their footing when the heat was on.

Together with Duncan and Sally, he had spent more time than he cared to waste during this past week in cutting back undergrowth and lopping branches to give a clear field of fire to each Gun, but there was little they could do to minimise danger from the chain of waterfalls and rocky pools that gave the Maiden's Leap drive its unique character.

As he led the procession of vehicles on the short drive from the Bellton farmyard to the Grange, Jericho tried to tamp down the mixture of anger and dread that threatened to overcome his judgment whenever he saw his wife and Hartzog together. He knew all too well that he was a dull dog, a plodding countryman, short on culture and lacking Hartzog's social accomplishments. He played neither bridge nor the piano; he could never be sure if he was looking at a Landseer or a Gainsborough; and he preferred reading *Farmers' Weekly* to the *Times Literary Supplement*. Hardly surprising, he thought despondently, that Marina with her cosmopolitan background and musical talent should find Hartzog a breath of fresh air in her circumscribed country life. Hardly surprising that her flashing smile when she spoke to him was one seldom directed at her husband.

None of which made him like Hartzog any better, or explained Hansi's compulsion to nark and niggle and needle him. Why was he always mentioning Marina, asking where she was and what she was doing?

Why? he thought; and back with the speed of a Google search came the answer: because he's in love with her, you dope. He's jealous of you. Yes, of boring old you. He may be loaded with money, talent, charisma and you may be the dullest dog on earth, but you're lucky enough to have something he wants – that he believes would make his life perfect: Marina.

Was he in love with her? Oh, no. Men like Hartzog didn't love – not in the sense that he, Jericho, loved. Hartzog was a collector, who coveted beauty in all its forms, and Marina's delicate blonde loveliness had excited that covetousness. He wanted to add her to all his other desirable possessions: the paintings, the debenture seats, the helicopter, the matched Purdey 12-bores, the polo team – or was it a football club?

A deep chill touched Jericho's heart, for when men like Hartzog really wanted something, they usually contrived to get it.

Butt out, Hansi! he thought angrily. Why did you ever come here? We were perfectly happy before you arrived and started throwing your weight around. As for letting you steal Marina, I'm damned if I will.

All the same, he could see that the next hour was going to be tricky. While he had his hands full with the Maiden's Leap drive, Hansi would be taking a back seat, chatting up Marina and no doubt dangling before her enticing offers of future entertainment that she would find hard to resist. The Royal Box at Wimbledon, perhaps? Adele at the O2? Seats at Salzburg? What could he do to stop him?

Get over it, urged the search engine in his head, but that was easier said than done. Yet, as he swung in under the big green-and-gold sign saying GRANGE FARM SHOP, his spirits rose. There she was, smiling and waving at the convoy of vehicles, backed by half a dozen of the Polish staff in their smart farmshop livery, standing at trestle tables loaded with urns of soup and quiches still steaming from the oven, baskets of chocolate bars and pyramids of shining home-grown apples.

'Well done, darling,' he said, kissing her and making introductions.

'You're spoiling us, Mrs Oak,' said Rodney with a dazzled smile as he tried to juggle gun, plate, and glass. 'The boys aren't used to this sort of treatment. We won't be able to hit a thing after this.'

The bespectacled twins Barn and Bas approached shyly and waited to be noticed. 'Weren't you – aren't you – the pianist Marina Bowaters?' asked Barn, who had done his own researches. 'Our Mum's a great fan. She's got all your records.'

Marina clasped their hands with both hers, in full diva mode. 'Oh, how sweet of you to tell me! But they're ancient, those discs. I haven't done any recording for years.'

'They're still the tops, according to Mum.'

'That's so kind – I'm really touched. Does either of you play an instrument?'

Cello and flute, it turned out, and the trio embarked on a well-informed musical discussion which quite excluded Hartzog, to Jericho's private satisfaction. But it was already noon and the sky was darkening, with clouds piling up in the west as the forecast had predicted. There was no time to waste before tackling the Maiden's Leap.

'This way, everyone,' he called after a bare ten minutes, and led the way through the sweet-smelling belt of mahonia and sarcococcus that concealed the farmshop's polytunnels from the hill above, through a wicket gate and up the winding path beside the Maiden Stream, which splashed from one rocky basin to the next in a series of small waterfalls.

The gradient was soon taking the puff out of Team Owen, who stopped talking to concentrate on putting one boot in front of the other. Uncle Thomas soldiered on manfully, breathing like a broken-winded horse and, unwilling to see him collapse before reaching the summit, Jericho sent Sally to guide him along a branch path to a flat platform of rock just above the lowest pool, while he and the rest of the party continued up the main path.

'Warn him to stay this side of the stream,' he said in a low voice as they separated. 'He won't have much of a field of fire, but the other bank's been undercut by the current.'

'Sure.'

'Once you've got him settled, come on up and join us at

the top. The beaters are moving in an arc, so we'll need you to keep them in line.'

'Sure,' she said again, glad of something concrete to do after spending the previous drives with the pickers-up, marking where birds fell. With Thomas following, she walked along the narrow path back to the stream and installed him on the rocky platform. He had abandoned the corkscrew dog-tether which had let him down at The Stubbles, and she saw him tie Mitzi to a sapling with a double knot.

'Don't want her running riot in the wood,' he muttered rather defensively. Sally passed on Jericho's warning about the undercut bank, and left to rejoin the others just as rain began to fall.

Robb had positioned himself and the game-cart by the gate to which the pickers-up would bring the bag, but looking through the fringe of the wood he could see only three of the eight guns stationed in the Maiden's Leap gorge since a shelf of rock hid the rest.

Rodney Owen, at Number One, kept fidgeting from side to side of his peg, and moving a few steps forward or back, as if uncertain of the best position. It was hard to tell at this distance, but Two and Three looked like the twins: he wondered if they had deliberately swapped numbers with someone else after the draw, so they could shoot side by side all day.

The horn had signalled the beginning of the drive five minutes ago, but nothing had emerged from the trees, and the rain was coming down harder every moment. Straining his ears he caught faint chirrups and whistles from the beaters, though they sounded a long way off still and then suddenly, clearly, a shout of 'Cock forward!'

Woodcock, he thought, as the bird zigzagged fast and high from the trees, and Rodney swung his gun up smoothly and brought it down with his first barrel only a couple of yards from his own feet.

'Well done,' muttered Rob. 'Cracking shot.'

As if at a signal, pheasants began to pour across the gorge, well spaced out and perfectly shootable, but either the Guns were too slow or they were having difficulty seeing in the downpour because Robb reckoned over ninety per cent of them escaped unscathed. After his initial success, Rodney did not hit another bird, though plenty flew over him, and when the beaters emerged into the open and the horn sounded, only half a dozen pheasants joined the woodcock in the game-bag.

Dripping and slipping on the steep path, the Guns scrambled up to rendezvous with the vehicles above the hanging wood, full of apologies and excuses.

'Sorry, sir. Your birds were too good for us there,' said Rodney to Jericho, who grinned and shook his head.

'Not your fault. As I said, this drive's well-known to be a challenge, and of course it's twice as difficult when it's raining cats and dogs. Now, are we all here? Better hop into the cars and we'll go back to Dunmorse.' He looked round, counting heads, 'Where's your uncle?'

They looked at him blankly. After a moment, Rodney said, 'He's not too fast uphill...'

'OK, we'll hang on here for a moment. You boys had better get into the cars. You're wet through as it is.'

Eric Lonsdale, a tall redhead who shared a desk with Rodney, said diffidently, 'Perhaps he's looking for a bird. I thought I heard two shots a couple of minutes after the horn.'

The twins nodded. 'So did we.'

'Or perhaps he thought it would be quicker to walk

back down to the house and get a lift from there,' suggested Number 6 gun.

Jericho bit back the answer that Uncle Thomas had no business adapting plans to suit himself, and said to Sally, 'Run down to where you left Mr Owen, and tell him we're waiting. Better take a dog in case he has lost a bird.'

Or lost Mitzi. The unspoken thought went through everyone's mind and Rodney, who was looking anxious, said quickly, 'I'll go too. Come on,' and set off at a run, followed by Sally and Pauly with his black labrador.

'This is where I left him,' she said five minutes later, standing on the rocky platform opposite the undercut grass bank. 'And that's the tree he tied the dog to.'

Here in the thickest part of the wood, where holly and laurels formed a tunnel over their head, rain drummed on the leaves and great gouts of foamy water swooshed from one ledge of the Maiden Brook to the next, but of Uncle Thomas there was no sign.

'Must have given up and gone back down the track,' said Rodney uncertainly.

'What's that?' said Pauly sharply, turning his head uphill. 'Listen – can't you hear it?' His labrador, ears cocked, was gazing in the same direction. The rain eased for a moment, and both Sally and Rodney heard what he meant: the dismal whining of a dog, interspersed with strangled yelps.

'This way.'

'Watch out,' warned Sally. 'The bank's liable to collapse.'

They battled a hundred yards uphill, keeping away from the water's edge since the brook was rapidly spreading outward, bent on becoming a river, and found Mitzi, sodden and miserable, lashed with her choke-lead to a sapling on the edge of the churning stream. Another ten minutes and she might well have drowned. She greeted her rescuers with ecstatic whining and wagging tail; but of Thomas Owen there was no sign.

'He's got to be here,' said Rodney. 'He wouldn't have gone off and left the dog.'

Sally was beginning to think there was no idiocy of which Uncle Thomas was incapable, but Pauly was more concerned with freeing Mitzi, whose struggles had pulled the noose under her chin past its "stop" and so tight there was no way of undoing it.

'Bloody hell,' he said, hacking away with his knife at the "stop."

The moment she was free, Mitzi bounded downstream and disappeared over the bank. 'Bloody hell!' repeated Pauly. 'Come on, but watch your step.'

They found the dog poised heraldically with one paw raised on the water's edge, peering down into the natural basin formed by a waterfall, on the lip of which Uncle Thomas half-sat, half-lay with one arm round a rock and his boots trailing in the water.

'Bust my leg,' he said through clenched teeth. 'Heard it snap. Damned bank gave way and down I went; gun's in the pool below.'

For a moment Pauly considered his options. Owen was a big man, probably sixteen stone, and though he was in no immediate danger it was far from certain that the three of them could lift him up to the bank without doing more damage to his leg. Air ambulance? Difficult in such thick woodland, and besides there was no mobile signal under the hill. Carry the casualty to Grange Farm? It was less than a mile, but they'd need some kind of stretcher.

He said, 'You stay with him here, Rodney; and Sal, you run back up and tell Jericho what's happened. I'll go down to the Grange and get a team to carry Mr Owen, and ask Mrs Oak to ring for an ambulance.'

Bloody old fool, thought Hartzog, watching the flashing blue light weave down the lane to the Starcliffe junction. Why couldn't he stay put instead of wandering in search of a better sight-line? His own agreeably flirtatious conversation with Marina had been brusquely interrupted by young Bellton's demand for manpower from the farm shop, an ambulance, and a hurdle on which to carry the casualty; all of which had entirely wrecked his carefully-planned schedule. It had always been tight, but now there wasn't a hope in hell of fitting in four drives before lunch. He would have to abort Skyscraper, which should have been Dunmorse's showpiece.

Time to reassert his dominance.

'Nonsense!' he had said briskly when Rodney showed signs of wanting to go with his uncle in the ambulance. 'He doesn't need you and you'll just be in the way.'

'That's what I told him.' Uncle Thomas had heaved himself up on the reclining seat. 'The last thing I want is to spoil the shoot for the boys. You carry on and enjoy yourselves and tell me all about it tomorrow. Oh – and ask young Bellton to look after Mitzi until I can collect her. Right, now, driver: we're off.'

With a lordly wave he lay back as the ambulance door slid shut and was borne away; for all the world, thought Hartzog, as if he hadn't done his level best to bugger up an operation that had taken nearly a year to organise.

It was a quarter to three, and though the rain had stopped the short winter day was already dimming. Despite their waterproof gear, the young Guns looked bedraggled and forlorn, standing about in groups with dripping hats and stamping clogged boots in an effort to keep warm. Hartzog rang Hagley's mobile, telling him to abort the Skyscraper drive and bring the beaters directly to the barn. Food and drink and warmth would cheer up the troops, and there was still Locksley Maude's evening duck-flight to round the day off nicely. Hartzog had insisted that the sporting press' representatives should stay for lunch: he certainly didn't want them reporting a debacle.

Nothing could have looked more welcoming than the big gabled barn, with light streaming through the open door and the warm smells of woodsmoke and spiced wine wafting into the courtyard.

'Come in, come in, you poor drowned rats!' exclaimed Anita, running out as the vehicles wheeled into a line. 'It's lovely and warm inside, and you can put all your wet stuff by the wood-burning stove.'

With chattering teeth and moving like stiff old men, Rodney's team invaded the lobby through the back door and stumbled straight into the L-shaped boiler-room, propping their guns against the walls or dumping them on the central table, before shedding layers of sodden jackets, hats, and boots on the slatted wooden shelving around the roaring stove.

'Help yourselves to dry socks,' urged Anita, producing a wicker skip filled with heather-mix shooting-stockings. 'You can't eat in those horrid wet ones.'

Gratefully the young men peeled the clinging tubes from their legs, which emerged as white and clammy as drowned men's fingers.

'Oh, lovely!' sighed Bas ecstatically, wiggling his toes in finest cashmere.

'Gorgeous. I thought I'd never be able to feel my feet again,' his twin agreed.

Ten minutes later, when they all trooped into the barn's hammer-beamed dining area, the boiler-room looked like a tip, and round the angle of the L, which concealed a row of basins and lavatory cubicles, the floor was awash with muddy water.

'Leave that as it is for now,' whispered Anita when Luz hurried in from the kitchen to restore order. 'Drinks first, then we'll get them to sit down.'

Hartzog was already handing out steaming glasses. 'An old family recipe,' he said as Team Owen sipped the spicy mulled wine, cautiously at first and then with abandon.

'Can we try it?' said Max hopefully, joining the throng round the bar.

Hartzog laughed and ruffled his hair. 'Over to you, Marina. Shall I give him some of this? It's not strong.'

'Certainly not!' she exclaimed. 'Buzz off, Max, and stop pestering the grown-ups. You and Pavel are eating in the kitchen – oh, and mind you stick to Coca-cola.'

'Boooring...' He trailed away.

Warmth and alcohol soon worked their wonders, and noise levels rose exponentially as the mulled claret went down. Anita and Luz hurried back and forth from the kitchen, carrying trays of tiny hot pork pies and grilled prawns and by the time the whole party was summoned to table in the next room the wet, cold hour-and-a-half that Team Owen had spent waiting first for Uncle Thomas and then for his gun to be retrieved from the pool, had been largely forgotten.

'Here, Rodney, you sit by me at the top of the table, and we'll put Marina next to you,' ordered Hartzog. 'Take the other end, will you, Jericho; and the rest of you spread yourselves out as you like.'

'Wonderful!'

'Fantastic!'

'Cor, look at that!'

To sportsmen accustomed to lunch on a couple of

sandwiches and a Mars Bar, the laden serving-table in Hartzog's refurbished barn was an astonishing sight. Freed from budgetary restraint, Anita and Luz had pulled out all the stops: dishes of sliced ham, Coronation chicken and turkey, steak and kidney pies oozing rich gravy, a whole salmon decorated with mayonnaise, together with bowls of buttered potatoes, quiches, vegetables ad lib, all crowded cheek by jowl on the snowy cloth of the serving table.

'Go on, lads. Dig in,' urged Hartzog. 'Remember we haven't got all day,' and with one accord the crowd surged forward to load plates and fill glasses from lined-up wine-bottles.

Expecting to eat with the other gamekeepers and beaters in the old cart-shed across the yard, Sally had brought sandwiches, but to her surprise found herself herded into the barn itself. 'Come and balance up the numbers,' said Anita in her ear. 'The boys will appreciate a bit of female company. If you want to earn your keep you can help me and Luz change the plates.'

Fair enough, thought Sally, though when the place beside her was taken by the whiskery, gingery, pointy-nosed correspondent from Euro-Gun she began to wonder if she'd made a mistake. He filled her glass with wine she didn't want, and immediately began to grill her about the degree of discrimination she experienced "as a woman in a man's world."

'But I don't. I mean I haven't,' she said rather indistinctly through a mouthful of ham.

He laughed. 'Oh, there's no need to be coy about it. I won't name names in my piece, but I'd just like a few examples of the kind of thing you encounter on a daily basis.'

'There's nothing to tell you,' she said more forcefully, swallowing the ham with an effort and wondering how to escape his questions.

'Let me put it another way, then. Are you a lezzie?'

'*What?*'

The ham had stuck in her throat. She swallowed again, coughing, and he patted her on the back in a patronising way. 'Steady on. I only asked if you are lesbian. You know? LGBT? Obviously it's the first thing a man thinks when he sees a pretty –'

A small hand plucked her sleeve, saving her from being rude to him. 'Where is toilet?' whined Pavel plaintively, jigging from foot to foot.

'I'll show you. This way.'

She jumped up and led him through the crowd still clustered round the serving-table, past the open kitchen door through which they glimpsed Anita and Luz speedily plating up tarts and trifles, and into the lobby with its heavily-encumbered coat-hooks. Just beyond it the drying-room was filled with a confusion of wet boots, guns, hats and cartridge belts steaming by the stove.

'The loos are just round the corner and on the right,' she said, pointing. 'Can you find your way back OK, or shall I wait?'

Pavel nodded, which could have meant either, and darted off down the passage, nearly colliding with Pauly as he emerged through the swing door. At the same moment Max came running towards her from the kitchen.

'Where's Pavel?'

'In the loo.'

'Is it down there?'

Before she could answer he trotted off to talk to Pauly, and Sally returned to the dining-room to find a seat as far as possible from Mr Quizzy of Euro-Gun.

Better luck this time, she thought, as white-whiskered Marcus Bellton, wheezing slightly, plonked a plate loaded with a substantial second helping on the place to her right, then lowered his portly self to the chair.

'Shame to let it go to waste,' he muttered, shovelling it into his mouth with gusto. Evidently his anger at Hartzog's duplicity didn't extend to boycotting his hospitality. From the end of the table Jericho caught Sally's eye and gave the tiniest wink, but even as he satisfied his enormous appetite, old Marcus still simmered like a volcano about to erupt, and as soon as he parked knife and fork on the empty plate, his grumbling broke out again.

'A thousand cows on zero grazing! It's unnatural, that's what it is, and that's what I tell the Planning Committee, but do they pay any heed to what I say? Hartzog's got half of them in his pocket, and the other half don't know their arse from their elbow. He tells 'em they've got to move with the times. There's no future in the old ways with livestock. It's all numbers now, and weighing and measuring every bite they eat.'

Jericho leaned towards him. 'They've turned it down once, Marcus. I don't think they'll change their minds.'

'Ah, but he'll try again. That's what he'll do: I know his sort. He'll keep niggling and pestering until he gets his way, and they won't have the guts to tell him to sod off,' said Marcus morosely. 'What with him and the bloody badgers, I dunno what farming's coming to.'

He pushed away his empty plate and Anita, hovering behind his chair, immediately substituted a large wedge of treacle tart, swimming in a lake of cream.

'Ta,' said Marcus absently, picking up his spoon.

'What about this environmental impact survey your son was talking about? Won't that help you?'

'Lot of high-flown nonsense, if you ask me.' Old Bellton was dismissive. 'My son Pauly's full of ideas but half the time they come to nothing. "Don't worry, Dad. I'll fix him," he says; but the truth is we've no way to fix him. I can't keep running to lawyers every time he puts in a new application, but he's got deep pockets, has Hartzog, and the gift of the gab.'

At the end of the room there was a flurry of activity and Sally saw Julius Lombard, who had been sitting halfway down the table, go across to whisper in Hartzog's ear and hand him a sheet of paper. After studying it for a moment he rose, rapping sharply on his glass. The roar of talk and laughter petered away into silence.

'Can I have your attention for a moment? Mr Lombard, who has been counting on his clicker every shot fired today, tells me the total so far stands at 778 shots. Now I propose that each of you makes a guess at what the total bag will be, and the one who comes closest gets an invitation to shoot here again next year. OK?'

Team Owen looked at one another and an assenting murmur ran round the room.

'Right, then. Mr Lombard will record your names and numbers. You first, Rodney.'

'Two hundred.'

'Basil? Barnaby?'

'Eighty. Seventy-six...'

The guesses varied wildly. Sally herself thought a ratio of one bird to every five shots would be about right, but some optimists on Team Owen were ready to believe nearly every cartridge had found its mark.

'Right,' said Hartzog, when everyone had made a guess. 'As you know, today's last hurrah will be flighting wildfowl on the lakes belonging to Mr Maude's shooting school. Locksley, is there anything you'd like to say?'

No answer. Sally had seen Locksley Maude slide out of the room ten minutes earlier.

Hartzog frowned slightly. 'He must have gone on ahead.

Never mind, he'll be there to put us in position. I'm sure I don't have to warn you not to talk as you approach the lake, and move as quietly as possible. All right? Now let's get going. Everyone boot up as quick as you can, and follow my car.'

A clatter of chairs scraping the wooden boards, a rush for the drying-room, and presently plaintive cries of, 'Where's my left boot?' 'Who's taken my jacket?' and, 'That's my gun-sleeve; yours is over there,' echoed through the building as Team Owen forced themselves into still-wet garments and laced their boots with fumbling fingers.

'Hurry,' urged Hartzog, pushing his way through the crowd and picking up his own gun. 'The daylight's going already.'

'Keep the socks,' said Anita, emerging from the kitchen to supervise the chaos. 'We'll have your own ones dry by the time you get back here. Now, has everyone got all his kit? Gun, cartridge bag, hat, coat, boots? Off you go, then, or the birds will be coming on to the lake before you get there.'

CHAPTER EIGHT

The Flight

The morning's heavy rain had cleared away, leaving gun-metal clouds underlit theatrically by the last rays of the sun as the party left the Dunmorse courtyard, and the temperature was dropping: a sharp frost was forecast.

Hagley had paid off the mixed team of beaters, retaining only three pickers-up with their dogs – all proven swimmers – to help with retrieving birds from in and around the lakes, so the procession led by Hartzog's Range Rover had been reduced to five vehicles carrying the Guns, plus the over-excited Max and Pavel, the keepers, and Julius Lombard with his clicker, while Robb pottered along behind with the game cart.

Though he had been sitting too long for the comfort of his reconstructed leg, he had enjoyed taking part in a shoot for the first time since he was a boy, when he had thought nothing of putting in twenty miles a day beating on Saturdays on North Yorkshire grouse-moors, while his father was stationed at Catterick Barracks. That had earned him the princely sum of a tenner, a pint and a pie, and though today's beaters probably earned three times as much, he thought neither the job nor the personnel had changed much since those far-off days.

He had also, though he was loath to admit it, enjoyed watching his daughter in her new role and couldn't suppress a flicker of pride at how quickly she had learned the ropes and dug herself a niche in this unfamiliar world. For the first time he had begun to think that this gamekeeping obsession of hers might lead to more than the dead-end job he had envisaged when she took it up. It could even be the foundation of a proper career: woodland and wildlife management was a political hot potato nowadays, and someone who understood it from the inside might find herself sought after by conservationists and landowners alike. Though he and Sally still treated one another with caution, their clashes during the past ten days had been minor, and he wondered now if any working father ever got to know his child properly until he was forced into its company without the diluting presence of wife or siblings.

Trouble is, we're too alike, he thought with a flash of self-knowledge. Neither of us can stand being pushed around, and though I've been forced to learn to button my lip, she hasn't yet.

The steep lane flattened out a couple of hundred yards short of the summit, forming a kind of platform, and there the motorcade halted in a lay-by.

'Don't slam the doors,' warned Locksley Maude, materialising from the shadow on a track overhung by trees. 'You stay here,' he said to Robb, and to the others, 'Quick, now. Follow me and try not to make a noise.' He was nervous, peremptory, even proprietorial: this was his big moment.

He hurried the party along the muddy lane and through a heavily chained but unlocked gate, and paused for a moment to let them take in the beauty of the scene. Before them lay the lakes, two four-acre crescents of shining black water, glimmering in the last light of the day. The pools were linked by a narrow causeway, with the many strategically-placed bays round the banks lined with clumps of alder and rhododendron. Concrete croys for fishermen extended into the bays, and each well-built hide of woven willow had a plank floor slightly raised above the swampy ground to give a secure footing.

A chain of small islands, some of them mere tufts of sedge and rushes, others with pebbled beaches and waist-high shrubs providing enticing nesting sites, speckled the dark water. It made a charming sight, and half-suppressed murmurs of admiration rose from Team Owen as they followed Maude to the hides around the lakes' perimeter; with Hartzog himself, Jericho and the two Belltons strategically placed on an outer crescent to shoot any birds going back.

'Changed a bit since I were here last,' rumbled Marcus Bellton with grudging admiration.

'Lovely job,' agreed Pauly.

When all were in place, Maude checked his watch. 'They should start flighting in twenty minutes or so,' he murmured to Sally as he hurried back to the gate where she and the other keepers were standing. 'Keep an eye on those youngsters. Don't let them start running around.'

Quarter of an hour crawled by and the boys had begun to fidget, looking up at the sky, and then –

'Reckon I hear 'em over yonder,' said Cecil Barley, cocking an ear towards the beech copse that sheltered Jackson's decrepit farm buildings, and as Sally strained her ears she, too, seemed to pick up a distant chatter and honking below the line of clouds.

'That's them,' said Maude, nodding. 'Now for it.'

A tense silence followed, broken only by the soft gurgling of water and occasional plop! of feeding fish. As always in moments of stress, Rodney's hand crept to his pocket to fiddle with his smartphone, worrying now that he should have gone with Uncle Thomas to A&E. What if he was left on a trolley all night? What would he tell his father?

Preoccupied with his thoughts, he failed to react fast enough to the whistle of wings as three teal glided right over his head within easy shot. Too late he fired towards the backmarker, but already two had alighted gracefully on the water, while the third flew back the way it had come. From his firing point at the oxbow lake's right-hand horn, Hartzog raised his gun, then lowered it without shooting.

Maude cursed. Wake up, you fucking idiot! he raged silently at Rodney, annoyed to find that his hands were shaking. Put your bloody mobile away and concentrate on what you're doing.

More spurts of flame from random shots erupted round the far side of the lake, then quite suddenly the air was dark with flighting birds as small parties of mallard, wigeon and teal zoomed in on their favourite islands. Fully alert now, Team Owen shot and reloaded, shot and reloaded until their barrels were hot and the parties of wildfowl had diminished to a trickle of solitary birds.

As the echoes of that bombardment died away, the Guns stared round, half-stunned, easing off their ear-defenders, eyes searching for where the birds they had shot had fallen.

'There's a mallard in those reeds. Shall I pick it up?' hissed Max, dancing on the spot, and was quickly quelled by Sally.

'Hush! Wait.'

'But it's not dead! It won't take a sec...'

'Wait!'

Hardly had she spoken before a V-shape skein of geese appeared above the trees, enormous targets magnified by the gloaming, zooming purposefully, to be met by flashes and staccato barks from the hides. More followed, and the guns thundered in response.

'Passchendaele,' gasped Basil to Barnaby in the hide they

were sharing. The sky was full of whirling birds, some landing, some getting up to circle the lakes, some plummeting into the water as shot after shot cracked out.

At its height the fusillade was deafening and seemed to go on for ever, though it probably lasted no more than three or four minutes before dying away into random shots and finally silence.

'That's it, then,' said Maude flatly, and put the horn to his mouth. He felt exhausted, wrung out with tension. His big moment was over. The Highflyers' Day was finished.

'Go on, boys. It's OK now,' said Sally, as the Guns emerged from their hides and dogs splashed about in the shallows, retrieving birds, 'and don't forget to pick up the cartridges. Where are your collecting sticks?'

Max and Pavel ran off, and she moved to help the twins, who were arguing over where they had marked birds. 'One's in the water just short of that island,' said Bas. 'Can you send a dog to fetch it?'

The lake shore was darkening by the minute, with figures silhouetted against the water, and dogs carefully carrying duck back to their whistling, shouting handlers.

'Good girl! Give... Thank you. Go fetch..!' they said as the retrievers worked steadily round the lake until every picker-up was weighed down by a beltful of wildfowl.

At the sound of the horn, Robb started his engine and drove up the track and through the gate where the Guns were gathering in a noisy, shifting group. Chatter and laughter, back-slapping and foot-stamping, boasts and laments: 'Couldn't hit a thing.' 'Must have shot a dozen.' 'Never seen anything like those geese.' 'My feet are like ice.'

Jericho joined them, and the Belltons; then Lombard strolled over with his clicker. 'I counted a hundred and fifty-seven shots,' he said, 'though I can't be sure I got them all.

We'll have to go back to the barn to tally up. It's too dark here. Where's Hartzog?'

Where indeed?

Jericho realised that subconsciously he had been waiting for Hansi's commanding tones to issue directions – orders, really – ever since the flight ended. It wasn't like him to let matters drift as they were doing now, with Rodney's team looking vaguely round, uncertain what they were supposed to do next. Were they meant to go back to the minibus for the long drive to London? Surely they should be thanking their host for his hospitality and for giving them a day's sport they would never forget? They were all longing to get home, but they wanted to do the right thing: they couldn't just disappear without a word.

Better take charge, he thought, since Locksley Maude didn't look as if he was going to. He was talking in a low voice to Cecil Barley, and seemed to have abdicated responsibility for bringing the day to a conclusion.

'Where did you ask Mr Hartzog to stand, Maude?' he called, and Maude broke off his conversation and walked over.

'He wasn't numbering, sir. He wanted to act as backstop, so I told him to cover the end of the lake between Marcus and Pauly.'

'That's right,' put in Pauly. 'I saw him when the first teal came over, but after that I lost sight of him. Isn't that right, Dad?'

'Never saw hide nor hair of him,' grunted Marcus unhelpfully. 'Time we got back to the farm, any road. Come on, Pauly. Animals want haying-up before dark and we can't go hanging about here any longer.'

For a moment it looked as if Pauly would dig in his heels, but after a glance at his father he shrugged and nodded.

They walked off and Jericho groaned inwardly. It had been a long day and the last thing he wanted was to make another circuit of the lakes looking for bloody Hartzog; but it had to be done.

'OK. The rest of us will go and look for him,' he said firmly. 'Leave your guns and clobber here on the cart, and split the party. He can't have gone far, and it shouldn't take us long to walk round.'

'Righto,' said Rodney, chilly now and glad of some action. 'Come on, lads, we'll go left-handed and meet Mr Oak in the middle.'

Max was tugging his sleeve, trying to get his attention. 'Dad! Look what we've —'

Jericho, who had quite forgotten the boys, looked round in search of help. 'Sorry to land this on you, Sally,' he said hurriedly, 'but I'd be glad if you'd take Max and Pavel back home now.'

'Oh, please let us come with you.'

'Absolutely not. You've been out quite long enough and Mum will be worrying. Go on with you, monkey!' He handed Sally his car keys, and added, 'Tell Marina I'll be back as soon as we get this sorted,' and hurried away after the others.

The cool, hypnotic notes of Beethoven's Moonlight Sonata rippled through the night air as Jericho approached the porch door and he paused for a moment on the threshold, unwilling to break the spell. Marina's ability to lose herself in her music was a marvel to him and he hated what he would have to do in the next few minutes, destroying her serenity by bringing news that was bound to distress her. Through the glass door of the porch he could see her seated at the piano, pale blonde head slightly bent over the keyboard in concentration, while her fingers flew from one crescendo to the next, one stabbing chord to another, with the haunting lyrical theme of the third movement singing through the chromatic runs and pyrotechnic brilliance right up to its triumphant resolution.

Taking a deep, steadying breath, he opened the door and in a single sinuous movement she swung round on the piano-stool and rose, hands clasped beneath her heart, questions bubbling out.

'What's happened? Why are you so late? Why didn't you ring me? I've been going mad. I couldn't make sense of what the boys were saying, and Sally just told me she had to get back to help look for Hansi. Is that true? How could he be missing?'

'Steady, steady,' he said, hugging her close. 'Yes, I'm afraid that was true enough.'

'Was?' Her face, always pale, was suddenly sheet-white. She stumbled and he caught her from falling.

'I didn't ring you because – well, he's always been a friend of yours and it's hardly something you can say over the telephone...'

Her eyes closed briefly and she drew a deep breath. 'Are you telling me that Hansi's hurt?' She read the truth in his face. 'He's dead?'

'I'm afraid so.'

'But what..? How? A heart attack?'

He swallowed hard, and said jerkily, 'Look, I'll tell you everything I know, but first I need a drink. Whisky. And so do you.'

Moving like a sleepwalker, she followed him into the kitchen and sat at the table while he poured them each a stiff tot.

'Tell me.' She shook her head. 'It seems unreal. I can't – can't take it in. He was fine at lunch. Really fine. Surely I'd have noticed if he wasn't well? I sat next to him, and he was in great form, joking away with those nice boys, saying the day was going brilliantly and he meant to hold another next year. And now you tell me he's dead.' Her voice trembled, and tears ran down her cheeks. Impatiently she brushed them away. 'I'm sorry. It's just such a shock.'

Still more of a shock for poor Rodney, he thought, who had stumbled over the face-down body some twenty yards back from the furthest hide, and attempted to turn it over. Fragments from the burst barrels had destroyed both Hansi's eyes, killing him instantly. The young man had been shaking from head to foot when his shouts brought Jericho and Hagley running; but he had mastered his horror and helped them rig up a floodlight attached to a long cable from Locksley Maude's workshop, and insisted on staying until the police arrived. A bad end to their special day, but in the circumstances he had to acknowledge that Team Owen had behaved extremely well.

'Drink up,' he said to Marina, downing his own whisky and pouring another; but her glass was barely touched as she re-lived her own last conversation with Hartzog.

'He was so well. So completely normal. I just can't believe there was anything wrong with his heart. Most of the time he was telling me how he had bought this special gun which had belonged to some dictator – president –'

He nodded. 'Enver Hoxha.'

'That's right. Hansi had the stock altered to fit him because he shot off his left shoulder with his right eye. Cast off, he called it.'

And it was this very special gun which had blown up in his face. Jericho sighed and said, 'Listen, darling, I'm afraid you've got the wrong end of the stick. It wasn't a heart attack that killed Hansi. It was an accident. A terrible accident.'

Huge-eyed, she stared at him, trying to take it in. 'You mean someone shot him?'

'No, no! Nothing like that.'

'Then what?'

Jericho said reluctantly, 'Well, in a way you could say he shot himself. We won't know exactly until we get a proper forensic report, but it looked to me as if the gun barrels burst when he fired.'

'How could they?'

'As I say, I just don't know. Maybe he fell over and they got full of mud. Maybe there was some flaw in the metal.'

'But he had just had the stock altered to fit him. Wouldn't the gunsmith have checked the barrels at the same time?'

'It's no good asking me, darling,' said Jericho wearily.

Marina bowed her head, her mind racing, testing theories, considering implications. After a while she said, 'Does Kelly-Louise know ?'

'Last heard of cruising in the Caribbean with the son from her first marriage. Luz is trying to contact her.'

'I suppose she'll inherit everything,' said Marina remotely, 'and that'll be the last thing she wants. Think of it: all that work, all that imagination, all that money that Hansi ploughed into Dunmorse – gone. Now it will go to someone who has said from the moment he bought it that she can't stand the place. Talk about irony!'

Jericho stared at her; this wasn't the reaction he expected, but although she looked dreamy, Marina was nothing if not practical.

'Steady on, darling. You're getting ahead of yourself. We don't know any of that. He may have left everything to a cats' home, or his second cousin once removed. All we can be sure of is that there's been an accident – a tragic accident. Hartzog is dead, and it's left to us to pick up the pieces.'

But even as he spoke he knew he was clutching at straws. He could think of only one way to make the barrels of a twelve-bore shatter when it was fired, and that was to ram some hard objects into them before it was loaded. Hansi had been by no means universally popular in Starcliffe, but who had hated him enough to do that?

PART TWO

CHAPTER NINE

The Boys

24th JANUARY

The icy gust of wind that blew in when Jericho opened the cottage door scattered the heap of letters which Robb was sorting through. Ten months since Meriel died, and still he hadn't replied to all of them, but with Sally out on the quad, checking damage from last night's storm, and Pilot sprawled snoring on the sagging sofa in front of the woodstove, he had determined to tackle them again.

'No, no,' said Jericho, hastily shutting the door. 'Please don't get up, I'm sorry to burst in on you like this, but I saw you were on your own and wondered if I could have a word?'

'Of course.' Robb sank back in his chair. Getting up in a hurry was still difficult unless he had something solid to press the back of his legs against. He was shocked to see how Jericho had aged in a few days. Deep new lines creased his forehead and his eyes looked heavy-lidded, as if he hadn't slept. It wasn't hard to guess what was worrying him, but for the sake of form he said lightly, 'I'm always ready to put off letter-writing. So how can I help? Fire away.'

'Here, budge over, old boy.' Jericho shoved Pilot into the

corner of the sofa, and plumped down where he could face Robb directly. 'I don't for a moment blame the police,' he began, though his tone suggested the opposite. 'They've got a sudden death to investigate, and naturally they want to know how it happened, who was involved, and so on. But the way it's going – '

He broke off, then said jerkily, 'My wife thought you might be able to advise us. God knows we need advice. We just don't know what to do, and she's worried sick that she may say something that will make matters worse. Are you with me?'

'About the accident? Of course I'll do what I can to help, just as anyone would,' said Robb. 'But you must realise I'm not here in an official capacity. I'm on sick leave. I can't influence the local police in any way.'

'No, no. Of course not. As far as I can make out, Robin Seymour, the solicitor, has got everything in hand – managed to contact Kelly-Louise –'

'Hartzog's wife?'

'That's right. They're not divorced: more of an amicable separation, and she's flying back from Indonesia, where she's been filming in the back of beyond, any day now. No, no. That's not our problem, and as I say, it's not the police's fault: they're trying to find out what happened, and it's pretty clear now what caused the explosion. The remains of twenty-bore cartridges on the ground near the body indicate that someone had slipped them into Hartzog's twelve-bore, so when he loaded the right cartridges on top of them, both barrels burst. Fragments of metal penetrated his eyes and into his brain, killing him. Now, how this happened is another matter. In other words, who put the wrong cartridges into his gun?'

Robb listened, his face impassive. Though Jericho sounded calm enough, there was a suggestion of tightly suppressed anger – or was it fear? – in his movements, and a tic beside his left eye was jumping. Let him get it off his chest first, he thought, and then we can go through it all properly.

Jericho said, 'Anyone will tell you the simplest explanation is often the correct one. If it looks like a duck and it quacks like a duck – you know? And the simplest explanation here is that our two youngsters who were mucking about with the guns while the grown-ups were eating in the next room thought it would be fun to try loading them. It's the kind of stupid thing boys do – but in this case it had tragic results. Right so far?'

Robb nodded. 'It's possible.'

'More than possible. I'd say it was likely. Boys showing off. Egging one another on. But then something went wrong. They could have put a couple of twenty-bore cartridges into Hartzog's twelve-bore gun, and because they were too small they slipped down the barrels and stuck, and the boys couldn't get them out again.' He paused. 'Does that sound feasible to you?'

Without waiting for an answer, he went on, 'If that had happened, I guess they would have panicked. Perhaps they thought they could shake them out by poking from the other end. And then perhaps someone came in, wanting the loo, and they scarpered.'

'Surely if that had happened they would have asked an adult for help?'

'I doubt it. They knew they were being naughty even touching the guns, and they did touch them. They told me so.'

'So...? Robb's eyebrows rose.

'So I don't – can't – blame the police for assuming they were the culprits. Open and shut case. Not looking for anyone else, they tell me.'

'But you don't think they are?'

'No. Marina and I have been talking, questioning, testing their story, off and on, ever since. We've questioned them, the police have questioned them, a child psychologist has questioned them both together and apart, and they absolutely deny trying to load any of the guns. They're quite happy to admit that they picked them up, and pretended to aim, and discussed the weight and the different bores, and which had the finest engraving, but nothing will make them say that they put anything into any of them.'

'Do you believe them?'

'Yes, I do,' said Jericho firmly. 'Max can be a little devil at times, but he's not a liar.'

'What about the other boy – Pavel?'

Jericho hesitated. 'Well, that's a bit different. I don't know him so well, obviously, but I'd say he takes his cue from Max. In any case, his father is pretty strict with him. His mother's back in Poland with four other children, and Tomasz works night and day to send her money and keep the family afloat. If Pavel steps out of line, he gets a clip around the ears and off to bed with no supper. It's a different mindset: they think we're soft with our children, and we think they're brutal, but it makes no odds because they all turn out much the same in the end.'

Robb nodded, thinking it over. On the face of it, the boys were far the most likely suspects; they had been in and out of the lobby and drying-room during lunch; Sally had even shown Pavel the way to the lavatories, and seen Max emerging from the kitchen.

He himself had eaten in the cart-shed with the beaters, and had seen both Max and Pavel from time to time, clearly bored with the length of the meal, sparring with their magnetic sticks, pulling faces for selfies, and counting the birds hung on the game-cart.

He asked, 'How old is Max? Ten-ish?'

'He'll be nine next month. Pavel is about six months older.' Anticipating Robb's next words, he went on, 'I know that makes them below the age of criminal responsibility, but that's neither here nor there. Max may be only eight years old, but he's no fool and perfectly capable of putting two and two together – even if in this case they make five.'

'Meaning?'

Jericho made an impatient noise. 'Meaning he can see where all this questioning is heading. He liked Hartzog, who sometimes gave the pair of them a joyride in his helicopter, and of course for the past three days it's been all over the village that Hartzog was killed because his gun barrels burst during that last drive. Now people keep asking him and Pavel whether either of them put anything down those gun barrels, so what conclusion do you think he draws from that?'

Robb said carefully, 'Obviously there'll be an inquest, but that won't be for about three months, and the Coroner is bound to return a conclusion of Accident. Even if the boys did tamper with Hartzog's gun, they couldn't be prosecuted.'

'What difference does that make? They would still grow up knowing that people thought they were murderers. Does that sound to you like the recipe for a happy childhood? It would be like a black cloud hanging over the pair of them. And besides –'

He stopped, gently pushing away the nose with which Pilot was exploring his pocket, then got up and walked over to open the front of the stove and put another log in.

'Besides?' Robb could see what he was driving at, but wanted it put into words.

'I don't want Max haunted by this. I don't want him to lose his confidence in people, and already I see signs that it's ebbing away. Making him more secretive: more... guarded. He's always said exactly what he thinks the moment he thinks of it, which can be maddening, I admit, but now if you ask him something – even nothing to do with Hartzog, or guns, or anything like that – he just clams up.'

He paused, looking searchingly at Robb as if wondering if he really understood. 'Think back to your own childhood. Can you remember an occasion when nobody would believe what you said? When you knew perfectly well that you were telling the truth but you couldn't convince the grown-ups? All right, I may be wrong and the boys may be telling a pack of lies, but it's worth considering this: if they didn't put the wrong cartridges into Hartzog's gun, someone else must have. Someone who knew exactly what the result was likely to be. And if the boys are blamed for the accident, that murdering someone will get off scot-free.'

For a moment they sat in a silence broken only by Pilot's snores. Then Jericho sighed and said, 'Marina and I have been going over this again and again, round and round. It's driving us crazy. I know you're on sick leave and not supposed to be working, but do you think you could quietly look into it? Talk to people? Try to get the whole picture?'

'I could hardly go over the heads of my colleagues here. Professional etiquette, you know.'

Robb knew he sounded like a self-righteous prat, but Jericho said quickly, 'Oh, no. Nothing like that. I wouldn't ask you to. But if you just thought it over, sort of below the radar, and chatted to people who were there and might have noticed something. Oh, I dunno...' he ended with a despairing shrug, and Robb wondered how much of this was calculated and how much real. By all accounts, Jericho Oak had not been Hartzog's greatest fan.

He said briskly, 'Just talking to people? Thinking it through? Well, I reckon I could see my way to doing that without treading on too many toes.'

'Thanks.' The relief on Jericho's worried face was too profound to be faked. 'Marina will be so pleased. She's sensitive, highly-strung. She gets very emotional, you know, being an artist, and Hartzog's death has hit her hard. He was – well, rather a special friend of hers. They shared a lot of the same interests, and to think that Max had anything to do with his death has really freaked her out.' He paused, then added awkwardly, 'I know, and she knows that Max is telling the truth, but we can't expect the police to see it like that.'

Special friend. Ho-hum, thought Robb, but that didn't necessarily make them lovers, though it might breed jealousy in the odd-man-outside the charmed circle.

He said, 'Tell me more about Max. Would you say he was obsessed with guns? Lots of boys are.'

Jericho considered for a moment. 'Obsessed, no. But interested, yes. Definitely yes. Obviously he knows quite a lot about them, he could hardly help it, living here. Guns and shooting – it's all part of the daily round, the common task. And he knows it will all belong to him eventually. Ever since he was quite small, he's been coming round the rearing field with me and Duncan. Helped us put out the pegs for shooting days, that kind of thing.'

'What about safety?'

'Oh, well – I hope that went in with mother's milk. He learned *Never, never let your gun, Pointed be at anyone* before *One, two, buckle my shoe.* And he knows the rest of it, too.'

'And Pavel?'

'Pretty much the same, I'd say. Tomasz, his dad, is what one might call a keen hunter-gatherer. More of a catcher-man than a fisherman, if you see what I mean.'

'A poacher, in other words.'

'You could call it that. Only for the pot, mind you. People round here tend to wink at it, though I've heard he's had some pretty sharp exchanges with Locksley Maude. Poor Maude! Not quite the way he wanted his duck-flight to end. I saw Anita this morning – you know, the girl who handled the catering – and she'd heard from Luz that he's really cut up about it.'

'So Luz is a friend of Maude's?' Robb made a mental note.

'She gives him a hand with his accounts, and I'm told he calls her in to help launch clays when he's short-handed at the shooting-school.'

'How does that work?'

Jericho shrugged. 'You'll have to ask him. Can't see the fun in it, myself, but apparently it's on the same lines as a round of golf. Clients go round a pre-set course, shooting clay pigeons from a lot of different traps designed to test their reflexes. Different speeds, different angles, like the flight of different birds. They call them High Pheasant, Springing Teal, that kind of thing. Some traps launch three birds at once and you have to shatter them all to score. Then the points are totted up and the best man wins.'

'I see.' Robb had never played golf, but he enjoyed fishing. 'So Maude runs these lessons and courses, and operates the catch-and-release as well? Busy man!'

'Pretty keen to make money, too, I gather,' said Jericho, nodding. 'The word on the street is that he had to borrow more than he bargained for to get the place up and running, and now we're leaving Europe, where most of his clients come from, he's having trouble paying it back. Losing a customer like Hartzog will hit him badly.'

'And Luz? Where does she fit in?'

'Oh, she's a girl of many talents,' said Jericho non-committally, pushing away Pilot as he competed for more space.

'Which are?'

'Anita's the expert on that. For myself, I'd say that survival is probably foremost among them. An ability to hitch her wagon to any star she reckons is rising – though choosing

Hartzog now turns out to have been less than brilliant.'

'Was she his housekeeper?

'Not exactly. From what I gathered, she did a bit of everything. PA, cook, you name it.' He gave Robb a sideways glance. 'I never listen to gossip, of course, but people say that when the boss was abroad, she's been seen driving away from that club-house of Maude's at some pretty unsocial hours. No doubt Anita could fill you in on that, too.'

He looked at his watch and got up. 'Sorry, I'm keeping you from your letters and Sally will be back any moment. I must go and put Marina's mind at rest. Thank you so much for offering to help us.'

I didn't exactly offer, thought Robb with some amusement. Aloud he said, 'Before you go, tell me: does Max know I'm with the police?'

Jericho looked surprised. 'Nobody knows except me and Marina. When I interviewed your daughter, she asked me to keep quiet about your profession. She said she never let on to her friends at school, because as soon as people knew her dad was a cop, they treated her differently, and she didn't want that here.'

'Good. Let's keep it that way for the moment,' said Robb briskly. 'One other question: what's Lombard's position with regard to the shoot? I didn't expect to see him out last Saturday, because Sal told me he's — and I quote — "an absolute pain to farmers who want to keep down the badger population," which doesn't quite square with supporting pheasant-shooting.'

'Quite a lot of Lombard's opinions don't square with others,' Jericho agreed. 'He's a clever chap and no doubt he can rationalise them to himself, but I must admit he often has me baffled. Sally's more or less right about the badgers. He has an ongoing feud with Pauly and Marcus Bellton because he thinks they bump them off quietly and get rid of the corpses by pretending they're road casualties – which may or may not be true, but personally I wouldn't blame them, seeing how they've suffered from bovine TB in the past decade. So he's anti-Bellton, pro-badger, but at the same time he's rabidly anti-deer, pro-foxhunting, and pretty well neutral when it comes to shooting pheasants.'

Robb groaned inwardly. Talking to Lombard would involve walking on eggshells. 'A mass of inconsistencies, then, to say the least. Why's he so anti-deer?'

'Because he loves his garden, especially his roses, and so do the local muntjac and roe.'

'Can't he scare them off? Shoot them?'

'Not so easy when you live cheek-by-jowl with neighbours who think they're adorable. They'd be up in arms at once if he shot one, and besides, he teaches in the local primary and has to get there at eight-thirty in the morning. He says that as he shuts the garden gate, the deer stroll in via the dustbins and there's not a damned thing he can do about it. Look, I really must be going.'

He stood up abruptly, patted the snoring dog, then turned at the door to say, 'As to why he was at the Shoot, I don't know if Sally told you, but he was blown up pretty badly in Afghanistan. Invalided out of the Army with PTSD. And then to cap it all, his wife left him. So Marina and I do what we can to keep an eye on him, invite him to lunch, that kind of thing. I asked Hartzog if he'd make him responsible for the clicker – tallying up the shots – since he's about the only local who can both count beyond ten and be trusted not to cheat... Joking,' he added, smiling.

'What does he teach?'

'Maths. IT. Technology. Games. The boys think he's great because he was in the Army. Do you want to talk to them after school? The bus puts them off around 4.20, and they're usually back before five, provided they don't spend too much time messing about in the woods. Amazing how long boys can spend dawdling on the way home.'

'Isn't it dark by then?'

'Oh, we make them take head-torches at this time of year and of course they've got their mobiles. They know their way like the back of their hands.'

Robb thought it over and said, 'Later, maybe. I'll keep you posted.'

'Excellent.' He sketched a wave and was gone. Robb heard him chatting to Sally outside as his footsteps scrunched away.

Jericho's question still echoed in his mind. Do you remember any occasion when you told the truth and nobody would believe you? Well, yes, he could clearly remember that happening when he was very much the same age as Max was now. The class rabbit had escaped on his watch, and everyone from Miss Evans to the boy who sat next to him insisted that he must have failed to fasten the door of the hutch. He knew very well that he had, and put the peg through the hasp, but no one believed him.

For a whole morning he had stuck to his story, increasingly miserable and defiant, while all the grown-ups and other children in his class told him he was wrong, he was dreaming, he had forgotten, that nobody blamed him for letting the rabbit out but naughty boys who told lies went to hell, and he had felt an awful overwhelming despair that nothing he could say would make them see he was telling the truth.

Then at lunchtime – the miracle. Two of the big girls from the top class told Miss Evans they were very sorry, but they had opened Cottontail's hutch to give her a carrot, and she had jumped out before they could shut the door again. Relief had washed over him, especially because he had been on the verge of admitting to something he hadn't done, just to stop the questioning... Were Max and Pavel feeling like that?

Mentally he composed a list, then pushed aside his letters and wrote it down. He'd have to talk to them all: Lombard first. As their teacher, he should have a pretty clear idea whether the boys' story could be trusted. Marina herself, whose attitude to Hartzog seemed ambivalent, to say the least; Anita, who apparently knew all the gossip; and then there was the anomalous position of Luz in the Dunmorse household, plus her relationship with Locksley Maude. Perhaps he should indulge himself in a day's fishing.

He felt energised, glad of the chance to do something other than sit around worrying about his future. 'Come on, Pilot,' he said and the dog stretched and yawned widely, sensing his change of mood. 'Time we went for a walk.'

Julius Lombard's cottage was the middle one of a group of three former millworkers' homes on the outskirts of the village. With their undulating roof-lines and tiny leaded window-panes, they were long on charm but probably short on mod cons, thought Robb, and on a Saturday morning after a storm, a man who loved his garden might well be clearing gutters and sweeping up the night's debris. Spot on, he thought, as he walked round the back of the building and discovered Julius Lombard with a stepladder and long pole scooping wodges of sodden leaves out of the hopper of the downpipe above the back door.

'Stand clear!' he warned, as Robb approached, and with a strong sweeping movement he dislodged the bloc obstructing the top of the pipe, sending a gush of water out of the bottom onto the concrete path. 'So satisfactory,' he remarked, climbing down the ladder. 'I think I'm really a plumber manqué. Hello, Robb, nice to see you down this way. Everything all right? How's the leg coming on?'

He was friendly; a brown-faced, brown-haired, six-footer with deep creases between the eyebrows, and the head-up, stomach-in bearing that to Robb shouted Army; and evidently glad of the chance to chat, as people who live alone so often are. 'Won't you come in? I was about to put on a kettle.'

'Sounds good to me.'

Robb kicked off his gumboots and left Pilot to guard them while he followed his host into the stone-flagged kitchen, where every surface was piled with school-books, the sink full of soaking saucepans and the draining boards with crockery. 'Sorry about the mess,' said Lombard, half-embarrassed, following his glance. 'As you see, I live alone, but it's one of Greta's days, so she'll do a big clean-up later. Will your dog be all right out there?'

'He's OK,' said Robb absently, gazing round, taking it all in. 'My wife taught him to guard, so he won't move until I do.'

Two or possibly three small rooms had been knocked together to form one large living area with the kitchen at one end. Beyond it were grouped scruffy but comfortable-looking chairs, several tables covered with photographic equipment and cardboard boxes and books, books, and more books heaped on stools, tables, and, more tidily, in bookshelves. A row of green filing cabinets and a stand of white wire baskets, a litter of large glossy prints, and a winking router hinted at more than a passing interest in technology, and complicated cats' cradles of flex snaked from a banana-shaped desk to multi-plugs on the floor. Old-fashioned radiators and a few bright handwoven rugs barely took the chill off the outside temperature.

'Tell me, how's the new knee?' said Lombard, handing

him a steaming mug. 'Sugar?' He hesitated, then said, 'Sally told me about the car crash. I'm so sorry.'

'Thanks.' Rob cleared his throat. 'Well, the physio warned me the knee would take a while, and said I must try to walk a bit farther every day, but to be perfectly honest I'm always glad to sit down.'

'Sit as long as you like. No ref duty for me today because the Waterstone Colts cancelled last night. Half their the team is down with some bug and we could do without our lot catching it. Pity, because the under-elevens is always a needle match.'

'Does Max Oak play for your under-elevens?'

'Max Vereker,' corrected Lombard. 'He's Jericho's stepson, didn't you know? But yes, he's our star player, and that mate of his, Pavel, is getting the hang of it by degrees. He's our IT whizz, and it's a shame his father can't afford a decent laptop for him. Typical Pole, though: flashes of brilliance followed by sudden complete collapses. Keen naturalist: mustard on bird recognition.' He leaned forward, very much the concerned schoolmaster. 'It would have done young Max a power of good to get out on the rugger field and forget his worries for an hour or so. Poor kid: he's had a bad few days.'

'They both have.'

'Well, yes, but I doubt if Pavel realises the implications as much as Max does.'

'Do you believe their story?'

Lombard thought it over, stirring his coffee into a miniature whirlpool. 'Well, yes and no,' he said at last. 'That to say, yes I believe they're telling the truth, but I think there's more to it than they are admitting. When I walked past that drying-room on my way to the Gents, I caught a glimpse of a man in some kind of a green fleece jacket or body-warmer, you know the sort of thing, bending over that long table they'd put the guns on, and I'm pretty sure it was

Pauly Bellton. Then when I came back past, a few minutes later, the boys were in the passage, heading out to the cart-shed where you had your lunch. You must have seen them. They were in and out all the time.'

'And Pauly?'

Lombard shook his head. 'I didn't see him, but that doesn't mean he wasn't there. The atmosphere was pretty thick.'

'But surely he wouldn't encourage boys that age to play around with guns?'

Robb suspected he was overdoing the surprise, but Lombard said grimly, 'You may be sure, but I'm not. Those Belltons are a law to themselves; think they can get away with anything. Old Marcus has had it in for Hartzog ever since he put in his application for a big dairy unit just down the lane from Castle Farm. Didn't you hear him breathing fire and brimstone just before Hartzog arrived in his chopper? If Pauly saw a way to do him a bad turn, he'd take it, I've no doubt about it.'

'Well, maybe. But booby-trapping his gun is rather more than a bad turn.'

Lombard said reflectively, 'Anyway, that's why I don't entirely trust the boys' story. If Pauly made them promise to keep quiet, hell would freeze over before they'd admit he'd been there with them. When it comes to *omerta*, a Mafia *consigliere* can't compare with an eight-year-old English boy.'

'Or Polish?'

'Or Polish,' said Lombard firmly.

Robb took a gulp of his coffee, crunched the accompanying biscuit, and said, 'Sorry, I must go. I'm holding you up.'

'Not a bit of it. To be honest, I've been wanting to talk this over with someone who hasn't got an axe to grind. The whole thing is so bizarre. Unthinkable in a place like this.'

The age-old comment – shocked, disbelieving, almost indignant – how often had Robb heard it from people caught up by chance in crime? It was no good pointing out that nasty, brutal incidents did take place even on the most bland and blameless doorsteps. Lombard had escaped from the kind of hell created by war, and now violence had invaded his quiet refuge. No wonder it preyed on his mind.

'How did you get on with Hartzog yourself?' he asked. 'Sal mentioned him now and then, but actually I saw him only that once, at the Highflyers', when it struck me that he certainly had a sense of theatre.' Just as it now struck him that the murmured phrase, 'Deus ex machina,' probably came from Lombard himself.

'Oh, yes. Bags of it. He missed his vocation: should have been an actor. He loved being the centre of attention, witness all the hoo-ha over getting the Press to cover his Shoot. In my mind that signals insecurity rather than confidence, but what do I know? I'm only a school-teacher.'

'Interesting,' said Robb.

'As to how I got on with him, our ways hardly crossed. From time to time I'd meet him when I walked in the woods, but of course I heard about him from other people.'

'People with an axe to grind?'

'Some of them. *De mortuis*, you know, but he wasn't exactly popular – threw his weight around too much. A force of Nature. Always wanted to be the biggest and best, and inclined to trample anyone who got in his way. I wasn't a threat to him, so he hardly rated me. In fact I was surprised when he asked me to count the shots last Saturday. I guess that was Jericho's idea – or Marina's, and since one of my younger colleagues had volunteered to referee the Cubs, I agreed.' The corners of his mouth twisted. 'Never turn down a free lunch, is my motto.'

'Sal said it was pretty lavish.'

'True.' Lombard rolled his eyes. 'More than true – it was ridiculous. Those young men would have been quite happy with soup and cheese instead of three courses and all that booze. Look at the time it wasted! I know they were all wet and cold, but it really wasn't necessary to cosset them to that degree. Dry socks – I ask you! No wonder there was a scrimmage when they all had to dress up again to face the elements, with Hartzog chivvying them to catch the last of the light. It was chaotic.'

And not much wonder then if in the chaos Hartzog didn't check his own gun barrels as he hurried off to the end of the lake, thought Robb, consulting his watch. 'Thanks for the coffee, and it's time I faced the elements myself,' he said with a smile, 'or my daughter will get no lunch.'

'Role reversal, eh? Well, do drop by any time. I've enjoyed talking to you.'

'Ditto,' said Rob, and took himself off.

CHAPTER TEN

Anita

In his own mind Robb was scrupulously avoiding the word 'interviewing.' These weren't interviews, with their overtones of police work and officialdom, but simply friendly chats in which he tried to work out the sequence of events which had led to Hartzog's death, while keeping an ear open for any suggestion or evidence that might put young Max and Pavel in the clear.

The question of who to have a friendly chat with next was decided for him when he found a white Citroen van parked in front of the gamekeeper's cottage, with a delicious aroma of freshly-baked pastry wafting from the open back door. Both side panels bore the words CLASSY COUNTRY COOKING in shocking pink Gothic lettering, with ribbon bows and curlicues fore and aft, and wedged in the door was a shapely female rump which he recognised as belonging to Anita Carew, bending forward to lift out a white cardboard tray loaded with sausage rolls.

'Hang on, I'll give you a hand with that,' he said automatically before remembering that both his hands were occupied with his walking poles, and if he discarded them he might easily fall on the steps.

'It's OK, Dad,' called Sally, skipping down the short flight. 'Anita's had a party cancelled at the last minute, and is offering us some of the fallout.'

'A wedding, actually.' Attractively flushed and dishevelled, Anita backed out of the van. 'A wedding which will not now take place. The marquee's up, the order of service printed, the flowers flown in from Kenya, but the bride has pulled out, so that's that. Some people! I've made all the food and they've paid for it, and now they tell me to get rid of it any way I like – so I thought I'd give you first refusal.'

'Lucky old us. Gosh! Take a look, Dad.'

Robb peered into the van. Cakes, sandwiches, stuffed buns, profiteroles oozing cream: none of it looked exactly slimming but he was hungry after his walk and even Pilot, notoriously picky about his food, raised his muzzle to sniff the air with interest.

'Come on,' urged Anita. 'Take what you like. It'll all freeze fine.'

She and Sally heaped cardboard trays onto the kitchen table until Robb said, 'Steady on. Only so much will go in that freezer. Leave a bit for other people.'

'Thanks so much, Annie.' Sally gave her a hug. 'You're a star. This'll keep us going for weeks.'

Robb added his thanks, pushing away his vision of canapés for breakfast, lunch and supper, and Anita smiled.

'Don't mention it. You're doing me a favour. God, it's all been such a rush. I was up half the night glazing and icing, and then I got this call at crack of dawn to say the whole thing's off.'

Sally glanced at the clock. 'I must go. Jericho's asked me and Duncan to meet him at the office to talk about Wednesday's Shoot.'

'So they're going ahead with that?'

'Jericho said there's no reason why not. I know...'

'It seems a bit – well – insensitive.'

'Um-hm.' Sally knotted her laces, wound on a scarf and grabbed her butcher-boy cap. The door banged behind her and Pilot, who had half-risen, sank back with his head on his paws.

Anita plonked herself on the sofa beside him, brushing dog hairs from her trousers. 'Mind if I stay and warm up for a moment?'

'Of course not. Do you want some tea?'

'Just now I think I never want to see food or drink again in my life.'

Robb allowed her a moment's silence, then said, 'That was a bad business last weekend.'

'One of my best clients,' she said mournfully. 'Lavish. Open-handed. Decisive. Appreciative. Not like this last lot.' She waved a dismissive hand at the boxes of food. 'No, he was nothing like them! He wanted nothing but the finest, no matter what it cost, though I must say he checked the accounts pretty carefully before he paid them.' She sighed. 'Mind you, he could be an absolute beast at times. You just had to stand up to him and then nine times out of ten he'd give way. He'd bully anyone weaker than himself – look at the way he treated Luz.'

'How did he treat her?'

'Like dirt. Worse. As I say, you had to stand up and fight your corner, and she wasn't in a position to do that.' She paused, seeing the question in his eyes, and added delicately, 'It's tricky for her because I don't think her papers are quite the thing.'

An illegal, then. Why wasn't he surprised? 'Tricky,' he agreed. 'How did she come to work for him?'

Gossip was the breath of life to Anita. She sat back, stretching her legs out comfortably, ready to spill beans. 'Right. Well, as far as I can gather, her mum was half-Spanish, scratching a living on the outskirts of Algiers with a succession of boyfriends, each nastier than the last, when some smoothie in a Mercedes passing through the village spotted her beautiful daughter waitressing in a café, and said he could get her a job in films. In England. The only snag was it would cost five thousand euros to smuggle her into the country. The mum fell for it, but of course she hadn't got the dosh. Smoothie said that was fine, Luz could pay him back when she began earning... and, well, that was it, really. The film job didn't exist. They'd taken away her passport, and she was in hock to the smugglers to the tune of five thousand euros.'

'So Hartzog stepped in?'

'Effectively, yes. You could say he bought her. King Corphetua personified. Picked her up in some nail-bar and said she'd be better off working for him. Paid off her debt to the smugglers, got her passport back: she thought she'd died and gone to heaven, but it didn't take long for her to fall back to earth. I've seen her literally crying with exhaustion after one of his weekend parties. Oh, yes. Hansi liked to get the most out of his investments. And then there was that horrid business about the hedgehogs.' She shuddered. 'That put me off him big time.'

Robb frowned. Sally had talked a lot about Hartzog, but never mentioned hedgehogs. 'What was that?'

'Oh!' Anita hesitated as if regretting having raised the subject.

'Go on. I'm interested. You hardly ever see them where I live.'

'OK,' she said reluctantly, 'I'll tell you though actually it still makes me sick to remember. Pauly Bellton – who else? – had taken rather a shine to Luz, and brought her two orphaned hoglets to look after until they were fat enough to return to the wild. It's the sort of thing he does.'

'So Sal tells me.'

'They were so cute, snuffling about like tiny bristly pigs. Adorable. She was really pleased with them, and showed them to me; but when I next asked about them she burst into tears and said they had died. So of course I asked What of? and she said that Hartzog had come into the kitchen and found her feeding them, and asked where she'd got them. When she said Pauly had given them to her he was furious, completely unreasonable. He said they had fleas, he wasn't going to have them in his house, and she must get rid of them. She said OK, she'd give them back to Pauly, but then –' Anita's voice suddenly wobbled – 'he said he didn't want Pauly hanging about here, keeping her from her work, so he would get rid of them right now, and he opened the Aga's top oven and threw them in. 'She sniffed and wiped her eyes. 'Sorry... It was such a horrible thing to do.'

'Vile,' he agreed, shocked. This was certainly a different side to Hansi Hartzog. No wonder there were people who had detested him.

'So that's why I say he could sometimes be a beast. But of course at other times he was completely charming.'

'What will she do now, d'you think?' Robb asked, and she blew out a deep breath, puffing her cheeks with eyebrows raised.

'That's the question. Poor Luz – she's never had much luck. She's free now, but she's seriously skint. I've said she can work for me a couple of days a week, but that's not going to keep the wolf from the door for long, and when Kelly-Louise finally gets here she'll need a roof over her head as well.'

'Mrs Hartzog, you mean? What's she like?'

Anita laughed, 'Oh, she's great gas! You'll see. Thin as a rail, tough as old boots, cropped hair, chain-vapes awful strawberry-smelling stuff through a long amber holder, swears like a trooper, and wore a red satin jumpsuit to her wedding, or so I'm told.'

'Sounds... er... unconventional.'

'You can say that again! But she's fun. In the advertising world, she's a Big Star. Spends her time exploring remote corners of the globe, on foot, with a mile-long train of porters, camels, baggage mules and armed guards tramping behind her, finding locations for photo-shoots; then she flies in top models to drape themselves over rocks or waterfalls in their flimsies and sells the result to American glossies. Quite crazy! She'd eat little Luz for breakfast.'

'Or perhaps let her stay on as housekeeper,' suggested Robb, but Anita shook her head.

'More likely she'll put the whole shebang on the market as soon as she can. Kelly-Louise is a nomad at heart, and the last thing she'd want would be a stonking great house in England.' She was silent for a moment, then said with a sigh, 'What Luz yearns for is a nice solid English husband to give her a nice solid English baby, so she can forget about papers and passports and live happily ever after.'

'You mean to say there've been no takers?'

She gave him a sideways glance. 'Takers, all right; but no stayers. My guess is that she's a bit too keen. Scares them off. To date, all the local lads she's targeted have backed off smartly.'

'You surprise me. Even Pauly Bellton?'

Anita laughed. 'Afraid so. Things looked promising for a time, but Pauly's a wily bird. Girlfriends – yes. The more the merrier, but 'taste and try before you buy' is his motto.'

'What about Hartzog himself?'

'Lord, no!' She shook her head emphatically. 'Strictly a business arrangement. To be honest, I always thought he was gay – rather too determinedly super-manly, you know – though when I said so to my cousin Jericho he thought I was raving.'

Robb reflected on personal relationships, and the layout

of the barn, and the comings and goings from dining area and kitchen. He said, 'That was a great lunch you put on for the Shoot. You and Luz must have been run off your feet.'

'We certainly were. Back and forth, to and fro, carrying drinks and food: I didn't even have time to pee. Of course it was mainly because everything got held up because of silly old Whatsisname. The one with the ginger HPR.'

'Thomas Owen. Rodney's uncle.'

'That's right. Pauly's taken in his dog. And then there'd been the storm. Those poor boys were wet through, and the thin lads with specs – the twins – were literally shuddering with cold. They didn't have proper wax jackets, so they got soaked. Luz found them a lot of dry socks from Hansi's wardrobe...' She laughed. 'You never saw anything like the state of the drying-room when they went in to lunch. Dripping coats everywhere, mostly on the floor. She said she'd do what she could to tidy up, but I took one look and told her not to bother. We were run off our feet as it was – we could have done with a couple more waitresses. Tidying the drying-room came pretty low on my list of priorities. Luz was afraid she'd get yet another bollocking from Hansi for neglecting her duties, but I told her I needed her in the kitchen and if he objected I'd deal with him.' She grinned. 'I would have enjoyed telling him where to get off.'

'Did you see Max and Pavel go in there?'

'Oh, I know what you're thinking. That's the way the police investigation is heading, too. Marina says they believe the boys fooled around with the guns during lunch, and put some of the twins' cartridges into Hansi's Purdey.' She shook her hair back and pulled a sceptical face. 'Well, I suppose it's possible, but frankly I don't believe it. Why should they?'

'As an experiment?'

She considered the question for a moment, then said thoughtfully, 'Max is a bit of a jackdaw, I know, and he collects cartridge cases, so it is a bit odd that the two twenty-bores that Marina found in the pocket of his anorak that night were live. They hadn't been fired. She asked me if I thought she ought to tell the police about them.' She shrugged. 'I said better not put ideas into their heads. Let them work things out for themselves; there's no sense in shopping your own son.'

It was a point of view, Robb acknowledged, filing the information away. Imagining the likely scenario, he said, 'I suppose she picked it up to put in the washing-machine and wondered why it was so heavy.'

'That's exactly what she said.'

'Would you call her an over-protective mother?'

'Not really. I mean, Max is her one-and-only, so I suppose she does a bit of heli-parenting; but unobtrusively, if you know what I mean. Jericho, too. They cut the boys a lot of slack in some ways. So long as they turn up for meals, for instance, they let them wander just about anywhere they like.'

'As we're told children used to in the good old days,' he said, and she laughed, feigning indignation.

'Well, I used to, and that wasn't so very long ago.'

But not exactly yesterday, either, he thought, looking at her more closely. Nearer forty than thirty, and built for strength rather than speed, yet even after the sleepless night, she had a kind of rosy milkmaid bloom which made her appear youthful. Nevertheless, a web of fine lines around mouth and eyes was there to give the game away.

She added, 'Of course, it's still pretty safe hereabouts, touch wood. Everyone knows everyone else, even if they don't particularly like them.'

'Who didn't particularly like Hartzog?' he asked, wondering if she would consider this outside the scope of a friendly chat, but instead she gave the question careful thought before shaking her head.

'Everybody and nobody. There's always a fair bit of jealousy when a rich man swoops into a place where no one knows him and begins to throw his weight – and his money – around, and since it didn't seem to occur to Hansi that the locals round here are a conservative lot and might resent being pushed about, he trod on a good many toes one way and another. Even when he got involved in charity work he couldn't help rubbing people up the wrong way. Always had to be the biggest and best, and make sure people noticed.'

Robb was nodding. 'I could see that when he arrived in his chopper last week. He wasn't quite shouting, "Look at me!" but not far off it.'

'That's right. It was as if a rock had been thrown into a pond, making a big splash and sending ripples right across the water. When he arrived, pretty well everyone living here was affected one way or another, and they weren't all delighted – not by any means.

'Take the Belltons for example,' she went on. 'At first they were pleased to see Dunmorse taken in hand. Fences, woods, buildings, fields, everything cleared and mended. No farmer wants thistles and ragwort flourishing on his boundary, not to mention deer and badgers doubling their numbers every few years. But then came the downside: this application to make the place pay for itself with a whacking great dairy unit planted right on Marcus's doorstep. Of course the Belltons have been opposing it every step of the way, but money talks – and Hansi has bottomless pockets. Had, I mean.'

She leaned forward, warming to her theme. 'Then there was some kind of ongoing hassle with Locky at the Shooting School. I don't know the ins and outs of that: something about a right of way? And even dear Jericho: well, he's a nice guy and extremely laid back, generally speaking, but I could see that the way Hansi targeted Marina was getting up his nose.'

'How did she respond to that?'

'Oh, you know how it is with Beauties. *O don fatal!*' she sang in a rich, fruity contralto, startling Pilot into an uneasy whimper. 'Sorry, old chap,' she said, patting him.'Is it as bad as that?'

'No, no,' said Robb hastily. 'Not a reflection on your voice. My wife and the girls used to sing while washing-up, and Pilot sometimes joined in – yow! yow! yow! – just like a wolf. It made us all laugh.'

He swallowed hard, remembering, and Anita gave him a quick, sympathetic glance. 'Where was I ?'

'Telling me about beauties.'

'Oh, yes. I was going to say that beauties like Marina are so used to chaps adoring them that they tend to forget the effect they're having. Perhaps they just don't notice. And when you add a kind, friendly nature and considerable musical talent, the combination is pretty devastating. I used to think Hansi was obsessed by Marina, but although she was perfectly civil she really didn't rate him.'

'Interesting. What form did his obsession take?'

'Oh, it was pretty blatant. I suppose the most obvious thing one noticed was the way he was always trying to undermine poor Jericho. Make him out more of a clodhopper than he is. Actually, he's quite bright: look at the way he's turned Grange Farm round. He took on a decaying family farm ten years ago and now it's a thriving modern business.'

'Impressive,' murmured Robb. 'So he and Hartzog weren't friends?'

'Lord, no. My impression was that Jericho thought him a genuine 24-carat shit, but was rather fascinated by him at the same time, if that makes sense to you. When I was asked to shoot at Dunmorse, he wanted to know every detail, and looked tremendously disapproving when I told him how they ran things.' She left the sofa to peer out of the window. 'The rain's easing off. I'd better go and hand out the rest of the food before the cream starts to go off. It's a pity the Care Home won't take it, but they're scared stiff of upsetting the old folks' tummies.'

'That reminds me,' said Robb as she picked up her coat, 'did you notice who else besides the boys went down the passage past the boiler-room during lunch?'

'You mean to the loo? Oh, pretty well everyone,' said Anita over her shoulder. 'Marcus Bellton came storming past twice — men are such hopeless lasters — and apart from us in the kitchen and Marina and Sally at table, the entire party was male.'

So really it could have been anyone in the party who tampered with Hartzog's gun, thought Robb. Someone with mischief in mind would have needed no more than one minute alone in the boiler-room, and could then have continued on to the lavatory with a perfect excuse for leaving the table.

Waving Anita on her way with renewed thanks, he reflected that so far his carefully-staged friendly chats had yielded a lot of background info but nothing hard except the inconvenient fact that Max had live 20-bore cartridges in his pocket that evening. It was looking more and more as if he and Pavel were lying. And yet, and yet...

If it looks like a duck and it quacks like a duck, as Jericho had said, it probably was a duck; but what if the culprit was a bird of another feather entirely? A carrion crow, perhaps, clever enough to shift its guilt on to an innocent? Someone who had factored in the age of criminal responsibility, and knew that although the boys would be blamed they could not be prosecuted?

It might be the slimmest of outside chances, Robb acknowledged, but the Oaks had been kind to Sally, they were worried sick about the effect of the investigation on their son, and he owed it to them to keep digging a little longer. He still needed to talk to Pauly and Marcus Bellton; Locksley Maude, Luz and the gamekeepers. Any or all of them might shed a light into some corner he had overlooked; and as soon as Jim Winter came back from his training session in the Atlas Mountains, he would ask him to run some names through the police computer and see what it came up with.

'Happy Birthday, Dad!' said Sally with a beaming smile as he clumped and thumped his way down the spiral staircase into the kitchen next morning, and he blinked at her in surprise. Could she be right? Was it really his birthday and had he really forgotten it? Meriel had always taken charge of family birthdays – remembering the date, how old everyone was, organising presents, outings, treats, cakes – while he took a benevolent but disengaged back seat in the whole anniversary scene. Now he felt touched that Sally appeared to have assumed that role, and managed to push through the fog of sleep and painkillers to produce a convincing smile.

'How sweet of you to remember.'

'As if I could forget! Claire and Hels and I have been emailing each other all week, trying to decide what to give you.'

'I never guessed. What dark horses you are!' he said, concealing his dread. Presents embarrassed him: he found it difficult to hit on the right words of thanks without sounding either curt or gushing, but whatever the girls had cooked up this time without Meriel to give them a steer, he must do his damnedest to look ecstatic.

'Come on, Dad, open your cards.' Now he noticed that the table had been laid with special care, a bunch of snowdrops drooping their heads in a tumbler next to his place, an eggcup suggesting something other than cereal and toast, and now Sally was taking a plate of what he greatly feared were warmed-up smoked salmon canapés out of the Rayburn.

Hiding his reluctance he took a knife and opened Claire's card, evidently home-made, with the superscription Happy Birthday! over a crudely drawn image of a tiny man with an enormous fish dangling from his rod.

'Can you guess what that is?' Sally was hopping from foot to foot like a small girl.

'Haven't a clue,' he said honestly.

'Look at the next one. It's from Hels and me.'

Another flamboyant Happy Birthday across a picture of a flat-capped sportsman aiming at an impossibly high bird. He stared at it helplessly, anxious not to say the wrong thing.

'Sorry, Sal. I'm completely baffled. You'll have to explain.'

She said as if she had rehearsed the lines, 'We all thought you must be bored of sitting around here while I'm working, so we've booked you a day's fishing on the lake and a lesson on how to shoot clay pigeons at Eastmarsh Country Sports. That's Locksley Maude's Shooting School. Special deal.'

It was the last thing he had expected, the last thing he wanted, but how could he say so without wounding her feelings and destroying the still-fragile improvement in their relationship?

'But, Sal,' he protested, 'it's wonderfully kind and I'm really grateful, but I can't have you girls spending your money on me.'

'Dad, I'm earning! I get the most enormous tips — and anyway this is from all three of us. We want you to have a bit of fun.'

Fun! He had almost forgotten what it was: pure, uncomplicated, undemanding enjoyment of some useless but agreeable activity. What a surly old brute he had become. How could he even contemplate turning down his daughters' desire to give him a bit of fun? Besides, in a practical sense, this needn't be useless at all, since it would give him exactly the excuse he needed to get an idea of where Maude stood in this affair, and what he felt about Hartzog.

Sally was watching him anxiously, afraid that her carefully hatched plan was going to flop. When he said, 'Well, thank you, darling, thank you all! It's a marvellous idea. I've been longing to do some fishing, and I haven't fired a gun since God knows when,' her expression cleared magically.

'Great! For a moment I was afraid you wouldn't be keen. I'll tell Locky and fix a date this week. Claire and Hels will be so pleased.'

Robb said, 'Don't expect me to hit anything smaller than a bus, and I'll need to borrow a shotgun. Yours will be too short in the stock for me.'

'Oh, don't worry: everyone says Locky's a good instructor. It's what he did in the Army, but he told me it damaged his hearing, so he left when his eight years were up. I know he keeps a few guns for his pupils to try out – side-by-side, over-and-under, and so on. He hires out fishing rods as well,' she said airily. 'He'll fix you up with everything you need. You might find a shooting-stick useful, and he keeps a special swivelling tripod for real cripples. Not that you are one,' she added hastily.

She went to consult the wall-chart diary hanging over the toaster. 'If I get organised today, we'll see if we can schedule your shooting lesson tomorrow at eleven, after I've done my morning round. Duncan will give me time off, I'm sure, because now we're so close to the end of the season, we're not nearly so busy. What are you laughing about?'

Hastily he rearranged his features. He couldn't admit to finding it amusing to see Sally – his rebellious, lippy and uncooperative daughter, always in trouble, always failing exams – suddenly taking charge, making plans, behaving like an adult at last. How Meriel would have enjoyed the transformation.

'I'm just thinking what fun it will be,' he said.

Mist blanketed the Starcliffe valley as Sally's mud-splashed Kawasaki Mule puttered up the steep hill behind Grange Farm, but as soon as they cleared the shrouded trees, a dazzle of brilliant light made them both them blink. Too bright for shooting, thought Robb, reaching for dark glasses.

Before them in a shallow natural bowl between two hills, the oxbow lakes which had been the scene of Hartzog's death looked very different in the morning sun. The water glittered enticingly as she drove past them and turned into the short gravelled drive that led to the main entrance of the Shooting School. A thick belt of conifers encircled the parking strip and beyond it a narrow path connected the sculpted hummocks and dips where the traps were positioned. Sally wheeled the little vehicle to park neatly in front of the central gable of the wooden clubhouse, with its two verandahed wings and double-width windows overlooking the traps and towers.

'Canadian cedar,' she said, pointing. 'It came prefabricated in huge sections, and the builders put it together in less than a fortnight. Electricity, running water, the lot. Store-room and office on the left, and the club-room on the right. Locky's workshop is round the back, so it's all very handy.'

'Quite impressive.' Robb wondered how much it had cost – indeed, how much the whole elaborate set-up had cost. In hock to the bank, Lombard had indicated: no wonder Maude was struggling to make the enterprise pay.

'Come on.' She jumped over the Mule's low door without opening it and nipped round to help her father disembark.

'It's all right. I can manage.' He disliked being so dependent on her, and strove to soften the words with a smile. 'It just takes me a bit longer than usual.'

Trim and businesslike in breeches, boots and padded waistcoat, Maude came down the two steps to greet them. 'Good morning, sir. Hi, Sally. Great to see you.' He smiled and his bold dark eyes rested on her a little too long for Robb's taste. 'Is it too late to wish you a Happy Birthday?'

'Only a day late.' Robb surveyed him thoughtfully. Good-looking in a lean and hungry way, wiry and clearly very fit, with well-dubbined boots and an easy competence in every movement. No wonder Luz had him marked down as a desirable husband. 'Did Sally tell you I haven't got a gun?' he asked. 'She thought you might be able to hire me one, just for this morning.'

'No problem at all. Come this way.'

They followed him into the office, where he opened a heavy steel cabinet. 'I take it you're not a complete beginner? Just haven't shot for a while, is that right?'

Methodically he took Robb through the paperwork. Licence, experience, insurance: sign here, sign there; then said, 'Right. That should cover it. Now let's look for a gun.' He sorted through the rack, murmuring, 'Medium height, long arms...'

'Like a chimpanzee,' teased Sally, but Maude didn't smile.

'We'll have a little more respect from you, young lady,' he reproved. 'Right, sir. Try this for size.'

The nervousness that had afflicted Robb all morning melted away the moment he hefted the Browning twelve-bore that Maude chose from the rack. The warm, satin-smooth stock cuddled between shoulder and cheek had the comfortable familiarity of an old and favourite boot, while the haunting whiff of gun-oil evoked memories of boyhood forays round the Shropshire hedgerows during Christmas holidays long ago.

Maude watched carefully as he mounted it several times. 'How does that feel?'

'Great.'

Maude wasn't satisfied. 'Not quite right. Here, try this Perazzi twenty-bore, it's one of my favourites. Ah, that's better.'

Robb felt the difference at once, and reflected that he had probably never shot with a gun that fitted him properly. 'Much better,' he agreed.

After trying out two more, they settled on the Perazzi, and after a short, no-nonsense lecture on safety, Maude led the way to the first stand. 'This is where I start beginners,' he said half-apologetically. 'I know you're not a beginner, but it'll give you confidence, and I'd like to see how you shape with some easy shots before we go on to more challenging stuff.'

'Suits me.'

'Right. When you're ready?'

'Ready.'

'Pull!'

The disc sailed in a high arc from left to right and, with an ease that surprised him, Robb shattered it. What fun! he thought, doing the same to the next five.

'Dad! Brilliant!'

Maude was smiling and nodding. 'Not much doubt about that, eh? Well done, sir. Now we'll try something in a different league.'

It was as if he couldn't miss. During the next forty minutes clays representing driven partridges appeared over hedges, high pheasants from left and right of the Meccano-like towers, and grouse angled low and fast over the stone-built butt: mount, swing, aim, fire and they disintegrated into tiny grey shards.

'Terrific, Dad,' said Sal, beaming the widest of grins.

'Excellent. Keep it up,' agreed Maude.

Then at the 'springing teal' stand two thirds of the way round the course, something went wrong. Five clean misses, one after the other, and confidence collapsed like a soufflé in a draught. Robb made tiny adjustments to his stance, cuddled the stock closer, tried swinging faster and slower: nothing worked, the magic had gone.

'Sorry, I've lost it completely,' he said. 'What am I doing wrong?'

It seemed extraordinary that what had appeared so easy had, in the space of a few minutes, become impossible. He couldn't imagine how, in the whole wide sky, he had ever managed to hit a fast-moving target.

'You're behind them, sir,' said Maude's calm voice at his elbow. 'Swing right through ahead of the target. Remember it's rising as well as going away and moving fast. Don't try to blot it out but give it a good bit of lead.'

Another shot. Another miss. And again. 'Still behind.' Maude thought for a moment, then said, 'Look, we'll leave the teal for the moment and try something else, then come back later.'

Pigeon came next, then rabbits. More my style, thought Robb, with relief, picking them off as his confidence returned. By the time they had looped back to his nemesis stand, he was shooting accurately again and arrived back at the clubhouse having completed his round of the traps with a storming six out of six springing teal.

'Thanks. I really enjoyed that,' he told Maude, handing back the Perazzi. 'It's a lovely gun. What's it worth?'

'Too much,' said Maude with a grimace. 'You handled it well, sir. With a bit more practice you'd be a fine shot. That's the key to it all – practice. Anyone who shoots four or five days a week, as some of the big landowners round here do, obviously has the edge over the sporting weekender, but if you want to improve your score, you're welcome to come up here any time. Have you ever tried target shooting? Completely different technique, of course, but I'm planning to install a range.'

Sally fetched coffee from the machine in the corner of the clubroom, and they sat on a slatted bench in the weak January sun looking out over the lakes with their little man-made islands. Robb wondered what Maude would think if he admitted that all his target-shooting to date had been done with a semi-automatic pistol in an underground gallery where human cut-outs were the targets, but it didn't seem quite the right moment to blow his cover.

'You've got a nice set-up here,' he said. 'Must have cost a fair bit.'

Maude didn't rise to the bait. 'Good of you to say so, sir. I'm getting there by degrees, but there's still a lot to do. I'd like to install a Promatic trap release system, so that regular clients could go round on their own, and of course we could do with a couple more towers.'

And what would all that cost? Given the empty car park, the silent lakes, it didn't seem likely that there was enough trade to support such grandiose plans. Was Maude a fantasist? Under the professional bonhomie Robb sensed anxiety and remembered what Jericho had said about paying back the bank.

He said, feeling his way, 'I suppose you get bookings from Gun Clubs? Charity Clay Shoots, that kind of thing,' and Maude nodded.

'Charity begins at home, where I'm concerned. But, yes: we do get very busy when the big boys from the Midlands' gun clubs decide they need a change of scene. I have to be careful not to double-book at times. They wouldn't like that – not at all. One has to be careful not to offend the paying customers!'

Over Maude's shoulder, Robb saw Sally's puzzled expression and knew she was thinking on the same lines. But before he could pursue the matter, Maude pushed back his chair. 'Excuse me a moment – that's the office phone. Someone trying to book a lesson, I expect.'

'Is he really so busy?' said Robb in a low tone. 'I mean, look around you.' His glance took in the empty room, the deserted grounds. 'I don't understand. Why's he trying to big it up?'

'Maybe he thinks you'll bring a lot of City fat-cats to shoot here.' She sounded unconvinced.

They sipped their coffee in silence until Maude hurried back. 'Sorry, sir. That was a call I've been waiting for: a gun club from Frankfurt who want to book a whole weekend. I said Yes, though it'll mean a bit of re-scheduling.' He paused, then said, 'Of course, without the usual parties from Dunmorse, I'm going to have some empty slots to fill.'

'That was a bad business,' said Robb.

'A bad business and bad for business. Hartzog did a lot to support me.'

This didn't quite square with Anita's account, but Robb let it go. He said, 'Such a tragedy! Having his own gun blow up in his face – how on earth could such a thing happen?'

Maude leaned forward, eager to make his point. 'I'd have thought it was obvious, sir. Letting boys that age mess about with guns – well, it was an accident waiting to happen. I saw them in the boiler-room myself when I went to the Gents, and chased them out, but by the time I came back they were in there again, along with Pauly Bellton. I'd have given him a piece of my mind, but I didn't want a row. It's my belief that half the time we were at table those lads were in and out of that drying-room, making free with the guns. Shouldn't have been allowed to touch them, of course, but cocky little tykes like that think they can get away with anything.'

Sally went pink and shifted uncomfortably, but before she could say anything in the boys' defence, Robb frowned a warning. 'No doubt the police will get to the bottom of it in time,' he said blandly, and drained his cup. 'Come on, Sal, we're holding Mr Maude up, and he's given us enough of his time already.'

Sally took a calming breath and forced a smile. 'You're right, we should go, but thanks, Locky. It's been great.'

'Don't mention it. You're welcome any time.' He waved as they drove away, and Robb watched him in the passenger mirror, a lonely figure on the verandah of his clubhouse, staring after the vehicle with a look of contained anxiety before turning back to his office.

Robb was aware that Sally, in the driver's seat, was simmering with indignation, and hardly had they cleared the gate before she exploded.

'Honestly, Dad! How could he say that about Max and Pavel! If you hadn't given me that look, I'd have let Locky have a real blast. I don't believe the boys had anything to do with it, and to blame Pauly was the pits.'

'Those two aren't bosom buddies, then?'

She shook her head emphatically. 'They had a fight over Luz.'

'Ah. And who won?'

'Hard to tell. She's pretty – what's the word? – enigmatic.'

'Blows hot and cold, eh?'

'That's about it. She plays them off against each other. All the same: to make out that Pauly was encouraging the boys to mess around with guns really was...well, despicable.'

'Mm–hm.' Robb glanced at her and took a decision. 'Look, Sal, while you were out the other day, your boss dropped in and asked me to do what I can to find out if there's any chance that those boys didn't cause Hartzog's death by fiddling about with his gun.'

'Ah!' she exclaimed, and then 'Oh!' After a moment's silence she said slowly, 'You mean someone else might have?'

'Right. And if so I want to know who. Now, I wasn't there in the barn for lunch, but you were; so I'd like you to think back carefully and see if you can remember who left the table and in what order.'

'But, Dad, that's impossible! People were coming and going all the time.'

But he could see her brain was already grappling with the problem, sorting and rejecting, trying to clarify her memories. 'It's surprising what you can remember if you think it over in order,' he encouraged. 'Go through it bit by bit, and by degrees it will make a picture.'

Sally said without much enthusiasm, 'OK, I'll try. I do remember that Mr Bellton kept getting up and down, but mostly for second helpings.'

'That's a start. He may have seen who else was wandering about at the serving end of the room. I'll have a word with him next and, of course, with Pauly.'

'You won't get much out of old Grumble-Guts,' she said with contempt. 'He's not interested in anything except his precious Ruby Reds. And, Dad, do take everything Pauly says with a grain of salt. He doesn't exactly tell lies, but sometimes...'

'He has a bit of a problem with the truth? OK. I'll remember,' he agreed.

'Good. And if you talk to him, the other thing to remember is that I do not, repeat not, want you bringing back any orphaned kittens, however sweet. Or puppies. Or hedgehogs. Pilot wouldn't like it, and nor would I.'

CHAPTER ELEVEN

The Belltons

Old Grumble-Guts stood in his farmyard in classic John-Bull-agin'-the-world pose, legs braced apart, brick-red face thrust forward, grubby waistcoat distended, one hand on a stout stick and the other resting on the top bar of the silage crush as he communed with his prized Red Ruby Devon bull, 2,200lb of muscle and power covered by curly long hair in a glorious shade of dark chestnut. Round his hocks swished a white-tipped tail, remarkable in that decrepit setting for its freshly washed fluffiness. Clearly a brush had been at work, and now he looked more closely Robb thought that the regularity of the coat's curls indicated titivation with a currycomb. On the left side of his neck were two small shaved patches, about the size of a 50p coin.

'What a magnificent fellow!' he exclaimed, standing back to admire him. The bull's clever bulging eyes sized up the interloper with a long considering stare before the great head dropped back to pick at his silage.

'He's a fine beast, right enough,' agreed Marcus gloomily. 'Four years old now and in his prime.'

'Did you breed him yourselves?'

'Aye, that we did. He's a true Ruby Red, line traces right back to Fairweather Red Ringan, Champion at the Royal in 1967 and then again at Smithfield. I'll show you the herd book, if you're interested. He's registered Castle Farm Garnet, but we calls him Bob.' With the tip of his stick he scratched the junction of neck and shoulders, and the bull turned sideways to offer the stick a bigger area.

'He likes being groomed, then?' asked Robb, moving a step to the side in order to escape the whisky fumes, and Marcus' mouth curved in a reluctant smile.

'Show me the man as doesn't. Sends him to sleep, half the time, while we're working on him.' He focused his attention, as if properly registering his visitor for the first time. 'You're little Sally Robb's dad, ain't you? I see'd you driving the game-cart at Hartzog's shoot. Heard you had a car-crash, killed your wife? I'm right sorry.'

'Kind of you to say so. Yes. A terrible accident.' Keen to deflect the conversation, Robb pointed at the shaved patches on the bull's neck. 'What are those?'

Wrong subject: back came the gloom with a vengeance. Bellton glowered and said, 'Bloody TB testing, that's what. At it all day yesterday, and back again Thursday. Only a year since we was cleared of restrictions, but with badgers plaguing us on all sides, what can you expect? They tells us to keep our cattle where badgers can't get to 'em, but I tell you every time I takes a look at our CCTV I sees them devils a-crawling over the barriers in the dark, eating from the mangers, drinking from the troughs. Keep 'em separate? Don't make me laugh.'

'It must be difficult.'

'Difficult? It's impossible. This here's an official cull area, but to hark at busybodies like that bloody schoolmaster, you wouldn't think it. With my hip so bad, I can't go out with the marksmen at night like my boy does, but every time I sets a trap, bloody Lombard springs what's in it afore I gets there.'

'You're allowed to trap them?'

An emphatic nod. 'That I am. My boy's a licensed shooter for the cull, and I'm AAP – Additional Authorised Person. Got Natural England paperwork and all, but with the trouble we get from every bloody anti who thinks he's the right to stick his nose into our affairs we don't shout it from the rooftops.'

'I quite understand.'

Once launched on his favourite rant, Marcus was hard to stop. 'There's too many townies come here wanting a bit of country life, then set out to change it to suit theirselves. Switch on *Countryfile* of a Sunday evening, watch a couple of wildlife programmes in the week, and think they knows it all from A to Z. They asks why they never sees a hedgehog aside from the skin, and curlews, skylarks and the like can't bring off their eggs round here, but tell 'em that's on account of too many badgers and they won't listen. They reckon us farmers is responsible for every trouble there is on the land – BSE, bird flu, foot-and-mouth, Schmallenbergs, you name it – and they could manage it better. Let 'em try, is what I says. Let 'em try calving a heifer on a February night in an open field in a hailstorm, with nothing but the tractor lights to see by. Let 'em muck out a byre after a cow's aborted and the vet's started yammering about bio-security.'

He stopped abruptly, staring at Robb, and now his eyes looked less angry than haunted. 'That's all they talk about, nowadays, bio-security. Wash this, disinfect that, put the power-hose on your vehicles, but I asks you, how the hell can I keep my cattle bio-secure when badgers are crapping in the feed-troughs and pissing all over the silage?'

They had gone full circle.

'Do the Dunmorse keepers help with the cull?' asked Robb, and Bellton gave a contemptuous snort.

'Ah, they sets their traps all right, but they're incomers, both on 'em. Don't know the woods like I does. Badgers like buildings, see: old buildings. Saves 'em trouble when they're setting up a colony if someone's done the spadework first, and there's a mort of old buildings hereabouts used to be part of Dunmorse estate, before everything was let go in Sir Philip's day. Time was when every cottage had its byre and every roof its storm-water tank, but most on 'em are under the brambles now.'

'So you put your traps round the old buildings?'

'That I do, but I'm not saying where.' Bellton's expression became mulish. 'Hartzog's like to have given Natural England leave to cull badgers in his woods, but that underkeeper of his, Cecil Barley, is too friendly by half with Lombard, and he and Hagley takes good care to keep me away from their release pens; but if you're wondering where the buzzards and ravens have gone from around here, I dessay them keepers could tell you, for all they'm meant to be protected. Toby Hagley was copped by the RSPB at his last place for shooting a hen harrier and destroying her tag, so he tries to keep his nose clean now; but old Barley's thick as thieves with the Fancy in Brum covered market, and every raptor he catches alive ends up flown out to Pakistan.'

It was the old story: the closer the proximity, the greater the mutual suspicion between neighbours, reflected Robb. No matter that Dunmorse Estate and Castle Farm must comprise a total of a thousand acres, of which quite a fifth must be woodland, the border between them was as rigorously guarded and enforced as that between North and South Korea. It was a depressing thought.

'What do you think happened to Hartzog?' he asked, hardly expecting a straight answer, but Marcus Bellton had little interest in the means, only the result.

'Whoever done it done me a right good turn, and I'd be proud to shake his hand,' he said robustly. 'There'll be no thousand-cow dairy unit at Starcliffe now, and I'm glad of it.'

'You don't think Mrs Hartzog will pursue the appeal, then?'

'Not she! Kelly-Louise is a nice lady, I got nothing against her, but she says it herself, she don't belong at Dunmorse. Super-yachts and fashion shows is more her style. And she's got an eye for the boys. There's some round here call her The Man-Eater, and say young Locksley Maude better watch his step.' He laughed throatily. 'No... I reckon she'll sell up here just as fast as she can, laugh all the way to the bank, and who's to blame her? Not us, that's for sure.'

He lapsed into ruminative silence, absently scratching the bull's back and peering at the small bald patches on his neck.

'See those marks? If one on 'em swells just a mite more than the other by Thursday, this fellow's done for. Makes you sick to think on it. Top one's avian tuberculin, and bovine's below it.'

'They look just the same to me.'

'Ah, but you ain't using callipers.' Another silence, then he patted the chestnut neck and said heavily, 'I must get on. Want to see Pauly, do 'ee? He'll be down in the flats by the river, training his dogs. Or he might have gone up the bank beyond. I'll ring his mobile, say you wants to see him. Go on through that gate across the lane and cut across the field. There's no cattle out now.'

As he turned to go, he said unexpectedly, 'Reckon Jericho Oak is glad as I am to see the back of Hartzog. Good riddance to bad rubbish. Pauly tells me they're blaming it on the boys, but it could just as well a bin Lombard, or the little furrin piece. I see'd 'em both come out the Gents in a hurry when I paid a call.'

157

'Luz? Surely not. In any case, she wouldn't have been in the Gents.'

'See'd her there myself,' said Marcus doggedly. 'Gender neutral they calls it. Makes no difference who goes where these days. Flittin' about the passage like a little brown moth, she was.'

Robb stared at him. It's the whisky talking, he thought, but couldn't rid himself of the nagging suspicion that Bellton might be right. Anita said Hartzog had treated Luz like dirt. Had she seen an opportunity to pay him back – and seized it?

'Good riddance,' repeated Marcus, and was gone, stumping across the yard, before Robb had the chance to ask any more.

Pauly was not down in the flats by the river, and after he had climbed slowly and painfully over two stiles and up a bank that commanded a view of the fields beyond, Robb's knee went on strike at the prospect of toiling any further uphill through thick rows of stubble-turnips rooted in liquid clay, completely obscuring the footpath, and he sank down on a handy log to consider whether it was worth pursuing his quest on foot when it would be perfectly easy to ask Sally to drive him to Castle Farm after lunch.

But one-to-one chats in the open air had the advantage of seeming spontaneous as well as confidential, and with the hazy winter sun dispersing the last of the river mist, it was agreeable to sit here quietly, listening to the muted but still distinct country noises – a steady distant chugging of tractors interspersed with the sharp rattle-crash of the Council's hedge-trimmer, mewing buzzards harassed by corvids and, far in the distance the occasional heavy boom of a timed gas-gun. England might be a small and crowded island, but out here in the sticks you wouldn't know it.

A shotgun barked suddenly near at hand, and from the copse at the right-hand corner of the field, his eye caught a glimpse of a cylindrical object flying low over the dull green leaves before disappearing into them. What was that? He reached for the small binoculars Sally had lent him, but before he had them focused there was a second loud bang and another cylinder thudded to earth fifty yards nearer him. A dummy: Pauly was training his retrievers.

Moments later a ginger streak rocketed through the hedge and began quartering the turnips with great bounds, head down, tail waving, and Robb smiled as he recognised Mitzi the HPR, homing in on the second dummy. She picked it up with an air of conscious pride and returned the way she had come, neck braced, dummy held clear of the ground, classic style.

Now, thought Robb, watching through the little binoculars, would she remember there was another to fetch?

She did. A second ginger eruption among the turnip leaves and Mitzi was back in action, working more slowly this time as she conscientiously zigzagged back and forth, raising her head occasionally for directions from what must be a whistle so high it was beyond his hearing-range.

Closer, closer... He leaned forward, willing her to pounce on her quarry, whose end he could just see protruding from the turnip-leaves. There! she nearly had it, but now – damn! she had overshot and was fruitlessly searching two rows beyond. It was as bad as watching small children play Hunt the Thimble, longing to assist but sworn to silence.

Mitzi paused, head up, ears lifted – and then, as if activated by a random puff of scent, began retracing her path with increasing confidence until finally she nosed down into the plants, drew out the dummy, adjusted it for balance, and set off back the way she had come.

Bravo! cheered Robb silently, and wished old Thomas Owen had been there to watch the performance. Plainly she was far too good a dog for a man of his ineptitude.

Evidently Pauly shared this opinion. He came swinging easily downhill through the turnips, with an assorted pack orbiting him like satellites round their planet, and the sun setting his hair ablaze. Flame-capped Apollo? thought Robb. Actaeon with his hounds? Or something wilder, more primitive: perhaps one of the less reliable members of the Celtic pantheon, inclined to transform into an animal at will ?

An aroma that combined silage, sweat, and trampled brassica wafted to Robb's nose as Pauly halted beside him, signalling the dogs to sit. He was in high spirits, glad of an audience.

'See that ? Reckon I'll make a Trialler of her yet,' he said boisterously. 'See her work for the second dummy? That dog's got a head on her, and the old boy says I can keep her as long as I like, because he's through with shooting.' He laughed infectiously. 'Suits me! Now, sir, what can I do for you? Dad rang my mobile, but the signal's crap on this bank and I couldn't make out half of what he said. Your daughter changed her mind about that kitten, has she?'

'She said I'd get no supper for a week if I brought one home,' said Robb, grinning.

Pauly planted himself on the log beside him, stretching out his legs and fishing in his pocket for the makings of a roll-up, while the five dogs – Mitzi, two black labradors, one old and fat, the other young and rangy, a sheepdog and a terrier – disposed themselves as close as possible to his boots. He blew out a cloud of smoke and heaved a sigh.

'Ah, that's better, that is.'

'Filthy habit,' said Robb equably, and Pauly grinned.

'You sound like my ex.'

'Well, at least one of you had some sense.'

For a moment Pauly smoked in silence, then he said, 'Dogs and I couldn't wait to get out the yard, after yesterday. Dad and I were with the vets all day, shoving beasts in and out the crush, students and pen-pushers getting underfoot, reading tags, filling forms, taking samples, shaving, measurements, jabs – God, what a shambles! And all to do again tomorrow.'

'How soon do you get the results?'

Pauly shrugged. 'Written confirmation? Could be a week, maybe less. They tell you as quick as they can, but it's the waiting that gets you – that and seeing the damned badgers crawling round the yard as if they own the place, and not a blamed thing we can do to stop them.'

'How's the cull going?'

Pauly looked sharply at him. 'Dad tell you about that, did he?'

'He did – and so did Sally.'

'Oh aye! She's a sensible girl, is Sal. So you're not one of those badger-hugging buggers like bloody Lombard – or bloody Maude, who puts out peanuts to draw them into his shooting grounds?'

'Why does he do that?'

'Because his clients –' heavy emphasis – 'and their women like watching 'em at night. Maude puts up an I/R lamp that comes up slow over the peanut trail, and charges his continentals a tenner an hour to sit in that lodge of his and watch badgers. Nice little earner, eh?'

Robb said nothing, and Pauly went on, 'Then he tries to get their husbands to buy guns off of him. I heard you had a go up there yourself, a day or so back.'

Robb shook his head.

'I hadn't shot for years. Half the time I couldn't connect at all.'

'That wasn't what I heard.' Pauly pinched out his cigarette and said reflectively, 'Strange about that gun of Hartzog's. I had a look at it myself: beautiful piece, real quality work, and just come from an overhaul. Seems to me the gunsmith will have to do some fast talking to explain why it blew up in Hartzog's face.'

'The gunsmith? Hardly his fault if 20-bore cartridges were blocking both barrels.'

'Ah, but were they?'

'That's what the police told Mr and Mrs Oak.' Robb didn't much like the way this conversation was going. He said, 'When did you look at the gun? Was it in the drying-room during lunch?'

'That's right,' said Pauly easily. 'Jericho's nipper and his pal were hanging about there, wanting something to do, so I showed them all the different makes and told them what to look for. Those twins, you know, the little chaps with glasses, were using a nice pair of Aya twenties, and the tall bloke – Patterson, was he? – had a Beretta over-and-under I wouldn't have minded trying. Hartzog's was the pick of the bunch, as it should be, seeing as what he paid for it.'

'How much?'

'Some say sixty, some say seventy thousand. Depends who you asks. All I know is there was nothing wrong with it when young Max and I looked. Barrels clean as a whistle. Less than an hour later, it blows up. Less than an hour,' he repeated. 'Makes you think, doannit?'

What it made Robb think was that either Pauly was being deliberately disingenuous, or he hadn't realised that every word he said made it clearer that not only had he himself had an excellent opportunity to tamper with the gun, but he had been one of the last people to handle it. Knowing that relations between them were strained, Robb had at first been inclined to discount Maude's claim of seeing Pauly and the boys messing about in the drying-room, but now that claim was confirmed by Pauly himself. Had he never heard of the Fifth Amendment?

'Did you tell the police this?' he asked, and was not surprised to see Pauly's left eye close in an elaborate wink.

'Wasn't born yesterday, Mr Robb.'

Omerta, thought Robb. Not confined to the Mob and eight-year-old boys, but in every nook and corner of everyday country life. Say nowt. Keep your mouth shut and you'll keep out of trouble. No wonder police forces struggled to engage the public's assistance. No wonder they were conditioned to treat with suspicion the rare person who volunteered unsolicited information.

At one level he was enjoying his present freedom from the stigma of belonging to the police, but he felt increasingly guilty at working under false pretences. In an attempt to square the circle, he said, 'Mrs Oak is worried about the effect of the investigation on her son. He says he didn't put anything into Hartzog's gun and she's sure he's telling the truth, but there's no way to prove it.' He hesitated, then added: 'She and her husband asked me to find out what I could.'

'Because you bin a copper, eh?' A slow smile crinkled Pauly's eyes. 'Still are, by my reckoning, for all you're off sick.'

Anonymity had been nice while it lasted. 'Is it so obvious?' Robb asked, and Pauly laughed wholeheartedly.

'Not so much you, sir, but I spotted that mate of yourn right off, when he drove you here, but since Sal didn't say nothing about it, I kept quiet. Reckoned you wanted to lie low and lick your wounds. Well, that's OK by me. Detective Inspector Robb, innit?'

'Chief Inspector.'

'Ah! Wonderful what you can find out on Google, though not all of it's up to date. Righty-o, sir. You go ahead and ask all the questions you want, and we'll see where that gets us. I don't think those nippers did it any more than Jericho and his missus do, though I'm blamed if I can explain it any other way. '

Where it got them was not very far, but it was better than nothing, thought Robb, limping back half an hour later to recover the Mule from the Belltons' muddy farmyard. On the one hand, Pauly confirmed that the boys had indeed been messing about in the drying-room and had handled most of the guns there before he found them and embarked on his impromptu lesson, but crucially he claimed to have chased them back to the company of the beaters before leaving the room himself; and he categorically denied that there had been anything wrong with the Purdey at that point.

So who else had the opportunity to tamper with it? Not Maude: according to Sally he had left the table while the rest of the party were still eating their treacle tart, and Pauly confirmed that he had seen him drive away while he himself was still talking to the boys. That left only a small window of opportunity for anyone else to enter the drying-room unobserved.

Anita had reported old Marcus tramping up and down the passage past the kitchen, but it was difficult to imagine his clumsy fingers abstracting cartridges from the twins' bags and deliberately pushing them into Hartzog's gun. Difficult – but not impossible. He had been in a simmering rage all day, and might have succumbed to a sudden murderous impulse. I'll teach that bastard to mess with us – that kind of thing. It was, after all, what he had been saying to everyone who would listen.

But if Pauly, who was sharper than he seemed, had even the faintest idea that his father was guilty, would he have volunteered so much just now? And how far could Pauly himself be trusted, when even Sally had recognised that he had a problem with the truth?

It was galling to reflect that he would have to report so little progress to Jericho and Marina who had invited him to drop in for a drink this very evening. On an impulse, he drove past the turning to Sally's cottage, and continued half a mile until he reached the left-hand fork in the lane that led to Dunmorse Hall.

It was time – high time – that he had one of his friendly chats with Luz and established her position in Dunmorse's sporting jigsaw.

CHAPTER TWELVE

Luz

From her lustrous black hair, caught up in a Spanish comb and spilling down her back, to her delicate ankles and slim feet in thonged sandals more suited to the beach than the winter countryside, Luz radiated the kind of vulnerable sex appeal that arouses a protective instinct in even the least chivalrous of males, together with a helplessness which was less likely to inspire jealousy than make competent women like Anita want to help her. Though her features were classically Spanish, with strongly-marked, high-arched brows and a proudly aquiline nose, Arab blood lent her complexion an extra warmth.

She was wearing yellow rubber gloves and a cotton overall in a vivid shade of green as she opened the back door to Robb's knock, and he guessed she was engaged in a major house-cleaning blitz in preparation for the arrival of Kelly-Louise.

'Yes, please?' Her voice was low and caressing as she looked him up and down, her large brown eyes with their hint of ingrained melancholy widening in puzzlement, as if she recognised him but couldn't place him. Then her face cleared in an enchanting, fleeting smile, and she pushed the door wider.

'You are Mr Robb, yes? Sally's papa?'

'That's right. Excuse me for bothering you when you're busy, but I wanted to ask if by any chance you'd found my daughter's coat? She thinks she left it here on the day of the Shoot.'

'Please to come in.' She undulated in front of him down a stone-flagged passage with utility rooms on either side – scullery, larder, walk-in freezer – and into an enormous kitchen which would, Robb calculated, involve walking at least a hundred yards to make a cup of tea. With its sombrely gleaming brushed-aluminium machines and double sink, its stark black granite working surfaces and severely black-and-white tiled floor, it looked more like an advertising fantasy than anything connected with food.

Slung from the ceiling and dominating the scrubbed-pine table was a stainless steel ring from which saucepans and frying-pans, ladles and colanders, all shining like new, were hung on metal hooks to revolve at a touch, with a tall tower of saucepan lids beneath them. The kidney-shaped island and breakfast bar were bare of all clutter, and the kitchen knives stuck in a large cedar block were so carefully graded in size that it was hard to believe they were ever used. No lists pinned to boards, no kitchen towels or racks of spices. It looked as sterile and clinical as an operating theatre, or a morgue.

Robb looked with distaste at the crimson four-door Aga which provided the only patch of colour. Even if Luz had snatched them out immediately, Pauly's hoglets wouldn't have stood a chance.

'Sit, please.' She waved him towards the table and as if on auto-pilot, switched on the kettle. 'Do you wish tea or coffee?'

'No, no,' said Robb hastily. He didn't want to get bogged down in cups and saucers and one sugar or two. 'I just dropped in to ask about Sally's jacket. It's one of those quilted affairs, dark blue, with a pair of gloves in the pocket. She thinks she left it there after the shoot.'

'Many people leave many clothes.' Luz shrugged theatrically. 'So much hurry and trouble after Mr Hartzog is killed. Come. I show you all I find.'

She unhooked a bunch of keys from beside the back door and led the way across the cobbled courtyard to the triple-gabled barn, its outer walls beautifully restored and repointed and still recognisable as originally an agricultural building, though this illusion vanished with one step through the electronically-operated glass door, which slid open at their approach.

Luz pressed a switch, and as the lights came up, Robb gazed around in wonder. This was a barn conversion to end all others.

'Good lord!' he said, and Luz nodded and smiled, pleased with his reaction.

'Come. I show you all. First we go this way.'

The entrance hall formed by the main gable was backed by a long bar with an impressive array of bottles, now locked away behind thick glass. To the right was the big dining-room, whose ceiling reached the barn's original cruck-beams, with swing doors leading to a serving-room beyond. He followed her past the kitchen and a walk-in refrigerator, and down half a flight of steps to the big L-shaped boiler-room lined with slatted pine shelves, a long wooden table, and two-by-two sets of batons on which upturned boots could be left to dry out. Every wall was provided with hooks, one above the other, on which to hang coats and hats, cartridge bags and dog-pegs. Round the angle of the L was a row of basins, mirrors, and lavatory cubicles.

Everything was spotless; shining clean and orderly now, but he could easily imagine the boiler-room filled with wet, shivering, hungry young men, shouting to one another, tearing off hats and cartridge bags, propping guns in corners, unzipping jackets with cold, stiff fingers, levering off sodden boots, and leaving a tangled mass of dripping clothes dumped in muddy puddles on the floor.

Hustle and bustle – and it was equally easy to imagine those same young men, hours later, sated with food and wine, probably rather sleepy and reluctant to leave the comfort of the barn, clumsily trying to collect their scattered their kit as their host chivvied them back to the vehicles in the fading evening light.

And Hartzog himself, dashing in, grabbing up the one gun left, with those deadly little cartridges stuck in the barrels.

Luz said, 'Here is where I put all that is left.' She opened the door of a cupboard with coats and jackets neatly hung from a rail. Maintaining the fiction of Sally's jacket, Robb rummaged through them, then shook his head. 'Don't worry. I'm sure it will turn up.'

As she accompanied him down the short passage that led to the barn's back door, he said casually, 'Your English is so good. Did you learn it at school?'

She smiled, gently shaking her head. 'Some at school, yes. But more when I am working here.'

'How long have you lived in England?'

The smile died. She flicked him a quick, sharp glance, her face suddenly wary. 'Oh, not so long. Two years and a half, I think.'

'You think?'

She said hurriedly, 'I mean, not all this time for Mr Hartzog. To start I am working in London beauty bar. Here is better – so much better.'

'You mean Mr Hartzog wasn't your original sponsor?'

'Sponsor? What is this?'

'I mean the employer who sponsored you to work in the

UK?' She stared at him blankly, her lower lip caught in her teeth, so he put it another way. 'Who got you your permit to work here?'

'Ah! No. Yes. Permit, yes. I have permit.' Obviously flurried, she took refuge in non-comprehension. 'I do not understand. Why do you ask such questions?'

'I'm sorry. I didn't mean to worry you. I was just wondering how you came to be working here?'

It was plain from her strained expression that she was at a loss what to say, and Anita's doubts about her papers were all too accurate; but before she could answer her mobile chirruped. She whipped it from her pocket, glanced at the screen and silently killed the call. 'Please excuse!' She forced a smile. 'I have much work to make all ready before Mrs Hartzog will arrive.'

'Of course you have. I'm sorry; I shouldn't be taking up your time like this. I'll be on my way, and thank you so much for looking for Sally's coat. Don't worry, I can find my own way out.'

He clumped away, limping more heavily than he needed to, and bent down to place the ignition-key on the cobbles half under the quad bike before quietly retracing his steps. Through the closed door he heard her speaking fast and fluently, a panicky note in her voice. '*Hola, querido*? What has happened? Why didn't you come last night? I waited so long for you. I must talk with you.'

Silence. Then: 'No, no. Not that. A man has been asking me questions. I don't know what to answer him.'

Another pause, then: 'Not police. No... Mr Robb – you know, Sally's papa, who drove the game-cart. Is he – could he be...? Wait. He is here still.'

She broke off abruptly, but by the time she had opened the door again, Robb was back by the Mule making a show of spotting the key on the cobbles and bending down stiffly to pick it up.

'Won't get far without this,' he called, giving her a cheerful wave as he manoeuvred himself awkwardly into the driver's seat. 'Thanks again, Luz. See you...'

'I couldn't help feeling sorry for her, sitting like Cinderella all alone in that big house,' he admitted as Jericho handed him a brimming gin-and-tonic that evening. 'I don't blame her for wanting to escape from whatever hellhole she grew up in, and she's obviously made a big effort to establish herself here. Once a pretty girl's in hock to traffickers they're not easy to shake off. Even if Hartzog bought her out, I imagine he kept her in line with threats to send her back where she came from.'

'More than likely,' Jericho agreed. 'So you're not planning to inform your colleagues?'

'Not really my business, is it?'

'No, but I wouldn't waste too much sympathy on her, if I were you. I guess you've been listening to Anita, right? She's always been a sucker for a sob story. Did she tell you about cruel Mr Hartzog lobbing Luz's baby hedgehogs into the Aga? Well, take it from me, that's a load of balls. Luz probably forgot to feed them, and didn't want to admit it. I'm afraid the long and short of it is that girl's what's politely known as a fantasist – in other words a bloody liar – and she's caused no end of trouble since she settled here. Kicked off by making a dead set at my manager, Tomasz, until she realised that everything he earns goes to support his wife and kids in Poland, and then would you believe it, she targeted old Duncan! Unbelievable. Fifteen years a widower, poor chap, so no wonder he was thrown when she started flashing her knickers at him. Pauly Bellton's a wily bird and realised what she was up to right away, and from what I'm told Locksley Maude has been cooling off lately too.' He smiled. 'I gather your daughter made you a present of a lesson with him on the clays. What did you make of him?'

'He's certainly a good instructor,' said Robb cautiously, somewhat disconcerted to have his reading of Luz so comprehensively rubbished, 'but it'll be a miracle if he can recoup what he's spent on setting up that business. You need a fair bit of backing to get an enterprise like that going, but when I was there with Sal, there wasn't another soul about. I suppose he decided to set up on his own after he left the Army, and thought his old mates would rally round to bring the money in.'

Jericho's mouth turned down. 'I'm not sure he left entirely voluntarily.'

'Oh?'

'His buddy was caught bringing unlicensed guns into the country, and tried to implicate Maude, but he managed to talk his way out of it. I don't suppose it did much for his chances of promotion, though.'

'Then how did he finance the shooting school?'

'I heard his brother left him money,' said Jericho vaguely, turning as the door opened. 'Ah, darling, here you are at last. All tucked up and asleep?'

'Tucked up, anyway.' Marina curled herself on the sofa. 'My poor baby! He looks so different – so anxious, as if he doesn't want to talk to me. I feel I'm walking on eggs. Oh, if only I hadn't let Hansi talk me into letting the boys help at the shoot!'

'Don't beat yourself up, darling. We all wish that, but it happened and there's nothing we can do about it now.'

'Except find out the truth,' said Marina fiercely, pushing back her hair. Like Jericho, she seemed to have aged in the past days, and looked pale and drawn. Nevertheless, small-boned and delicate-featured as she was, she reminded Robb of a cornered cat with claws unsheathed, ready to lash out in defence of her kitten.

Robb said, 'I'm told you found a couple of live cartridges in your son's anorak pocket after the Shoot. Twenties – is that right? Did you ask why he had them?'

'He said they looked so sweet, and he wanted them for his collection,' she said reluctantly.

'Can I have a look at them?'

'I'm afraid I binned them.' She glanced at her husband and added, 'The bags are collected on Tuesdays, so they're gone for good. '

No doubt on Anita's advice, thought Robb. Aloud he said, 'Can you remember what they were called?'

'Something like Black and Gold, I think. I didn't look too carefully: I just wanted to get rid of them.' She thought for a moment, then added, 'I did look through Max's collection afterwards, and I don't think he had any others like them. He must have picked them up because they were different.'

Just like I used to collect birds' eggs at his age, thought Robb as he turned to Jericho, 'Do you know what cartridges the twins were using?'

'I could get in touch with them and find out.'

It might be quicker to ask Pauly, thought Robb. He admitted handling their guns, and might well have taken a look at their cartridge belts as well. It was galling to have to admit to the Oaks that nothing he had discovered so far put Max and Pavel in the clear – in fact rather the reverse. He repeated Marcus Bellton's claim to have seen both Luz and Julius Lombard come out of the boiler-room after the boys had left, but it was a very slender thread on which to hang any hope and, as he expected, Jericho was immediately sceptical.

'After the amount of booze he'd put away over lunch, I doubt if Marcus could recognise his own mother, let alone a girl he'd only seen a couple of times,' he said despondently. 'As for fingering Julius, we know the Belltons would say anything that might make trouble for him. They blame him for mobilising antis to disrupt the badger cull, and I've heard it said that Julius has been spotted opening cage-traps at night, which doesn't make him exactly flavour of the month at Castle Farm.'

'I was down there this morning,' said Robb, 'and both of them were pretty much on edge.'

'Hardly surprising,' said Marina. 'Anita told me they've had an APHA team testing their cattle for bovine TB this week, and just one reactor will be enough to put their entire herd under restrictions again. At this time of year when fodder's getting tight, not to be able to move cattle between farms is the very devil.'

'Have they got another farm?'

'Oh, yes. Another two hundred acres over beyond the main road, and that's where most of their feed is stored. A standstill on movement would mean transporting silage, straw, concentrates – everything needed for the rest of the winter – across to Castle Farm, and then when they wanted to turn the cattle out there wouldn't be enough pasture here for all of them.'

'A logistical nightmare,' said Jericho. 'Let's hope it doesn't come to that. Say what you like about old Marcus, he's the best stockman most of us will ever know. He really cares about his animals. Knows them through and through: what they want, what they need, how to keep them in the best nick. What was it your father used to call him, sweetie?'

'Wasn't it "the Nonpareil" – something of the kind?' she said, searching her memory. 'That was in Daddy's speech after Marcus won both male and female championships at the West of England Show. We all teased him about the silver polish he would need.' She turned to Robb. 'He's got the most amazing collection of cups and trophies in that little office of his. Every show he went to ended the same way: Bellton and Son first; the rest nowhere.'

Jericho nodded. 'That's right. A real, old-fashioned stockman – that's Marcus. One of a dying breed, unfortunately. All that experience and know-how doesn't count for much in the agricultural scene nowadays. Instead you get a lot of bright youngsters coming into farming fresh from college, where they've been taught that science can deal with anything, and they should rely on regular testing and vaccinations against every known disease rather than observation and the kind of hands-on treatments farmers have used since time began – and yet when there is a real national calamity like the outbreak of foot-and-mouth in 2001, the only answer the government can come up with is wholesale slaughter and burn the carcasses.'

'And bio-security,' put in Marina, wrinkling her nose. 'Most of it totally impracticable in Marcus's case, plus an avalanche of forms to fill in with twelve-digit numbers. Think of it from his viewpoint. Specs on. Specs off. Where's that biro? Hold her head still while I check the ear-tag... No wonder it drives him half-mad.'

Jericho nodded. 'Quite honestly, that's the main reason we ourselves decided to give up livestock and turn over to horticulture ten years ago. A: we were barely scratching a living from the cows; and B: the regulation demands from DEFRA – aka Brussels – were becoming quite absurd. You know,' he went on contemplatively, 'it's my guess that Marcus's principal objection to that planning application of Hartzog's for the thousand-cow dairy unit wasn't the disruption it would cause to his own farm – he could deal with that – but the way those thousand cows would be treated. They'd be machines, not animals. No amount of scratching posts and scientific feeding would compensate for their loss of freedom to graze and behave like cows.'

He gave a short, half-embarrassed laugh. 'Sorry! I'm bending your ear. I just wanted you to know that although old Marcus is a roughish diamond, his heart's in the right place and there's more to him than meets the eye.'

CHAPTER THIRTEEN

Maude

'Can't wait to see my Lucky Locky again. We'll have ourselves a ball!'
Kelly-Louise had texted as soon as she got back to Jakarta, and
when the message popped up on his screen, Maude had felt
the kind of surging delight tinged with disbelief that winners
of Euromillions must experience. Did she mean it? Did she
remember those three sunlit afternoons in his little green boat
moored under overhanging gorse-bushes on the island in the
middle of the lakes where no one could see them?

Or at least where he had hoped no one could see them,
because there was no way of ignoring the fact that it was shortly
after she had left Dunmorse to embark on filming the first
travelogue in her Desert Songs trilogy that Hartzog's solicitor
had begun to harry him with questions about his right to access
the lakes and shooting school by crossing Dunmorse land. It
was possible that the timing was pure coincidence, but powerful
men like Hartzog seldom appreciated horns, and Maude had an
uneasy suspicion that Kelly-Louise's husband meant to make
life uncomfortable for him.

Slashing away with a billhook at the invading hazel
saplings and brambles that inhibited backcasting, he allowed

his mind to stray to the image of Kelly-Louise sprawled naked against the thwart of the green boat, sun glinting on her tightly cropped lint-pale hair as her wicked green eyes challenged him to come again.

'Don't keep me waiting,' she breathed huskily, and swivelled in one sinuous movement to offer him a different view of her perfectly tanned body. 'Come on, hero. Try it the Turkish way.'

A shiver ran over him, remembering how she fought and moaned as he mastered her, forgetting all his frustrations and anxieties as together they surfed a wave of pleasure. Making love with Kelly-Louise was champagne and caviar compared to Luz's brand of bread-and-butter sex, and a world away from taking possession of Marlene's resentful doughy body.

Since that brief idyll, two years had passed with never a word from her; two years in which he had felt himself being sucked ever deeper into trouble and debt, but now it was as if the stars had relented. Hartzog, the nemesis who had overshadowed those silent months was no more, and here was Kelly-Louise suggesting they took up where they had left off, as if those silent months had never been. There was no doubt in his mind that she had the power to make his problems vanish. A word from her to that over-zealous solicitor would sort out his right of access, and her recommendation would bring clients – the right sort of cosmopolitan sportsmen – flocking to fish in his lakes and hone their marksmanship on his targets.

He had attracted her once, and if he'd had the guts to seize on her invitation to come away to Paris for the weekend, who knows how much he could have profited? But when he'd said, half joking, half in earnest, 'I daren't. Your husband would kill me,' a blank, impenetrable expression had come over her face and she'd left him without another word.

Bottled it! he'd thought, cursing himself as he watched

her red Maserati sweep away into the woods, and that was the last he'd seen or heard of her until now. Her text message had brought hope sweeping back. If he got a second chance, he would not let the opportunity slip through his fingers again.

But first he must settle the question of Luz. Schemes flashed through his mind only to fizzle out like expended fireworks. She'd always been clingy, which at first had excited him, but since Hartzog's death it had begun to cloy. Not only cloy, but also alarm him as she became more insistent and resorted to bargaining, offering silence against the promise he now regretted.

How could he have been such a fool? What would Geoff have told him to do? But then, he reflected bleakly, canny old Geoff would have sniffed danger long ago. He would never have landed himself in such a fix.

Every time he saw her working with Anita, chatting with Anita, he had visions of Luz blabbing, blurting out that she was pregnant with his baby. Just a couple of sentences on those lines could scupper his chances with Kelly-Louise.

Flinging down the billhook, he sat on the bank and breathed deeply, scrabbling for a cigarette. Somehow he must find a way out of this before everything he had risked, everything he had worked for, vanished in a puff of smoke.

When the last of the cattle had been herded back into the yard and his team had finished hosing down their boots and stripping off their blue coveralls, Andrew Sawyer said quietly, 'Well done, team. Carry on, boys and girls. Load up your stuff and get on back to base. I won't be far behind you,' and crunched across the smashed ice of the farmyard towards the lighted window of Marcus Bellton's office.

From the railed passage leading to the crush, Pauly watched him go, hesitated a moment as if to follow, then bit his lip and went back to his job of closing gates and securing bars. He didn't envy Sawyer the next few minutes.

'Mr Bellton? May I come in?'

'Go on. Tell me how many,' grunted Marcus without turning round. In one hand was a tumbler of very brown whisky, and an open bottle was planted among the papers on the desk.

One wall of the small room was lined with shelves filled with spring-arch folders and box files; two tall metal filing cabinets flanked the desk, and the rest of the wall-space was crammed with flamboyant rosettes – red, blue, red-white-and-blue, orange and green, the occasional white or yellow – denoting prizes and championships at every agricultural and fatstock show in the country.

In front of the rosette-wall stood a six-foot display cabinet, and that, too, was crammed with engraved silver cups and trophies. Sawyer steeled himself and said steadily, 'Just the one. Everything else was clear.'

'I knowed it. I bin watching that lump grow and there wasn't a damned thing I could do to stop it.'

'It's a shame. A real shame.' He hesitated, watching Marcus's back, then added, 'You'll get written confirmation, of course, but I wanted to tell you myself how sorry I am.'

'Much good that'll do.'

'I know.' Sawyer racked his brain for some way to soften the blow. 'At least you've got some cracking calves from him, that's the best that can be said.'

There was a long, painful silence, then Marcus swung round at last. 'Listen to this, man. I been breeding Ruby Reds these fifty years, best bulls put to the best cows no matter what they cost, using top bloodlines all the way, and now when I've reared near-as-dammit the perfect animal – this happens. Dog-meat. Not even dog-meat. He'll go in the incinerator like any other rubbish, all because of Ministry rules and they bloody badgers. Why don't you take those calves with you! Think I want to go through it all again? Makes you sick, it does.'

'I'm more sorry than words can say.'

'Then say nowt. Gah! Come on, man, sit down and have a drink. You need it as much as I do.'

Reluctantly Sawyer shook his head. 'Thanks. I'd like to but I can't. I've got a couple more calls to make before heading back to the surgery, and my assistants will need my signature before they send off the samples.'

Marcus gave another incomprehensible grunt, and the vet added, 'I see your son's out feeding now. I'll have a word with him before I go. '

He held out his hand, and after a perceptible pause, Marcus shook it. Through the window he watched the vet trudge back towards the row of vehicles parked by the cattle-yard, pause to speak briefly to Pauly, then drive out of the gate...

The winter sun was setting in a red blaze, underlighting the flocked grey clouds with extravagant pink and purple flounces when Marcus roused himself from his chair and pulled on his boots and heavy Barbour coat. There'd be another frost tonight, and already the broken ice-puddles were skimming over again, and the breath of the yarded cattle made an edging of misty vapour along the feed-troughs. Glancing round to check that the yard was human-free, he backed his mud-caked Land Rover into the old Nissen hut which served as a refuge for surplus vehicles, and hitched up a light alloy trailer with a removable tailgate. Into this he lifted a long weldmesh cage, specially adapted by the agricultural engineers for trapping badgers, and secured it with elasticated straps to minimise its rattling on the woodland tracks.

Finally he fetched the shrouded carcase of a badger which Pauly had shot the previous night, and hoisted it into the back of the Land Rover. Without switching on his headlights, he drove slowly out of the Castle Farm yard and turned down the bridlepath through Scaffold Wood.

Newcomers to Starcliffe village often assumed the wood had some association with executions ordered by Judge Jeffreys at the time that the Duke of Monmouth's rebellion was so ferociously put down, but in fact the name had a more recent origin. Before Dunmorse Hall was built in the 1850s, several alternative sites were considered for the big house, and an elaborate stable complex complete with coach house and haybarn was under construction in the spinney then known as Allansgrove before the Dunmorse of the day quarrelled with his architect, scrapped his plans, and translocated the whole project half a mile farther down the hill.

For years the unfinished buildings, complete with scaffolding, stood abandoned as trees, brambles and rhododendron smothered human handiwork, creating a wildlife haven of which deer, foxes and badgers were not slow to take advantage. Acquisitive local builders carried away loads of good quality stone for their own purposes, and generations of Starcliffe children played hide-and-seek in the ruins or, as they grew older, experimented with tobacco and sex away from parental supervision. The name stuck, even though the wooden scaffolding had long rotted away, and by the late twentieth century nothing remained of the original Hall's structure but a few broken walls through which elderbushes sprouted, as well as the underground drainage system, plus storm-water tanks whose contents had long leaked away, still positioned where the run-off from guttering would have flowed into them.

It was here that Marcus Bellton, who had himself as a child explored every inch of the ruins, carefully positioned his cage-trap in a tangle of brambles which he knew concealed a storm-water tank some thirty feet deep.

'That'll sort out the bastard,' he thought vindictively, hauling the dead badger out of his vehicle and unwrapping the shroud. Arranged in a curled position by the door of the trap, as if trying to escape, it looked remarkably lifelike in the fading light as he swung the Land Rover in a circle and drove home, unaware of the dark, curious eyes watching from the shelter of a thicket of rhododendron fifty yards away.

Back at Castle Farm, he returned the trailer to the Nissen hut and parked his Land Rover beside his office before returning to his desk and the whisky bottle.

'Bloody shame,' he muttered, sipping as he rearranged the tiers of winning rosettes in order of importance. Triple layers of coloured ribbon denoted Championships, double layers for Best in Show, Red for First, Blue for Second, Yellow for Third. County shows, National shows, International Shows: over the years he had won them all.

Two glasses in, and unable to focus any longer on sorting his trophies, he unlocked the middle drawer of his desk, feeling at the back until his fingers encountered a flat black case. He flipped up the lid and stared at the old Greener Bell Gun's chamfered muzzle before loading the single round-nose lead bullet and slipping it in his pocket.

In the feedshed he switched on the yard lights, filled a scoop with cattle coarse-mix and added it to the bull's chopped fodder, absently scratching between the dark-red shoulders while peering at the raised bumps of tuberculin. There could be no doubt which was larger, no question of reprieve.

Damned if I'll let them cart him off to the abattoir, he thought, imagining the rattling stock-lorry backing up to the lairage, with its aura of stress and smell of trampled straw; the impassive slaughtermen driving Castle Farm Garnet into the railed chute, metal gates clanging, the ineradicable scent of death.

Bob's massive head nosed into the trough as he sought the last grains then raised it, still chewing, as he looked for more.

'Good lad,' said Marcus, in his usual tone.

With a hand that betrayed no tremor, he placed the Greener's muzzle between the bull's eyes and squeezed the trigger.

'Good old lad,' said Marcus again, as Bob slumped to the floor of the pen, his head in the concrete trough.

For a few moments Marcus stood watching until the involuntary twitching of the carcase stopped, and the cattle in the adjoining barn, who had lumbered to their feet on hearing the sharp crack, went back to their peaceful cudding, before stumping back to his office to sit down at his desk. With some idea of not letting good whisky go to waste, he swigged down what was left in his glass and screwed the cap on the bottle. Then he reloaded the Greener and placed the muzzle firmly against his own temple before squeezing the trigger.

A hundred yards before she reached the bus stop, Sally spotted the two small figures standing forlornly by the sign, and glanced at her watch. Eight-twenty: the bus must have gone past ten minutes ago. She swerved into the lay-by and as soon as they recognised her maroon 2CV, the boys snatched up their backpacks and ran towards her, waving frantically.

'Want a lift?'

'We missed the bus.'

'Only because Pavel was late,' said Max crossly, plonking himself in the front passenger seat.

'I was looking for my stick. I know I gave it to you.'

'You didn't.'

'I did.'

'Shut up, both of you,' said Sally, 'and do up your seat belts.' She eased off into the rush-hour traffic, and said, 'What would you have done if I hadn't come along?'

'Pauly picks us up before the bus comes past,' said Max.

She glanced at him in surprise. 'Always?'

He wriggled in his seat. 'Well, ever since... You know.'

Since before the accident. She nodded, and Max said in a hoarse whisper, 'Some kids on the bus call us murderers. I don't care, but they say Pavel should be deported. '

'That's rubbish. Don't listen to them. They don't know what they're talking about.'

Max was still wriggling about, fiddling with the pockets of his backpack as if looking for something, and finally tipping the contents on to his knees.

'Don't do that,' said Sally. 'There's enough mess in my car without you adding to it.'

'Sorry.' He crammed handfuls of sweet papers, pens, bits of string and unidentified objects back into the pockets and said plaintively, 'I don't know why Pauly didn't come. He's usually early because of feeding the animals.'

What should she tell him? How she and her father had been interrupted at breakfast by a breathless Pauly, wild-eyed and choking with sobs, blurting out that his father was dead in his farm office, and pleading with Robb to come and take charge quickly before his mother saw what had happened?

'It's blown my mind – can't seem to think straight – but you'll know what to do, seeing as it's your line of business. He's dead all right, sat there in his chair with his head on the desk and all his cups and rosettes laid out and scattered round about, and the old Greener bell-gun on the floor. Looks like he been there all night. I could tell there was summat wrong

185

the minute I come in the yard this morning. Cattle bellowing for their grub, the bull dead in his pen and the light still on in Dad's office.'

He had scrubbed at his eyes. 'Shouldn't a done it. There was no need. Not without saying a word. We'd a got through it somehow. It wouldn't of bin the end of the world. Oh, Dad, you bloody old fool! It's that Lombard drove him to it, sure as if he'd put the muzzle to Dad's head hisself. Him and his sodding badgers.' His voice choked and faltered. 'It's knowing Bob was done for finished him. Dad didn't love much, but he loved that bull and say what you like, I knows that bull loved him back.'

'Hang on a tick. I'll get my coat.' Robb lurched to his feet, and briefly gripped Pauly's shoulder. He said quickly to Sally, 'You stay here while I go and sort things out. Better get on to the police and tell them there's been an accident up at Castle Farm. OK?'

'I'm coming with you, Dad.'

'Better not. Just do as I say.' It was an effort not to add "for a change," but he managed to bite it off, and followed Pauly out of the porch...

None of which made a suitable answer for Max: Sally said at random, 'Something must have delayed him. Perhaps there was a new calf last night.'

'Not in January,' he said crushingly; and then, 'I'm too hot.'

'Then take your scarf off.'

Pavel leaned over from the back seat and whispered something Sally couldn't catch. Again they began the low-level wrangling, and she was heartily glad to turf them both out in front of the school gates. Pavel thanked her politely, but Max still looked aggrieved, and as they went off across the tarmacked car-park, she saw them shoving one another about before scampering out of sight as if suddenly aware of the time.

It was not a good start to the day.

'Mu–um,' said Max on Friday evening, putting on a baby voice and drawing the word into two syllables, 'if I can't go with Dad tomorrow, can I sleep-over with Pavel instead?'

'Oh, I don't know,' said Marina distractedly, wanting him to have a bit of fun, but instinctively trying to keep him close to her. 'Tomasz will be busy in the shop – you know there's always a crowd on Saturday – and after a tiring day I don't suppose he'll want both of you under his feet all evening.'

'We wouldn't be under his feet,' said Max indignantly. 'Come on, Mum. Don't you remember, they're running off the heats for the mountain bike races on Fiddler's Folly? Heats in the morning and the Final after lunch. We want to go and watch.'

'Well...' She couldn't think of a good reason to veto this plan. The annual mountain bike races down the steep track through the Starcliffe woods known as Fiddler's Folly drew daredevils from all over the country. Starting from an almost vertical chute behind the Eastmarsh Sports entrance, these lurex-clad dragonflies faced an obstacle course full of sudden humps and dips, concealed tree-roots and water-splashes zigzagging down a precipitous three-mile descent before zooming out onto the coned-off lane at 30-40 miles per hour. It was a thrilling spectacle which Max had watched every year since he was five, and he always began reminding her about it months ahead. This last week it had completely slipped her mind.

'All right,' she said at last. 'So long as you promise – absolutely promise – you won't be a pest and will do exactly what Tomasz tells you to.'

'No problem.'

'And come home straight after breakfast. I've got a PCC

meeting after church, but Anita has very kindly offered to give you a lift to your football coaching. No, darling, don't make that face. Mr Lombard says if you don't do the practice, you can't play in the match.'

'OK. Will Pavel come for coaching, too?'

'You'll have to ask his father. Now promise me you'll behave and do as Tomasz tells you.'

'I've already said I would.'

'That's not good enough, darling.'

'OK, then. I promise. Thanks, Mum.'

He hugged her and trotted off. He had stayed overnight with Pavel before, and anticipated no difficulty with Tomasz, whose usual evening routine was to wolf down whatever his son prepared for supper – baked beans were a strong possibility – and telephone his wife Magda in Warsaw, after which he would retire to the cramped little front room with a couple of mates and a bottle of vodka, leaving the boys to amuse themselves as they saw fit. With the mountain bike races to look forward to and an unsupervised evening ahead, Max felt that the weekend looked full of promise.

'Anybody home?' called Detective Sergeant James Winter, pushing open the porch door and putting his head into the kitchen.

'Jim!' Sally jumped up from the table and gave him a big hug. 'How lovely to see you. You look terrific.'

A fortnight training in the Atlas Mountains had indeed done wonders for Winter's fitness; he had always been wiry and muscular but now he seemed to have filled out and grown a couple of inches. Compared to winter-pallid English complexions, his tan was striking.

'Good to see you, Jim.' Robb shook his hand warmly. 'I expect you've heard what's been going on here while you've been conquering the peaks?'

'I've kept a long-distance eye on it,' Winter admitted. 'Small boys and shotguns are always a bad combination.'

'True enough, and hardly surprising that's the line the police are taking. But...'

Winter's attention sharpened like a dog winding game. 'Are you saying there's some doubt about it?'

'I've got doubts, and so – unsurprisingly – have the boy's parents.'

'Go on.'

'Sit down and have a cuppa and I'll tell you all about it.'

Winter was a good listener and though he frowned once or twice during Robb's account, he said nothing until he heard about the failed TB test and Marcus Bellton's suicide.

'So that explains the Incident tape at Castle Farm. Hi-vis jackets everywhere, as well as blocking off the road before the mountain bike races. My first run is at eleven-fifteen.' He turned hopefully to Sally. 'Are you coming to watch?'

'Can't this morning. I've got work to do – unlike some.' She saw the disappointment he tried to conceal and added, 'But providing you don't break your neck in the heats, I might come and watch this afternoon. Let me know if you make it into the final.' She glanced at her watch. 'Hey, look at the time! Duncan will skin me. 'Bye, Dad. See you, Jim.'

With a wave she was gone, and the two men settled back in their chairs, while on the hearthrug Pilot drooped his ears and rested his long muzzle on his paws. The cottage seemed very quiet without her.

'Now,' said Winter, 'let's go through it all again. You say that Pauly Bellton and the boys were the last people seen handling guns in this boiler-room – drying-room, whatever

189

– before the general exodus?'

'Right.'

'And this chap who topped himself, Mr Bellton senior, had been breathing hell and damnation at Hartzog all morning, because of some planning application?'

'Right again.'

'And Bellton had been seen to visit the Gents, which adjoins said boiler-room, at least twice during the meal, so why couldn't he have boobytrapped the gun?'

Robb said patiently, 'If you'd met him, you'd have seen why not. He was a clumsy old sod, not to put too fine a point on it, and none too steady on his feet after a G&T followed by a skinful of wine. I agree, he does look the most likely candidate, apart from the boys, but I just can't see him having the dexterity – or getting the timing right.'

'Anyone found shot in the head would be of interest to me,' said Winter doggedly. 'Say he stuffed the twenties into Hartzog's barrels when he was boozed to the eyeballs, and regretted it when he sobered up. Consumed with guilt; shot his bull then blew his own brains out. How about that?'

Robb shook his head. 'I don't buy it. Bellton wasn't the type to get consumed by guilt. Not in his nature. He was glad of Hartzog's death and made no bones about telling me so. Said he'd like to shake the hand of whoever had done it.'

'OK, then.' Though unconvinced, Winter abandoned his theory and said, 'Who else? Oh, by the way,' he added, 'I checked some of the names through the computer, as I promised, and came up with a few interesting results.'

'Such as?'

'Well, Hartzog's headkeeper, Tobias Hagley, was not only sacked from his job on a grouse moor in the Borders, but also prosecuted by the RSPB for shooting a protected bird – a hen-harrier – and destroying the identifying tag.'

'Ah, someone did mention that. Go on.'

'RSPB couldn't make it stick, but word got around and Hagley was out of a job for five years, because none of the Scottish landowners would touch him. From what you tell me about Hartzog, I should think he set some pretty stiff conditions before he agreed to take him on.'

Robb thought it over and nodded. 'Anyone else? What about Luz Fernandez?'

'Nothing on her. Seems to have slipped under the radar. But as your Mr Oak indicated, the shooting-school proprietor's got form. His mate Staff Sergeant Bill Creedy, a moron if ever there was one, had his bags searched after a tip-off, and said he'd only put two H and K machine-pistols in as a favour to Maude, who hadn't got room in his kitbag. Of course Maude denied it.'

'One man's word against another?'

'That's about the size of it.'

'Who did the court-martial believe?'

'Who do you think? Bill Creedy was dishonourably discharged and got two years. Maude sounds a plausible bugger, and he got off scot-free, but left the Army as soon as his time was up. Then blow me down if his big brother, who owned a garage of some sort, didn't keel over within the year and leave him enough money to set up here on his own. Talk about luck.'

Robb wondered how much Luz knew about Maude's early career. 'Never been married, then?'

'Divorced. Two children. They'll be teenagers now, but the wife hasn't remarried, so he's still supporting them to some degree, I imagine.'

And if he was as deep in debt to the bank as Jericho seemed to think, Robb reflected, he was hardly in a position to take on new commitments. He thought that it might be worth digging a little deeper into Maude's past; but Winter was pursuing a different line.

He said, 'However you look at it, boss, those boys are the most likely culprits. No motive, I give you that; unless you accept that the mere fact of being nine years old and male makes you incapable of leaving guns alone; but from what you tell me, they had opportunity in spades.'

Robb gave a discontented grunt. 'Don't go telling me what I already know, Jim. What I need from you is fresh thinking. Some way of showing that young Max and Pavel are telling the truth, and the villain is right here under our noses, although we can't quite see how he did it.'

'OK. Let's try this for size,' said Winter promptly. 'Knock 'em out one by one. We can eliminate the Belltons first. Old Mr B because he's dead; and Pauly Bellton because he made a full and frank admission of handling Hartzog's gun, and swears that both barrels were empty when he and the boys left the room. And for some reason I can't quite fathom, you believe him.'

'Never mind, Jim. We can't all be psychic. Just take my word for it, all right?'

Winter's sniff showed what he thought of such unprofessional reasoning. 'So we'll eliminate Pauly, too; and Mr Oak, because he's the boy's father –'

'Stepfather,' corrected Robb, and for a moment Winter's interest flickered.

'Wicked stepfather?'

Robb grunted again and shook his head. 'No. Strike him out, too. Right, now who have we left?'

'You haven't given me a lot of choice,' said Winter, shrugging. Mentally he reviewed all the information Robb had relayed. 'It's got to be young Lothario – the gun-runner, hasn't it? But you say both Sally and Mr Oak – what do you call him, Jericho? – saw him drive away from the barn well before Pauly and those boys came out of the boiler-room. Maude hadn't even left his own gun there, according to your friend Anita. It was on the rack behind the driver's seat of his pick-up. So if he shoved twenty-bore cartridges into Hartzog's twelve-bore, he must have done it by magic. And as you probably know, boss, I don't believe in magic. Or else –'

'How else?'

'Collusion,' said Winter with slow certainty. 'That ticks all the boxes. Remember how he got his mate Bill Creedy to carry illicit firearms for him? Same pattern.'

'Now you're getting somewhere,' said Robb with satisfaction. 'Keep at it, Jim.'

'So he gives the cartridges to his girlfriend – the 'little furrin piece' old Bellton saw flitting about near the Gents ¬– and tells her he'll marry her and live happy ever after if she'll slip into the boiler-room while everyone's listening to speeches, and put them down the barrels of Hartzog's gun. Then off he drives, well ahead of everyone else, to give himself an alibi. How about that?'

Robb nodded. 'That's exactly what I think must have happened. Well done, Jim. I've been mulling it over for a week now, and you've reached the same conclusion in – what? – half an hour. Snag is: how can we prove it?'

'Would she confess if she knew Maude had been two-timing her?' As if the mention of time had galvanised him, Winter looked at his watch and jumped up. 'Sorry, boss. I must go. My first run is scheduled for 11.15 and it'll take me twenty minutes to get kitted up. What's the quickest way to the Shooting School? The Fiddler's Folly course starts round the back of it.'

'Don't break your neck,' called Robb as he clattered out. 'I'm going to need your input when I put all this to the CS team.'

CHAPTER FOURTEEN

The Races

SATURDAY 27th JANUARY

Quite half the fun of watching downhill races comes from the very real possibility of seeing some spectacular falls. After four years' experience, Max had worked out how best to maximise his chances of being at the right viewpoint when these occurred and, since the obstacles on the course remained much the same from year to year, he liked to divide his time between the grandstand halfway down the hill, from which to watch the race's early stages, and the one overlooking the finish and final watersplash through the Arne Ford which often caused competitors disproportionate grief, being deeper than it looked.

As usual, the races attracted a large crowd. Favourites to win the team trophy were the Co. Durham raiders who had triumphed last year, though there was rumour of fresh talent in the Norfolk ranks. Individuals were harder to predict, with strong support for Bruno Bellini, a neck-or-nothing Italian who was said to have broken the record for a Black-graded descent in the hills above Trieste.

It cost the two boys a good deal of wriggling, provoking disapproving comments from their elders, to wedge themselves into Max's chosen position on the central grandstand, and the criticism redoubled when he decided this viewpoint wasn't good enough and retreated through the packed rows in order to take up his preferred station near the end of the course.

'Settle down and stop pushing!' growled an exasperated marshal as they forced a passage through the tiered seats. 'You won't see any better from anywhere else.'

'It's Jericho's nipper. Let them through,' said a fat woman, turning sideways to make room, but they were still standing on tiptoe trying to see past people's heads when Winter came flying downhill on his second run. His first had clocked up an impressive time which placed him fourth on the leader-board, and it was with new confidence that he wheeled into the chute and thrust down on the pedals.

Although he had walked the course early in the morning and had a fair idea of its shape and pitfalls, on his first run the corners and hazards seemed to come up with such bewildering speed that he was constantly on the brink of losing control. Now, however, as he threaded between the trees, using his knees to iron out the bumps, he was able to anticipate each obstacle and adjust his balance over the rapid succession of drop-offs, berms, and steps that bounced his wheels into the air, to swing effortlessly round the big boulders and shoot the sudden humps without a thought of braking.

This is terrific! Best Red course ever, he thought, sneaking a glance at the stopwatch strapped across the back of his glove. Six seconds off his earlier time at this point, and he was experiencing the heady exhilaration of feeling in complete harmony with his bike, his body, and the track – its myriad obstacles and convolutions mere blips in his headlong descent. Nothing it threw at him had the power to hamper or throw him off course. Together he and the bike were invincible. In any other situation he would have yelled with sheer delight, but this was serious. He really wanted to win.

Below him stretched the wide Starcliffe valley, with the silver thread of river snaking through its water-meadows, and ahead the course took a long loop through clear-felled woodland, where a single-track board-walk abruptly replaced the narrow leaf-strewn path.

Speeding up on the smooth surface, he nearly came to grief as the board-walk doubled back on itself and reverted to muddy ruts, then packed gravel over which his extra-wide tyres laboured, threatening to skid. He survived a tricky chicane, took the shortest route over three logs which had felled earlier riders, and as the track dived into thick woodland once again, he caught a distant glimpse of colour: the red-and-white cones marking the final furlong along the road.

R U winning? Sally had texted half an hour ago; and for one incalculably brief instant he believed he might be able to answer Yes. Was it that tiny lapse in concentration that did for him? he wondered later. Did he allow his attention to wander at the critical instant?

Whatever his state of mind, the primary cause of his downfall was clear enough. A startled cock pheasant rocketed noisily from beside the track and struck his front wheel squarely, pitching him over the handlebars into the brambles, with the bike on top of him.

Felled by a fucking pheasant so no final he texted grimly when the marshals had pulled him out and dusted him down, but before he pressed Send he decided it looked self-pitying and deleted the expletive. After all, the collision was hardly the pheasant's fault: he was the interloper.

The bird was still crouched a couple of feet away, making ineffectual fluttering movements. He picked it up, amazed by the beauty of its warm, soft plumage, the startling contrast between iridescent blue-green head and clean white neck-ring, the bright chestnut cape and long barred tail feathers. What a work of art! He had never handled a cock pheasant before, and found it hard to ignore the mute appeal in the red-ringed eye; but the right wing, hanging uselessly, showed there could be no question of a reprieve.

Oh damn! Not my scene, he thought.

'Give me. I do,' said a stout red-bearded man, taking the pheasant from him and breaking its neck with a quick, practised twist. Trailing after him, two boys stopped a couple of paces away to stare at Winter with admiration.

'You were the quickest,' said the pale, taller one. 'We hoped you would win the prize.'

'Is your bike OK?' asked the other, whose round face was pink with excitement.

The three of them inspected it. Apart from mud and festoons of brambles, it had suffered remarkably little damage.

'Not too bad,' Winter decided. 'At least it's still rideable.'

'We were sure you'd win,' said the round-faced boy sadly. 'We were cheering like mad.'

'Ah, well. These things happen.' Winter mounted cautiously as various aches and twinges made themselves apparent. 'Thanks for cheering, anyway,' he called and rode off.

Three hours later, as the light began to fade, Tomasz decided to go home. Young Mariusz, his sister Kinga's skinny, earnest son who was anxious to improve his spoken English, had been persuaded to take his place and act as manager all afternoon at the Farm Shop but although seldom over-active, Tomasz's conscience now dictated that he should check the takings and lock up himself before heading for home.

His decision provoked an immediate outcry. 'But we want to see who wins!' Max protested hotly. 'We can't go yet.'

'Come now, or walk home,' said Tomasz stolidly. 'You choose.'

The boys exchanged agonised glances and Max consulted his much-creased copy of the running order. 'Bruno Bellini is coming next.'

Pavel nodded. 'OK, we walk.'

And walk they did as soon as Bellini had received his trophy and completed a lap of honour in the dusk. Cars were flicking on their side-lights as they entered the wood, but in the open there was enough light to see Starcliffe church on the far side of the valley, with the Castle Farm cattle-yard below it and the outlying cottages belonging to Dunmorse Hall just showing round the shoulder of the hill.

Pavel strode along easily, but Max was tired and regretting his decision to stay when Tomasz left. Any fool could see that when James Winter was knocked out Bruno Bellini was bound to win, he thought despondently, and now he was faced with a long walk on the road followed by the usual slog through Scaffold Wood and up the drive to the cottage where Pavel and Tomasz lived. His short legs were aching already, and his runkled sock rubbed his left heel.

'Can't you slow down a bit?' he whined, searching his pockets for forgotten Haribos and finding nothing.

'No. I wish to show you something. Is not so far now —'

Before Pavel could complete his sentence, an all-too-familiar pick-up braked to a halt beside them, and an all-too-familiar voice said: 'You little idiots! What on earth are you doing, walking in the lane in the dark? Come on, hop in. I'm on my way to the Hall, so I'll give you a lift as far as the bus stop and you can walk home from there. At least in the wood you won't get run over.'

He leaned over and opened the door, and Max scrambled in eagerly. 'You, too,' said Maude as Pavel hung back. 'Get a move on, I can't hang about here all night.'

'Bossy beast,' muttered Max, not quite sotto voce enough.

'What's that you said?'

'Nothing.'

'You should be glad I saw you before the police did. Then you'd have really been in trouble. I mean, more trouble than you are already.' He accelerated away, passing a mud-spattered quad bike with feedsacks on the carrier which had squeezed into a lay-by to make room for him. Max recognised Sally on her way to check the pheasant-feeders, and waved as they drew level.

'So your dad didn't take you shooting today, eh?' needled Maude. 'Didn't want you messing about with firearms, I expect. Not like you were last Saturday in the barn.'

Pavel gritted his teeth and was silent, but Max leaned forward and said hotly: 'We weren't messing about. Pauly was teaching us about the guns.'

'Ha! Teaching you – is that what you call it? That's a laugh, that is. And just what was he teaching you, if I make so bold as to ask?'

Max knew sarcasm when he heard it, but his temper was rising, and he said, 'He was teaching us lots of things we didn't know.'

'Such as?' When Max didn't answer, Maude added scornfully, 'See, you can't even remember anything he said.'

From the back seat, Pavel came to his rescue. He said solemnly, 'Pauly showed us which guns cost a lot, and how to know who made them, and how old they were.'

'So you've got a tongue in your head after all,' said Maude mockingly. 'Go on. Tell me more. Which gun cost the most?'

'Mr Hartzog's,' they said together; and Pavel added, 'But I like the small ones better. They are not so heavy.'

'You shouldn't have touched them.'

For a moment or two he drove in silence, but Max was simmering with resentment at the rebuke, and finally burst out, 'Then why was Luz touching them?'

'Don't talk rubbish,' snapped Maude. 'Luz was in the kitchen. She wasn't anywhere near the guns.'

'Yes, she was. Pavel saw her. '

'Stop talking, Max!' Pavel leaned over the seat in his agitation. 'Don't say more.'

'Why not? You told me you saw her picking up the guns.'

But Pavel was remembering how Luz had whipped round when she caught a glimpse of him in the mirror, and her face had gone hard and ugly, like a witch. She had put down the gun she was holding and caught hold of him by the front of his pullover, jerking him so close that her face was inches from his as she hissed, 'Bad boy! Wicked boy! Why do you spy on me?'

'I'm not!' he had protested, trying to get away, but she held him tightly.

'If you tell anyone – anyone – that you see me here, I will know and I will tell English police how your papa is stealing many fish secretly in the night. Then he will be deported from UK, and you too. You understand me?'

Trembling, he had nodded, and she let him go. He had bolted back into the lavatory and been sick again. He hadn't told anyone then, not even Max; but later on when they were looking at the photographs he had taken of the Shoot, Max had spotted it and asked why Luz had been looking at the guns and Pavel had told him how she had threatened to get him and his father deported.

'Tell him, Pavel,' Max insisted. 'You told me you saw her in the drying-room when you went to the loo to be sick.'

'Liar!' said Maude, his mouth suddenly dry.

'He's not! It's the truth. He took a photograph of her.'

'Show it to me.'

There was a long pause, then Max said sullenly, 'I can't. I've lost the bug.'

'What do you mean?'

'He put it on a bug and gave it to me and I've lost it.'

'Where did you lose it?' said Maude, his heart-rate returning to normal.

'If I knew it wouldn't be lost, would it?'

Max knew such pertness would bring a sharp reprimand from his mother, but Maude was too relieved to scold him and said only, 'That's true enough, at least. Look, here's the bus stop. Out you hop, and if you hurry you should be home before it's really dark.'

Hurrying home, however, was the last thing on Pavel's mind. He had been waiting patiently for the chance to find out what Mr Bellton had been doing in Scaffold Wood at dusk on Thursday, and now to Max's dismay he turned abruptly off the main track through the wood and followed the faint traces the Land Rover and trailer had left as it passed through the frosty scrub towards Allansgrove plantation.

'Where are you going?' demanded Max, tripping over roots as he tried to keep up.

'I show you something. Is not too far.'

'But it's nearly dark. What is it, anyway?'

'Quiet! You will see...'

As the wood grew thicker, the Land Rover tracks became easier to follow. It had smashed through clumps of brambles, and bent back ash saplings, leaving a trail which Pavel followed confidently.

'Here is where I watched him,' he said at last, halting beside the rhododendron thicket.

'Watched who?'

'Pauly's papa. He put a cage in the...' He pointed, stuck for the name.

'Over there? In the ivy?'

'Ivy. Yes,' Pavel whispered. 'Now we go quietly.'

They crept forward until they could see the dull metal of the trap showing above a dense blanket of ivy which had smothered a ruined wall. Brambles snatched at their clothes as they approached it, treading softly. An acrid feral whiff reached their noses.

'It's caught something,' whispered Max. 'Looks like a badger.' He began to move forward, but Pavel touched his sleeve warningly.

'Wait.'

They stood motionless, staring at the yellowish-grey heap of coarse hair curled up against the door of the trap. It did not move and again the feral whiff drifted to them, now with a distinct undertone of decay.

'Is dead,' said Pavel with finality.

'Come on, let's have a look.'

Abandoning caution, they approached the trap and Max lifted the catch to pull at the self-closing door. 'It's...stiff! Try from the other side.'

They were both struggling to open it, gasping with effort, when without warning the ground subsided under them. The cage-trap tilted, and for an instant they clung to the metal mesh before their fingers were torn from it and, with terrified yells, they plummeted into blackness.

CHAPTER FIFTEEN

Tomasz

SATURDAY NIGHT

Tomasz was in a hurry. After locking up the afternoon's takings in the safe and setting the farmshop alarms, he barred the doors and locked the carpark barriers before mounting the bright red Yamasaki Monster moped which was his pride and joy for the short journey home. The boys were not back yet, but then he would have been surprised if they had torn themselves away from the downhill races before the trophies had been presented, and Pavel, at least, was perfectly capable of getting supper on the table.

Nevertheless, even with a busy evening ahead of him, he did not entirely neglect his parental duty. Unwrapping the golden-crusted veal and ham pie he had taken from the farmshop display, he hacked it into quarters, two of which he put on his own plate and one for each of the boys. Then he scattered a handful of cutlery on the kitchen table, added plates, glasses, and a jug of water and, remembering they had a guest tonight, he opened a tin of baked beans which he placed beside the two-ring stove.

Duty fulfilled, he retired with his own plate to the cottage's second room, from which he could see up a narrow gully to the Eastmarsh clubhouse. Half an hour earlier he had seen its lights extinguished, and Maude's long-wheelbase pick-up emerge from the lane, heading down the narrow, winding road that led to the Hall. Now, as he wolfed down his pie, Tomasz considered where he could best launch his raid tonight.

Like every successful hunter, he believed in studying the habits of his quarry. He knew how pheasants followed the sun in their daily perambulations, how fallow buck chose the same traditional rutting stands year after year, and where and when rainbow trout preferred to feed.

He knew how Hagley, the headkeeper, would take corn to his pheasants and go round his traps every morning, and then spend half an hour watching porn on his smartphone in the plucking shed, and he knew of the hollow tree by the release pen gate in which he cached his bottle of Johnnie Walker; he also knew a good deal about Cecil Barley's dealings with Pakistani falconers and their middlemen in Birmingham's poultry market.

Another thing he knew was that on Saturday evenings Locksley Maude was in the habit of picking up Luz from Dunmorse Hall and taking her clubbing in Lower Langley, the nearest town where legal highs were readily available, together with less legal but more powerful substances such as Big K and Meow-Meow; and that this was a propitious moment to pay a visit to the Eastmarsh lakes.

'Where's Max?' asked Jericho as he came in from seeing off the last of his Guns. 'I thought he'd like to help Duncan in the game-larder. I don't want him to feel left out of the shooting scene altogether.'

'Oh, darling, I feel just the same – as if he's deliberately separating himself from us,' said Marina, pushing back her hair with a tired gesture. 'It really worries me.'

'I'll call him. Is he in his room?'

Marina shook her head. 'Tomasz took both boys to the mountain-bike races at Fiddler's Folly this afternoon, and Max asked me if he could stay for a sleep-over at the cottage.'

'And you said Yes? Honestly, darling, is that a good idea? Have you seen the state of that cottage?'

'A bit of dirt won't hurt him,' she said, shrugging. 'At least he'll have company, rather than kicking his heels here alone while we're out to dinner. And we've got Communion at 8.30 next morning –'

'*You've* got –' he interposed quickly.

'– with the damned PCC meeting following on at 9.30. That usually drags on for over an hour, so Anita, bless her, has offered to take Max to his football coaching. I should be free by eleven to fetch him home.'

'In other words, a really peaceful Sunday morning,' said Jericho, laughing. 'Well, I'd better have a shower and change if we've any hope of getting to the Rawlinsons' by 8.30. No doubt we'll all meet up tomorrow at lunch.'

'Never touch the bait with your fingers,' Dziadziu used to tell the six-year-old Tomasz. 'Never be in a hurry. Never be greedy...' There were a lot of prohibitions in his grandfather's fishing lore, but who else could have kept his whole family fed and fit during the terrible hungry years after the war with nothing but a few baited hooks and lines tied to an otterjack? His skill was legendary, and though he had been dead for fifteen years, Tomasz still followed his advice to the letter.

How Dziadziu's clever dark eyes would have sparkled if he could have seen the spreading rings on the still black surface of Eastmarsh's bigger oxbow lake tonight under the bright half-moon, showing where trout were busy near the reedbeds, and how he would have gasped at the size of them!

The hunter is Nature's truest friend, was another of his maxims, and in a country overflowing with game like England, he would have scorned a grandson who fed his family on shop-bought meat and fish. Nevertheless, mindful of his condemnation of greed, Tomasz took only enough for his own needs – plus those of certain selected friends who could be relied on to pay up and keep their mouths shut.

Or so he hoped. It was a worry that the friendly landlord of *The Rising Sun*, Dave Dymoke, who had always been glad to buy a couple of fresh-caught rainbow, had recently taken up with stout, bosomy Trish, daughter of Cecil Barley, who had effectively forbidden Tomasz to bring fish to the pub's back door. An embarrassed Dave had directed him to the farthest corner of the car-park and asked him to conduct his business there. It was not so convenient a spot, smelt of petrol and urine, and worst of all, Trish's presence had encouraged some of the Dunmorse Hall beaters to transfer their allegiance from the *King's Head* to *The Rising Sun*. Although it would mean setting up a whole raft of new connections, Tomasz thought he would find somewhere else to dispose of his catch in future.

Tonight he had orders for six fish, one of which he planned to keep for himself. After setting his fixed lines across the narrow neck of a little bay, he waited patiently until he felt the thrilling bump and jiggle that told him a fish was interested – and an instant later, that it was hooked. Gently drawing up the jack while slipping his long-handled folding net below and behind it, he lifted it from the water and in one smooth movement swung it on to the bank. A fair-sized rainbow, not one of the 12kg monsters but over 3kg at a guess and well worth keeping: he killed it quickly and slid it into a polythene bag before gathering up his jack and moving to another favoured bay.

Five times he repeated the operation, putting on surgical gloves before baiting his hooks with neat little balls of Dziadziu's infallible compound – meal, egg-yolk, insects and worms mashed together and baked hard – and meticulously obliterating all trace of his presence from each spot where he had lingered. When the last line he set caught two fish simultaneously, he conscientiously removed the extra one from the net and returned it to the water, then carried the bag to where he had cached his Yamasaki and arranged the gleaming, iridescent fish, nose to tail, in the big cool-box on his carrier.

With a last careful check that nothing had been left behind, he puttered away downhill towards *The Rising Sun.*

It was half an hour before closing time, and though the car-park was far from full it was darker than usual because the lamp-post in his allotted corner had blown its bulb. Nevertheless, he set the moped on its stand, and unstrapped the cool-box, then settled himself on the low surrounding wall to wait for customers.

Five minutes passed; then another five, but no one approached him. What had happened? More cars drove out. He heard the landlord call Time, and there was a sudden exodus which left only half a dozen vehicles grouped close together near the door to the Public bar.

Tomasz skin prickled: where were his customers? Something was definitely wrong. He replaced the lid of the cool-box, clicked the catches, and was about to hoist it on to his carrier when the pub door burst open shedding a stream of light on the remaining cars, one of which he recognised as the beat-up van belonging to Cecil Barley.

No need to panic, he thought. Why shouldn't Barley visit the pub where his daughter was landlady? There, indeed, was the stocky underkeeper coming through the door, stick in hand as usual; what was unusual was that the group of men he headed were all carrying sticks, fanning out to form a half-circle and moving purposefully towards Tomasz. In order to leave the car-park he would have to ride right through the cordon.

'There he is, the dirty thief,' said Barley roughly. 'Come on, boys. Let's see what he's been stealing tonight.'

With a confused growl, the men surrounded Tomasz and broke his grip on the handle of his cool-box, wrenching it away and spilling the contents on the tarmac. Furious, he lashed out and caught Barley a heavy blow on the chin, sending him stumbling backwards, following up with a kick that doubled up another of his attackers, who sank to his knees, moaning.

Tomasz had learnt self-defence in a hard school, and at 6ft 2 and seventeen stone he was no weakling, but even Polish fire and fury could hardly improve odds of five to one, and when a movement behind him warned of reinforcements joining from the rear, he knew the game was up.

Nevertheless, like an embattled bull elephant beset by wild dogs, he continued to kick, punch, and grapple, chopping the edge of his hand at the throat of one attacker, and even biting off half the ear of Barley's cousin, who had come along anticipating an enjoyable scrap and found himself getting more than he bargained for.

Inevitably, numbers told. Tomasz was blown and bleeding, clothes torn and woollen beanie missing though still striking out like a man possessed, when Barley, moving behind him, brought down his cudgel with maximum force on his exposed skull, and the Pole crumpled to the ground.

This was the signal for the jackals to move in with boots and cudgels, first on the unconscious man, and then on his moped, whacking off lights and mirrors, slashing the tyres with Stanley knives, crumpling the front wheel, tearing off cables and bending the exhaust-pipe. They scooped up the contents of the coolbox, smashing the jack and lines and scattering the fish into the shrubbery behind the car-park. After stamping the cool-box into shards, Barley poured a flask of rum over Tomasz before shouting to his daughter to ring the Starcliffe police.

'Say the Grange Farm Poles been fighting again and you need them to sort it out. Come on, boys. Leave him now, and let's be going.'

Ten minutes later when the police van's headlights picked out the battered figure sitting beside his wrecked Yamasaki, Tomasz was mumbling aloud in Polish and English, but making no sense in either.

'Nothing broken – just cuts and bruises and a lump on his head. No prizes for guessing how he came by that,' said the police surgeon after a quick check. 'Doesn't know if it's Christmas or Easter.' He took a step backwards. 'Faugh! Smells like a distillery. What time is it? Quarter to midnight? Put him in a cell and let him sober up before we decide what to do with him.'

CHAPTER SIXTEEN

Sally

SUNDAY 28th JANUARY

For even the least car-proud of owners, the winter accumulation of mud, salt, moss in window crevices, and spiders' webs on wing-mirrors, combined with a gently decaying interior compost of dog-hair, leaves, ancient Polos, car-park tickets, old shopping lists and scraps of silver paper eventually becomes intolerable, and on that bright crisp morning Sally looked her car over with disgust and announced her intention to do something about it.

'What's the point? There's rain forecast tomorrow,' grumped her father, who made a point of listening to the 7am news. 'It'll be just as dirty in a week's time.' He had forgotten to take painkillers before going to bed, and having woken in extreme discomfort at 3am and swallowed them down, found it impossible to get back to sleep.

'No, it won't. From now on I'm going to look after it properly. After all, it's the last thing Mum gave me and Hels.'

Too late she realised this came dangerously close to rubbing salt into the wound, and was hardly surprised when

Robb said dryly, 'Not that your sister gets much chance to use it.'

'Dad! That's unfair. You know she said she couldn't get behind the wheel when she was pregnant, so that's why I've got it here.'

Silence from Robb was comment enough on this explanation, and with the truce between them still fragile, neither risked further discussion. Determined to make good on her resolve, Sally drove down to the old rickyard immediately after breakfast, connected up the power-hose, and gave the little 2CV the wash of its life, prising great chunks of dried mud from the wheel-arches and blasting away every scrap of moss that had lodged round the windows.

'Worth sixpence more now,' commented Anita with a smile. She was sitting on the old milk-stand and had pulled her knees to her chin to avoid the flood of muddy water. 'Do you want to borrow my hoover to finish the job?'

She fetched it from her flat above the old cart-shed, and watched as it noisily sucked debris from the Citroen's cramped interior.

'It's not pulling properly. Sounds like you've got something stuck in the pipe,' she said after a minute. 'Switch off and it'll fall out.'

A couple of brisk shakes brought a bright green USB bug rattling down the pipe. 'Not mine,' said Sally, picking it up.

'Your dad's?'

Sally laughed. 'Unlikely! I do all the techie stuff for him.' She switched on the vacuum cleaner again and tackled the mess between the seats.

Anita was looking at her watch. 'Max is late. He'll miss his footie coaching if he doesn't get a move on. He was having a sleepover with Pavel last night, and of course Tomasz has Sundays off. I wonder if they've all overslept. Perhaps I ought to drive up to their cottage and roust him out.'

'I bet if you do he'll turn up the moment you've gone.' Sally regarded her car with satisfaction but the mention of Max had triggered a memory. 'I also bet that USB stick is his. He was hunting for something he'd lost when I gave him a lift to school. He left his scarf in my car, too. I found it on the floor. It sounded to me as if they'd missed the bus on purpose.'

'I heard that Pavel gets horribly teased, poor kid. Max does his best to stick up for him, but once the "Poles out" brigade get going, they're impossible to shut up.'

Sally pulled a face. 'Little brutes! So cruel – it's hard to know how to help. And what's up with Luz? She looks terrible, have you noticed? Really unhappy. She told me she wanted to go back to London.'

'She told me she's pregnant.' Anita pulled a face. 'Frankly, I don't see Locky falling for that one.'

They were silent for a moment, then Anita said, 'Twenty past nine. I think I'll nip up to the house and have a word with Jericho. There may have been a change of plan.'

As expected, Jericho was in his gun-room, rodding through his beloved Atkin twelve-bore, a present from his father on his 18th birthday, watched by two interested spaniels. He was singing along so loudly to Verdi's Hebrew Chorus on Classic FM that Anita had to tap him on the shoulder to get his attention.

'Sorry!' He spun round, flushing to the roots of his hair. 'Marina's out, so I was rather letting rip.' He frowned. 'I thought you were taking Max to his coaching session?'

'Well, yes. I thought so too – but look, I don't want to worry you, but do you know where he is? I've just been up to Tomasz's cottage, and there's no one about. Door locked, curtains drawn, but not a sign of life.' She paused, then added, 'The van's there, but no sign of Tomasz's moped.'

'Oh, lord!' He thought for a moment, then said, 'I'd better ring round the farm staff. Ask if anyone's seen either of them. And Pauly Bellton. He might know: he's always about with his dogs. They can't have gone far.'

'Police?' said Anita hesitantly, but he shook his head vigorously. Sirens, flashing top-lights, a helicopter hovering over the valley...? The last thing Marina would want. In truth, the last thing he would want himself, and the idea of Max being questioned all over again revolted him.

'Not until we've had a good look round ourselves. Ten to one, the little wretch simply forgot about football coaching. He seems to have lost his enthusiasm, more's the pity. I'm so sorry to have messed up your morning, Annie.'

She put her arm round his shoulders and hugged him tight. 'Don't give it a thought. Now, if you're going to ring round the farm staff and Pauly, I'll alert Duncan, and also drop in and tell Sally on my way back. Between us we'll find them all right, don't worry.'

She left, and Jericho was just reaching out for the telephone when it rang, and an uncertain voice said, 'Mr Oak? This is Mariusz. Can I speak with you?'

'Yes, of course. Go ahead. What is it?'

'It concerns my... my uncle. Tomasz, you know.'

'Yes, I know Tomasz,' said Jericho sharply. 'What about him?'

There was a pause as if Mariusz was struggling with his English. Go on, spit it out, thought Jericho impatiently, but he didn't want to scare the young man, whose lugubrious tone suggested that any news he had would be bad. In fact, he could almost predict what the next words would be.

'The police –'

Spot on, thought Jericho with a lurch of his heart. 'What about them?'

Mariusz said carefully, 'They ring my mobile because Tomasz was fighting in the night, and his head is broken. The doctor say he has con – er –'

'Concussion?'

'Yes. Concussion. They need to tell someone of his family before they make a scan.'

'Is he badly hurt?'

'Not bad, no. But his Yamasaki is broken –'

'Never mind that. Look, Mariusz, I'll deal with it. Leave it to me. Did they give you a number?'

He scribbled it down and broke the connection, then sat for a moment, heart hammering. Damn, damn, damn! Should he or should he not mention the missing boys? Marina would certainly be very upset if she came back to find the place swarming with rozzers, and what a hysterical fool he would look if Max and Pavel had been playing in one of their dens and had simply forgotten the time.

No, he decided. Much less hassle to look for them ourselves, once I've sorted out what Tomasz has been up to. He stretched out his hand for the telephone.

'Max? Are you awake?'

It was a long time since either of them had spoken, and Pavel had a deep fear that if Max drifted into a doze he might not wake up again. He remembered his mother's story of her little sister, Isa, who went out on the porch and let the door slam behind her. She had been found curled up in the dreadful snow-sleep, frozen to death.

He, Pavel, knew how to fight the cold, rubbing his hands and breathing down the neck of his jacket, but Max seemed too stunned to move. They had shouted until they were hoarse, and argued about whose fault it was until both realised it was futile. They were stuck in the dark at the bottom of a deep hole, with no mobile signal and nothing but a faint, faraway glimmer of starlight to remind them that the world they knew was still there above them. By the weak light of Max's smartphone they had explored their prison, discovering that the walls were of brick, from which plaster had fallen in patches, and the cone-shaped heap of soft earth on which they had landed, saving them from serious injury, must have showered down through the hole at the top. Though huddled together, they were chilled to the bone, and Max's battery was low.

'My leg hurts,' he moaned.

'I think part of my arm is broken,' countered Pavel, moving it cautiously.

'I'm really, really hungry.'

Pavel dug in his anorak and found an old, dry, chunk of venison-jerky, home-smoked by his father and so tough that you had to gnaw at it like a rat. He passed it to Max and warned, 'It makes you thirsty.'

'I don't care.' Silence again, broken only by the gritting of Max's teeth against the dried meat. Presently even that ceased and Pavel knew that despite his nudges and questions, Max had fallen asleep.

Hours passed and the sky had begun to lighten before he spoke again in a faint, fretful voice, 'I'm so cold. Why hasn't anyone come to find us?'

Because they don't know we're here, you dope, thought Pavel. He could guess only too easily what his father had been doing all night, and how unlikely it was that he would look into the boys' room when he finally staggered home.

Would he notice that the food on the kitchen table had not been eaten? Probably not until he woke with a sore head and stumbled to the kitchen tap for a drink. In the same way,

Mr and Mrs Oak would not expect their son to return from a sleep-over until after breakfast, and hadn't Max said something about Anita driving him into Starcliffe for coaching? That put the time the alarm might be raised back another hour, and by then the bone-chilling cold might have overwhelmed Max beyond recovery.

Suppressing his own panicky thoughts, he said as steadily as he could, 'Soon it will be day. Then they will come.'

Sally drove her spotless car back to the gamekeeper's cottage, glad to find that Robb had recovered his spirits enough to admire her handiwork. 'What a transformation! I hardly recognised your old banger.'

'Clean inside as well as out,' she said, preening, glad of the olive branch. She took the green USB from her pocket. 'I suppose this doesn't belong to you? No? Then it must be Max's. And this is his scarf, too. Honestly, that boy! He drops things wherever he happens to be and expects other people to pick them up for him.'

Robb restrained himself from pointing out that her mother used to level precisely the same charge at Sally herself. 'Actually, Anita came here a couple of minutes ago to ask us to keep an eye out for the boys. No one seems to know where they've got to.'

'Pestering Duncan? Watching Pauly train his dogs?'

'Apparently not. In fact,' said Robb slowly, 'no one seems to have seen them since they left the mountain-bike races yesterday.'

'But surely they must – ?'

'Hang on. According to Anita, Max wasn't allowed to join the shooting party yesterday – quite understandably Jericho didn't want a repeat of last week's shenanigans – so he asked his Mum if he could go to the races with Pavel and Tomasz. Then, because his parents were going out to dinner, he got permission for a sleep-over at Tomasz's cottage. OK so far?'

Sally nodded, but something else flickered at the back of her mind. When she had pulled over to allow Locksley Maude's pick-up to squeeze past her on Fiddler's Lane, Maude had raised a finger in acknowledgement; but hadn't she seen a smaller hand waving from the passenger seat?

She still had her morning round of the feeders and traps to complete, but it would be the work of only a moment to look in on Locky at the shooting-school and check this out. While listening to her father with half an ear, she stuck the green bug into her laptop; as she expected, it contained Pavel's photographs. Quite good, too, she thought, flicking through. Close-ups of spiders' webs. Silly selfies of him and Max; an excellent image of Hansi Hartzog on the helicopter ladder; retrievers carrying pheasants; more selfies; a good shot of Pauly by the river, and another of the pony-cart bringing bottles and hampers...

She had a sudden sense of urgency. The morning was trickling away and she had work to do. She could look at the rest later. She said, 'Dad, I've got to pass the shooting-school, so if Locky's there, I'll ask if he's seen anything of the boys. If Jim Winter happens to come round, will you tell him I'll be back about midday?' She added rather self-consciously, 'I'd like to see him before he leaves for London.'

'Will do.'

'Thanks.' She smiled. 'It might amuse you to look through Pavel's pix of the shoot, too. There's a good one of you driving the game-cart.'

With a wave she was gone. The Mule's engine gave a couple of recalcitrant chokes then spluttered into life; and as silence descended on the cottage, Robb moved around restlessly, wishing he could help with the search, do something useful. He was worried that Jericho's determination to minimise contact with officialdom might be putting the boys in danger. No one knew better than he did how intrusive a police search could be, but an airy insistence that Max and Pavel would turn up as soon as they felt hungry was, he felt, leaning too far in the other direction. Should he overrule Jericho's decision and call in his colleagues himself?

I'll give it until lunch-time, he compromised and, for want of something better to do, sat down at Sally's computer, flicking rapidly through the images until a familiar flash of green caught his eye. Luz, with her thick black hair and emerald overall, standing with her back to the camera, bending over a long table with a shotgun in her hands. He stared at it with a sense of shock. Carefully he enlarged the picture and examined it minutely.

The photographer had been intent on capturing himself in the mirror above the basin, but since there was no door between it and the boiler-room he had also photographed the area where some of the guns were propped against the walls in their slings, and others – mostly broken to dry out – laid on the table. Just the scenario he and Winter had envisaged, with the 'little furrin piece' old Marcus had described flitting about between boiler-room and Gents, handling the guns, giving them the evidence they needed.

Bingo!

Robb reached under the table to find the multi-plug socket, connected the lead and switched on Sally's printer. Back and forth rattled the carriage, but instead of offering him a print menu, it stopped midway, and up came the picture of two empty cylinders and the predictable message: Out of ink.

Hellfire! he thought. Where amid this clutter of paper,

biros in jam-jars, small ornaments, clipboards and agricultural catalogues did his scatterbrained daughter keep replacement cartridges?

He was hunting through the drawers of the work-table when he saw Mrs Cunningham's herd of alpacas, who had been leaning over the railings gazing with longing eyes at the shrubs just out of reach of their long necks, whirl round and canter away as a familiar Land Rover ground noisily past the window and parked beside the front steps.

Pauly jumped out, bounded up to the porch, and stamped his feet on the mat.

'Mr Robb! Are you there?' he called urgently..

Abandoning the laptop, Robb went quickly through to the kitchen. Beneath the tousled copper mop, Pauly's face was pale and strained.

'Pauly! How're you doing? Your mum bearing up OK?'

Pauly shook his head distractedly. 'Can't seem to get it in my mind that he's gone, poor old bugger, and Ma's the same. Don't seem real, and that's a fact. They'd been married nigh on forty years, and now he's gone without a word.'

Robb gave a sympathetic grunt, and Pauly said quickly, 'That's not why I've come, though. It's about the young lads.'

'Have they been found?'

'Not a sign. We bin searching everywhere they're like to be and nowt to show for it. But I've found something - ' He stopped.

'That's to say, found something missing.' He took a deep breath. 'I was looking round our sheds where we keep bits and pieces of machinery. Old stuff, you know. Out of date. Things that don't get used from one year's end to the other, so I don't check that often.'

He paused and Robb said, 'Go on.'

'Well, that's where Dad kept his cage-trap that he'd set

219

pretty regular for badgers. Knew the best places to put it, seeing as how he'd grown up round here, and liked to keep 'em to hisself in case those bloody antis came snooping and carried it away.'

'And that's what's missing? The trap?'

'Aye, and that's not all,' said Pauly doggedly. 'I see'd Dad back the trailer with the trap into the shed just a couple of days ago, so I know it was in there then; along of a badger I'd shot for the cull and put in a bag. The Ministry tests 'em for TB, same like the cattle only dead, but because we was knee-deep in vets that morning and everything all to blazes, it'd got left there.'

'And now it's gone?'

'Aye.

'What makes you think that's connected with the boys?'

'Well, sir, Dad was always on about losing badgers from his traps. Reckoned it was that schoolmaster and his mates, letting 'em out, on account of being against the cull; but I said a bloke like Lombard wouldn't risk doing anything illegal. With all the people walk these woods, someone would see him. Word would get round, like it always does, and bang would go his career. Sure, he talked about protecting badgers, and your daughter found him having a right barney with them diggers from Taunton – everyone knows who they are – but as for springing a neighbour's traps... Well, I don't see him doing it.'

Robb was nodding. 'So you think it was Max and Pavel?'

'I don't say it were,' Pauly began to backtrack, 'but it could a been. Lombard teaches those kids. They could of done it to please him.'

Yes, that was possible. At the back of Robb's mind sounded the echo of Jericho's voice. "The boys think he's great because he was in the Army." Would they have absorbed Lombard's views on saving badgers from the cull along with Maths and IT?

Pauly had moved to the stove, bending down to stroke Pilot who was lying in his usual place on the hearthrug. 'So by my way of thinking, if we find where that trap's got to, we may get a line on where the youngsters are, too. And seeing as how you're police, and this here's a police dog, what I came to ask is – did he ever do any tracking?'

CHAPTER SEVENTEEN

Eastmarsh

Frost etched every twig of the low-hanging branches fringing the lane that led from the back of Grange Farm to Folly Wood, looping past the scene of yesterday's races. The Fiddler's Folly course zigzagged through the wood, carefully designed to make the most of its natural undulations and obstacles, and where it crossed the lane the grandstand was still in place, though all Diversion and Road Closed signs had already been removed.

It astonished Sally that anyone – let alone Jim Winter – should want to ride a bike at full speed down such gradients. When he first joined her father's team she had thought him a bit of a prig, an ultra-correct letter-of-the-law man and a townie to boot. She could even remember her father describing how Jim had refused to eat a game pie because he disapproved of shooting. And, of course, he never touched alcohol. Yet underneath this measured exterior she had begun to recognise and even admire a cool courage that got its kicks from challenges that made her shudder. Rock-climbing. Surfing off the coast of Portugal. And now hurtling downhill through trees at breakneck speed. There was no doubt that he was disappointed not to have won yesterday, but equally there had been no complaints, only rueful laughter when he rang to give her father the results.

'Wretched bird was lying in wait. Must have put his money on Bruno Bellini,' he explained. 'I don't know which of us got the biggest shock, but the pheasant came off second best, poor creature. It was lucky for me there was someone who knew what to do with it, because I hadn't a clue.'

No, she thought. Killing wounded birds would not be Jim's forte. She wondered if a morning in Duncan's company would do anything to change his perceptions.

At the top of the hill the mist, thick as drifting cloud, hit high ground for the first time since leaving the Bristol Channel. She pulled over into a shooting ride and bumped a hundred and fifty yards along the slope to where a three-legged corn-dispenser had been knocked over, probably by deer, and the contents scattered – a bonanza for rats and squirrels. Duncan had spotted it yesterday, when he was bringing the game-cart back to the larder but had no time to right it for fear of keeping Jericho's guests waiting for their customary brace of birds.

Now Sally moved it to a new patch of ground and lashed all three legs firmly to stakes which she hammered into the leafmould, using the heavy mallet from the Mule's toolbox. After re-filling it with tailings, she cleared the yellow dispenser tag of mud and leaves and checked that it was moving freely, then set two rat-traps in home-made wooden tunnels before turning the Mule to bump back to the lane.

Another half mile brought her to the fourway intersection known to local shooters as 'Spaghetti Junction.' Here one lane crossed several other tracks which marked the boundary between Dunmorse territory and Grange Farm's ground, and Duncan had placed more pheasant feeders along it to discourage his birds from straying. This was the nearest she would get to the Shooting School without going round three sides of a square to the entrance on the main road, and for a moment Sally hesitated. Should she complete her morning round by topping up Duncan's feeders before going on to ask if Locky had seen the boys? Robb's anxiety about their non-appearance had communicated itself to her and, having worked at Grange Farm for three months, she knew better than he did the spirit of laissez-faire that characterised Tomasz's approach to parenting, and his fatal fondness for poaching.

After a moment's thought, she compromised by turning down the green lane, opening the gate at the end, and driving cautiously along the marshy verge of the larger lake until she could see the cedarwood clubhouse through a gap in its sheltering surround of conifers. The grassy track was alarmingly squashy, with puddles filling every dip, and after a particularly soggy patch set the Mule's wheels churning uselessly, rather than get bogged she backed it up against the bank and continued on foot.

A light from Maude's little office shone yellow through the mist, and as she drew nearer she was aware of an engine's beat and a strong smell of exhaust coming from the workshop at the back of the building. Guessing he would be in there, she pushed open the small door set into the roll-back garage entrance and closed it behind her. The only illumination was an arc-lamp suspended over the work-bench against the office wall. In the dim light she could make out the shapes of half a dozen vehicles and machines, the big ride-on mower and brush-cutter he used to keep the paths between the traps clear, his Toyota pick-up, and a neatly ranged row of power-tools: hedge-trimmer, chainsaw and heavy-duty branch-loppers with telescopic handles.

The pick-up's engine was running, and in the enclosed space the smell of carbon monoxide was overpowering.

Sally was about to call out to Maude when she saw him emerge backwards from the office, dragging a long bundle wrapped in a patterned duvet cover. A white breathing-mask covered his nose and mouth, and something indefinably furtive about his movements made Sally freeze, while her heart hammered against her ribs. For a moment her mind refused to accept what she was seeing. Rooted to the spot, she watched as Maude half-lifted, half-pulled his burden towards the pick-up and hoisted it on to the back seat. Then he slammed the door, brushed his hands together, and went quickly back to the office.

A wave of nausea – part shock, part lack of oxygen – washed over Sally. Her mind raced. She needed air, clean air, but first she must force herself to open the pick-up's side door and see if what she dreaded was true. She had little doubt that it was Luz wrapped in the patterned duvet-cover; the question was whether she was alive or dead. Had she been attempting to blackmail her lover with a claim of pregnancy? If so, she had chosen the wrong man. "I don't see Locky falling for that," Anita had said with a wry grimace, and Sally herself had reached the same conclusion, but she hadn't expected anything like this.

How long would Maude leave his victim to breathe noxious fumes before coming to check? Cautiously Sally moved towards the pick-up, keeping out of sight of the office door. She pulled up her scarf and breathed as shallowly as possible, but as she threaded her way between the machines and vehicles a stabbing pain began to drive through her head, her eyesight blurred and dizziness threatened to overcome her.

She reached the side door and tugged at the handle, but it would not budge. Locked. Standing on tiptoe, she peered through the back window, but all she could see was the vague outline of bedclothes heaped along the seat and back footwell. At one end the cover had been pulled back to expose a mass of dark hair. Luz's hair.

Her head was bursting. Useless to think she could confront Locky on her own. Get out! Get help! clammered her brain. Abandoning caution, she ran to the door she had entered by and wrenched it open, gulping down great lungfuls of cool, damp, misty, clean air; but even as she slipped through she saw the light from the office brighten suddenly and a figure outlined against it.

'Who's there?' demanded Maude sharply. Fighting nausea, she fled across the gravel, seeking somewhere to hide.

Running footsteps thudded on the concrete floor, but before Maude reached the outer door Sally was already in cover, wriggling into the thicket of brambles that concealed the High Pheasant No 1 launcher. Careless of ripped skin and clothes, she worked her way into the very middle of the clump, trying to stifle her panting breath and thanking her stars that Locky had no dog to give away her position.

Gently she eased out her mobile and flipped the cover. Though she could not see Maude, she could hear his crunching tread on the gravel, ranging about so scarily close that she dared not speak.

SOS LUZ MAY B DEAD EASTMARSH IM HIDING SOS she texted with shaking thumbs, and prayed that Jim Winter had his mobile switched on.

CHAPTER EIGHTEEN

Pilot

Like most old dogs, human and animal, Pilot was set in his ways. He was used to travelling in Sally's 2CV, in which he had travelled many hundreds of miles when it belonged to Robb's wife Meriel, who had adopted him at the end of his service life, and he refused categorically to get into Pauly's Land Rover. It smelled of too many other animals: canines, possibly unfriendly; and of alien humans, dead badgers and manure, none of which appealed to a long-retired police-dog who chose to spend his declining days snoozing as close to the fire as he could get.

He lay at the top of the steps with ears flattened, thick tail straight behind him, 80lb of resistant fur and muscle, and when Pauly took hold of his scruff and tried to pull him forward, he growled.

'Hang on,' said Robb. 'Better take Sal's car. He'll get into that all right, and you can drive. It'll get us as far as the bus stop, and we'll just have to walk the rest of the way.'

He had unearthed Pilot's old harness and leash from a tangle of equipment in the porch, and Pauly had produced a yellow mitten, clumsily hand-knitted, that he thought belonged to Pavel. In a flash of inspiration Robb remembered the green-and-white school scarf that Sally had hung on the kitchen door, and Pilot had sniffed it obligingly, though without any particular enthusiasm. It was clear he considered his working days were long past.

'If the dog can pick up their line somewhere in Scaffold Wood it will show us which path they took after leaving the bike-races,' said Pauly hopefully, though even he had begun to sound dubious about Pilot's tracking ability. Meriel's dogs had worked mainly in airport baggage areas, and his speciality had been the detection of drugs.

'Did your wife handle him on raids?'

Robb shook his head. 'She was more of a trainer than handler. Her dogs came from all over: I think Pilot was imported from Germany – or was it the Czech Republic? Abroad, anyway. I wish now that I'd seen him working, but I never did. He got shot in the shoulder during a drug bust, and that's why they retired him. Actually, at one moment it looked as if he'd have to be put down – you may have noticed he still limps, but the vet did a brilliant job, and my wife offered him a home for life. He even got a pension to help with the bills, though that ran out of steam a while back.'

'How old is he now?'

Robb gave him Sally's keys and got into the passenger seat, trying to work it out. 'Six when he was shot, and we've had him – what – another seven years? I'd say he's roughly thirteen, but he's gone downhill since my wife was killed.' He could say it now without faltering. 'Sort of lost interest in life, you know.'

'Maybe he needs a challenge,' said Pauly, the optimist.

They bumped in silence down the lane and parked in the bus-stop lay-by. 'Come on, lad,' urged Pauly, jumping out and opening the door; but Pilot waited until Robb had manoeuvred himself and his stick to the back of the car before consenting to move.

'Now what?' asked Robb.

Pauly had been working it out. 'Say they came down the lane from Fiddler's Folly, they'd a crossed the main road here where we are, and cut through the wood by the main track. A couple of hundred yards in, there's a clearing my dad called 'Seven Dials,' with footpaths going off every which way. It's where those boys would meet up of a morning, going for the bus. Now if young Max had a bin making direct for Grange Farm, he'd a gone straight ahead. But since he was planning on staying the night with his mate, they'd a turned left and followed the path to the stile at the end, hopped over and there they'd be at Tomasz's cottage. Clear so far?'

Robb nodded.

'Now our land – Castle Farm land, that is – runs down to the Scaffold Wood by another track with a gate in it, and that's where Dad's like to have driven to set his trap.' He rubbed his nose with the back of his hand. 'I can't get no nearer to guessing jest where he put it...'

'He told me that badgers liked to dig under old buildings,' said Robb tentatively, and Pauly laughed.

'Ten a penny round here, those are. Remains of cottages, barns, sheds, middens, all gone back to jungle.'

'Abandoned?'

'That's about the size of it.' He added seriously, 'You want to watch your step round some of them ruins. There's wells, and back in the old days folk wasn't so choosy about where they dumped fallen stock. Many an old flesh-pit in them woods to give foxes and badgers a living.'

Pilot showed no interest in the bus stop, and slunk behind Robb on a loose lead as they walked in silence along the rutted main track to the clearing where smaller paths radiated in all directions. Here Pauly showed him the scarf again.

'Go on, good boy. Go seek! Hey-lorst!'

No response. Robb tried in vain to remember a phrase – any phrase – with which Meriel used to encourage a dog, but all he could think of was how she, so small and slight, had to loop the leash round her hand to prevent the trainee pulling her over. What was it she used to say as she did it? Something a bit odd... It had begun to nag at him even before Pauly said: 'D'you reckon he was trained in Germany? Or wherever you said, was it Czechoslovakia?'

Robb stared at him and nodded as the echo of his wife's voice came to him at last. Even then, it had seemed an odd way to address a dog who was clearly male.

'Lady, she used to say. Lady. Something like that. Or perhaps a bit more Welsh – Hl-lady.'

'Look at 'im!'

Pilot had cocked his ears, looking expectantly at Robb. His whole demeanour had changed.

'Show 'im the scarf again. There! Look at that. Now say it again.'

'Hl – ledey!' said Robb with more authority, and let go of the leash as Pilot put his nose to the ground and began to work back and forth across the clearing, his tail waving in a way it hadn't done for months. Without glancing back, he settled on a line that took him right-handed through some rhododendron bushes and headed for the thickest part of Allansgrove wood at a purposeful trot.

'After him,' said Pauly, and set off at a run.

Day had succeeded night, but the glimmer of light filtering into the storm tank hardly alleviated the gloom where the boys huddled together, Pavel hugging his companion tightly, fearing that at any moment the spark of life would go out. From time to time during the long hours of blackness he would rise to stamp his feet and bang his arms round his ribs as his mother had taught him to combat the cold. Taking a deep breath he would huff it down the collar of his padded jacket, and try to encourage Max to do the same, but without success.

'It's boring,' he complained.

'It makes you warm.'

'It doesn't,' said Max flatly. The venison jerky had given him a raging thirst, and he found that by sticking out his tongue he could catch a few drops of the water that trickled down the sides of the tank.

'That is not clean water,' Pavel warned, though tempted to do the same.

'I don't care.' Nevertheless, he stopped licking the stones, and the conversation died.

Now it was hours since they had spoken. Even Pavel was losing hope that they would ever be rescued, and only his occasional convulsive shudders showed Max was still alive. Down here there was no sound of wind through the branches, no cawing of corvids or cocking-up of pheasants. The silence was so complete that when Pilot's urgent whining reached his ears, Pavel thought it must be a dream. Then his heart leapt wildly as he heard a shout.

'Mr Robb! Quick – over here! Your dog's telling to the trap. No, he's not. It's a hole – a bloody big hole –'

Scratched and panting, Robb lumbered towards him. 'Max! Pavel!' he shouted. 'Are you there?'

And gathering all his remaining strength, Pavel cupped

his hands round his mouth and shouted in a thin, wavering voice, 'We are here. Please get us out.'

'Are you hurt? Is Max with you?'

'He sleeps. He will not wake. And I have something with my leg.'

The men looked at one another. 'Sounds bad,' said Pauly, and Robb nodded.

'Get the fire brigade.'

Crouching in the heart of the blackberry bush, Sally waited until Maude stopped prowling about the car park and went back into his workshop before wriggling out and running as fast as her cramped legs would carry her into the thick shelter of the conifer belt. She had no way of telling whether he had concluded that wind had blown the workshop door shut, or whether he was still watching for an intruder, and took a long cast away from the lakes, keeping below the skyline and using every scrap of cover before angling her course towards the far end of the oxbow where she had left the quad.

Apart from that one brief text to Jim Winter, it was no use relying on her mobile to summon help. Though her overwhelming desire was to get back through the gate to the green lane and thence to the road, as soon as she left the top of the hill the mobile signal petered out. *No Service* reported the tiny screen as she re-entered the notorious "not-spot" of the Starcliffe valley.

As she knew well, the big windows of the wooden lodge commanded an extensive view of the fishing water, but unless Maude were to walk right round the perimeter it was unlikely that he would notice the little green-brown vehicle tucked up against the bank. Frightening though it had been to see him patrolling the gravel at such close quarters, she found it almost equally unnerving to have him out of sight. Was he on the verandah, scanning through binoculars, or had he decided to reconnoitre on foot? Would he see that the gate to the green lane was open, proof of an unauthorised visitor?

Slipping and stumbling on the long wet rushes, she slid down the last twenty feet to the fishing path and paused to catch her breath. One more attempt to raise a signal, but no: unresponsive and dead. Cautiously she walked the sedgy path beside the water, keeping close to the bank and trying to remember exactly where she had parked. The shore had been carefully sculpted into bays, effectively giving each fisherman a private stretch of water. Was it round the next corner? The one beyond?

She glanced back over her shoulder to re-orientate herself and realised with dismay that despite the drifting mist she was now in full view of the clubhouse. Hurrying on, she saw the dull green of the bonnet outlined against the low sandy cliff and ran towards it, abandoning caution. Her hand with the key in it was already reaching for the ignition when a kammo-clad figure rose from the rushes where he had been kneeling. Over his arm he carried a gun.

'What's the hurry, Sal?' said Maude.

Her heart gave a tremendous bump and then started racing. For a moment she struggled to speak.

'I saw on the monitor that the back gate was open and came to check who'd come in. I've been having a fair bit of trouble with poachers lately. I didn't expect it to be you.'

He sounded so normal, so reasonable, that she could hardly believe what she had seen in his workshop half an hour ago, yet in her heightened state of awareness she detected a menacing note. Monitor? Had he been watching her on CCTV?

'Y-yes,' she stammered, trying to control her voice. 'I'm

sorry I left the gate open. I didn't want to stop on that steep slope but don't worry, I'll shut it on my way out.'

'Of course.'

'I came to ask if you'd seen the boys — Max and Pavel?' she went on hurriedly, unnerved by his curtness. 'They didn't turn up for football coaching this morning, and no one seems to know where they are. Jericho's got half the staff out looking for them.'

He shook his head dismissively. 'I shouldn't worry. They'll turn up all right when they're hungry. What made you think they might be here?'

'Oh, it's just that when I passed you in the lane last night — do you remember? — I thought I saw one of them waving from your pick-up.'

He laughed, though his eyes were wary. 'So you did. I found them walking down the lane on their way back from the races. Young fools! It was almost dark and they hadn't even got a torch. So I took them down to the bus-stop and told them to make their way home from there. I was in a bit of a hurry or I'd have taken them right up to the Grange.'

He paused, then added confidentially, 'You see, I'd promised to drive Luz to the London train. She's got a job interview lined up this morning.'

'In London?' The easy fluency of the lie took her breath away. 'When will she be back?'

He shrugged. 'Depends whether she gets the job, I suppose. Between you and me, I think she wanted to be well away before Kelly-Louise starts counting the spoons, and I can't say I blame her.'

He moved a step nearer and she steeled herself not to retreat. 'So you thought you'd pop up here on the q t and fetch those young tykes home before I caught them stealing my fish, did you, Sal? Well, I can tell you this for free: if that bloody little

Pollack thinks he can start helping himself from my lakes like his old man does, he'll get a clip around the ear and find himself back at the Grange so fast his feet won't touch the ground. I've had a bellyful of Jericho Oak's thieving Poles. Time and again I've complained to him, and all he says is that its just part of their culture. Culture be damned. It's bare-faced robbery and I won't stand for any more of it.'

Sally blinked, taken aback by this sudden bitter outburst, so far removed from his usual obsequious manner. What had happened to change him? Why did he suddenly feel able to put civility aside and reveal the feelings he habitually hid beneath the need to please paying customers?

His casual, even familiar reference to Hartzog's absentee wife gave her a jolt too. "Thinks he's God's gift to women," old Duncan had warned. "They say the husbands are always the last to know." Had Hartzog been one of those husbands? How different had been Maude's tone to her father last week: "Yes, sir; no sir; three bags full;" every inch the respectful professional with a client. In the past she had wondered at the way he complied with Hartzog's frequent demands for fishing for his female guests and shooting lessons for their menfolk, and supposed it was part of some quid pro quo, one of the ways he kept his precarious business afloat. Perhaps he had been getting his own back in a different way.

Even Jericho, who was closer in touch with local opinion, was inclined to be dismissive of Maude. In his eyes, shooting clays scarcely registered as sport, and fishing for farmed trout was little better than shrimping. He tended to view Tomasz's night-time forays with amused indulgence. "He doesn't take much," Sally had heard him say. "Surely Maude doesn't grudge him the odd brace of fish?"

A misjudgment, she thought. A serious misjudgment. In how many other ways had people underestimated his simmering resentment and the chip on his shoulder? Somehow she must play him along until she could get away and raise the alarm.

She said quietly, 'They're only children, Locky. I'm sure they wouldn't try to steal your fish. I just thought you might have an idea where they might be.'

'So that's why you came sneaking in by the back gate instead of using the proper entrance? So you could have a good snoop round without me knowing?'

'Of course not.'

'Then where have you been this past half hour? Why did you leave the quad down here if you wanted to see me? What have you been doing?'

He was working himself into a rage.

She said, 'I was afraid I'd get bogged, and anyway, I've only been here a few minutes.'

'Liar,' he said with contempt. 'The engine's cold. What were you doing on the hill? Did you go into the clubhouse? Did you —' he leaned forward, eyes boring into hers — 'look for me round the back? In the workshop?'

He knows, she thought with a chill of fear. He heard the door bang shut and went back and watched the CCTV tape. He saw me go round the building, out of sight of the camera. He thinks I went into the workshop, but doesn't know for sure.

She shook her head, attempting a laugh. 'Honestly, Locky, all these questions! I climbed the hill to get a better signal, so I could ring Jericho and tell him they weren't —'

Bad mistake. 'Give me your phone,' he said and now the menace was plain. If he saw her text to Jim Winter suspicion would become certainty.

'But why? There's nothing...' She leaned against the quad, pretending to fumble in her pocket. Over his shoulder, far away on the main road, she saw lights twinkling through the mist. Blue lights.

'Come on, hand it over.' He raised the shotgun.

'Locky! No!' she stammered.

'Give it here.'

'Hang on, I'm trying to find it. Here, catch!'

As the barrels drooped, she feinted to the right, then flung her mobile as hard as she could over his left shoulder and into the lake. Even before it splashed he had whipped round to run after it; by the time he turned back to her she had swung herself onto the quad and started the engine.

With a cat-like spring, he grabbed at the loaded carrier and let it pull him along with great strides. He was struggling to slow her down and climb aboard, but suddenly the remaining sack of pheasant-corn toppled off, breaking his grip as it burst. 'Stop!' he roared.

Heedless of puddles, humps and dips, Sally gave the Mule full throttle, hell-bent on getting through the gate and down the green lane. Her mouth was dry and her heart pounded as she concentrated fiercely on keeping to the slippery thread of path and stopping the little vehicle from sliding towards the water. On such terrain she was going too fast for safety, but didn't think of slowing until she skidded between the gate posts and faced the steep downhill slope where two muddy channels had been carved out of the lane.

Careful, she thought, touching front and back brakes lightly at first, then more forcefully as they failed to respond. Instead of resisting the pressure, they revolved uselessly and both footbrakes went flat to their full extent. Terror seized her. Twist and stamp as she might, she could not slow the rocketing quad, plunging downhill at ever-increasing speed. Should she attempt to throw it into reverse? Switch off, jump clear and roll?

Trees flashed past, and tears blurred her vision. At this speed she could never negotiate the sharp corner a hundred yards ahead, which skirted the lip of the old quarry. Her only hope was to fling herself off before she reached it. She killed the engine, pushed her whole body sideways, bracing herself for the impact, and shoved herself away. For an instant she thought she had fallen clear, then a sharp pain shot through her leg as her boot caught the footboard, dragging her along with the runaway vehicle for a dozen yards before the boot came off and her foot slipped free.

Seconds later, a tearing crash followed by a series of metallic crunches told her that the Mule had gone over the edge and was rolling through the trees on to the stones below, while the momentum of her fall carried Sally, half-stunned and semi-shod, into a tangle of deep bracken some thirty yards below the green lane.

Shaking all over, she tried to stand and immediately fell over since her right leg would not support her. She curled up in the nest of bracken as pain spread from ankle to knee, and from neck to shoulder. Blood streamed into her eye from a gash on her forehead, and her ribs were scraped where her jacket had ridden up as she was dragged. She lay still, waiting for the shock to wear off, listening hard. He would follow the tracks and come looking for her; she had no doubt of that and, helpless as she was now, she had no way of escaping him.

'Sally? Where are you?'

Go away, she prayed. Oh, God, make him go away. Make him think I've gone over the edge with the Mule and am lying down there in the rubble. Give the police time to find me.

She was sure that twinkling blue light meant Jim had alerted the rapid response team, but how long would it take them to get through the locked main gate, check out the clubhouse and workshop, find poor Luz and come looking for her?

'Sal?' His voice was urgent, confidential – and far too close.

She pressed her face into the dead bracken, thankful for its cover but afraid its crackling would give away any movement. How far from the lip of the quarry was she lying?

'Cok-cerok cok-cok!'

Go away, you blasted bird, she thought; not daring to stir but knowing an inquisitive cock pheasant must be standing just yards away, neck stretched and eye fixed on the alien object that had invaded his territory. 'Cok-cerok!'

Sure enough, it attracted Maude's attention. She heard the slither of boots down the slope, felt the pressure of hands on her shoulders, turning her to face him.

'You shouldn't have run away,' he said softly. 'I didn't want to have to do this.'

Keep him talking, she thought. Play for time. 'You killed her,' she said through a mouthful of mud. Her voice shook and her limbs felt floppy. 'You were afraid she'd tell on you about the gun.'

'Oh, clever little Sal,' he mocked. 'You can't prove a word of it, and you're not going to get the chance.'

As he seized her under the armpits to drag her towards the quarry, she grabbed hold of a sapling and clung to it, refusing to let go even when he kicked her in the stomach. She could hear a confused babble of chatter coming from the green lane above them, and she managed two shrill screams before Maude clamped his hand over her mouth and crouched beside her in the bracken, holding her so tight she could scarcely breathe.

'Quiet, everyone!' barked a familiar voice. 'Listen!'

'Jim!' screamed Sal through the muffling hand.

Disturbed pheasants were rocketing out of the trees with loud alarm calls. With brutal force Maude wrenched her hands from the sapling and began to drag her along the slope towards the precipice.

'Try down there!' shouted a woman's voice, 'but watch out, there's a big drop.'

Bracken, ivy, dead branches – Sally kicked and wriggled, clutching at anything she could reach to slow Maude's progress, digging her heels into the leaf-mould, but it was no use. He was far too strong. On reaching the lip of the quarry he flung her to the ground, and seized one arm and one leg.

'Over – you – go!' he grunted, and she felt him tense for an extra effort. Forty foot below she saw the twisted metal of the quad, wheels uppermost, and a tumble of sharp-edged rocks among the nettles.

'Please...no...' she whispered.

'Stop!' Scarlet in the face, with leaves and twigs in her dishevelled blonde mop, Anita burst from the thicket of hazels and confronted him. 'Drop it!' she ordered, as if to a dog.

'What the fuck – ?' As Maude turned towards her in a fury, Jim Winter stepped swiftly up behind and felled him with a precise, effective karate-chop just under the ear. Without another sound, Maude crumpled.

'Nice – one – Jim!' gasped Anita. She bent swiftly to pull Sally away from the edge, then stood with open mouth and hands pressed to her sides, struggling for breath. Shouts and crashing in the trees above them heralded the arrival of a panting Mariusz, with two Community Support Officers in hi-vis jackets hot on his heels.

'Nick of time, Josh!' said Anita faintly, and Sergeant Josh Evans grinned.

'Right, sir,' he said briskly. 'Well done. We'll take over from here.' As the recumbent Maude began to stir and mutter, he cuffed his hands and pulled him upright.

Winter knelt down in the leaves beside Sally, who clutched his hand as if she would never let go. 'Did he hurt you? Is anything broken?'

'Oh, Jim,' she whispered, 'I thought you'd never come. I thought I was going to die.'

'You're all right now. You're safe with me,' he said.

Anita took one look at his face, and turned away to hide a smile.

CHAPTER NINETEEN

Jericho

FRIDAY 2nd FEBRUARY

'Got to look ahead. No use wishing it hadn't happened,' said Jericho, puffing up the steep path from the Grange and wondering how Marina, who never took any exercise, could glide up a one-in-four slope as if it was as flat as a putting green, while he who never stopped moving from the moment he got out of bed to the moment he lay down in it was already blowing like a grampus two-thirds of the way to the top field above the Maiden's Leap waterfall.

'Of course, I do wish it hadn't happened,' he added, halting and hoping her love of an argument would bring her back to join him.

'And of course if anyone had listened to you, it wouldn't have had a chance to happen,' she said. 'All the same, I do beg you won't go around saying, "I told you so." Some people – quite a lot of people – might think it showed a lack of feeling.'

'But I did say right from the beginning it was a bad idea.'

'Oh, darling, I know.' With a quick change of mood, she shuddered and said sombrely. 'Just think: we could have lost Max. The doctor said neither of them would have lasted much longer down that hole. If it hadn't been for Pavel hugging him all night, and that good old dog... and Pauly...' She swallowed and closed her eyes. 'I can hardly bear to imagine it.'

It was four days since Locksley Maude's arrest, and the Starcliffe valley had been galvanised out of its state of stunned disbelief by the whirlwind of Kelly-Louise's arrival. Helicoptered in with a retinue of two sons and a daughter from earlier marriages, a solicitor, financial adviser and hairdresser – 'though why she needs one when her hair's no longer than a toothbrush,' marvelled Mrs Cunningham at the Community Shop – she had booked the whole first floor of the Starcliffe Arms for her entourage and set about sorting out affairs at Dunmorse with dispatch and efficiency.

'She's amazing!' said Jericho, half-admiring, half-appalled. 'A steamroller crossed with Genghis Khan.'

'Nightmare woman. No wonder poor Hansi was insecure.'

Bloody funny way he had of showing it, thought Jericho, but he said only, 'Now the question is, what happens to Eastmarsh? Maude was up to his neck in debt, and the Bank wants its money back asap.'

'You have been keeping your ear to the ground!' she said in mock admiration, but he remained serious.

'Got to, when it's so close to home. That's what I want to discuss with you. Kelly-Louise says she'll buy it to secure the Dunmorse boundary before putting the whole estate on the market, but only if we don't want it ourselves. Decent of her, I thought. So what do you say? Shall I make a bid?'

'No, no, and again no!' she said vehemently. 'Let her have it. I could never walk round those lakes again without thinking of poor Hansi and Luz; or looking at the quarry without imagining Sally being thrown over the edge.'

'As she would have been if Anita hadn't shown our gallant detective sergeant the short-cut up through the wood. She was feeding him and Mariusz doughnuts and coffee in The Caff when he got Sally's SOS, and after calling up the rozzers he had the sense to ask Annie the quickest way to the lakes. You can't beat local knowledge, but it was a close shave, she says. They got there just in time.' He shook his head, frowning. 'Lombard warned me that Maude was a wrong 'un, but I never thought he might be a killer. Well, we live and learn.' He patted the smooth trunk of a fallen beech. 'Come on, love, sit down and I'll tell you about the reshuffle I'm planning for next season.'

'But you've hardly finished this one,' she complained, 'and that log is not only sopping wet but covered in fungus.'

'Never hurts to look ahead,' he said cheerfully. 'I've been talking to Robb and Sally, making plans, and we've agreed that she'll stay on through the spring and summer to help Duncan with the hatching and rearing, by which time she'll have completed her year's practical and be ready to finish her course at the Ag. Coll.'

'With a glowing report from you.'

'Correct.'

'Leaving Duncan to carry on alone?' she said, frowning. 'He's been here as long as I remember and he's getting on a bit. Will you recruit someone to help him?'

'Ah, that's where we come to the reshuffle. Duncan tells me he's good for another year at least so long as we let him have an underkeeper to do the heavy lifting, and he pointed out that we've already got someone suitable working here. Who do you think he had in mind? I must say, I was surprised myself.'

She thought it over, blue eyes abstracted as she gazed out across the valley while tendrils of blonde hair crept out from her hooded parka. At last she said slowly, 'It sounds ridiculous, I know, but my guess is he was thinking of Tomasz. Whenever I see him serving in the Farm Shop he makes me think of a bird in a gilded cage.'

'Or a bull in a china shop,' Jericho chuckled. 'Spot on, darling. I haven't said anything to him yet, but I think he'd jump at it. The classic role reversal: poacher turned gamekeeper. I'll give Mariusz an upgrade to Manager, and of course Pavel's already got the makings of a naturalist...'

We're playing God, thought Marina with a superstitious shiver. We're moving people about our little chessboard when we haven't the least idea of what they really want, or what is really going to happen in a day, a month, a year's time. Who would have thought, when Hansi proposed this idea of a Starcliffe Highflyers' Day, that it would result in two deaths, one suicide and an arrest for murder? Or that our precious boys would be entombed in a cold dark hole for more than twelve hours?

'Just look at those fellows!' Jericho pointed to a sunny glade some twenty yards from their log, where two cock pheasants were sparring aggressively with ruffled hackles and open beaks. Feigning indifference as they watched from a short distance was a group of hens, their muted creamy-brown feathers contrasting strongly with the cocks' flamboyant plumage. 'They don't think it's too soon to think of next season,' he said with a laugh. 'It amazes me how they know exactly when shooting's finished and they're safe to strut their stuff with the girls in full view of us.'

Only for a few weeks, she thought, gripped by a fresh wave of melancholy. After that they'll be knocked on the head to make way for their successors. You could say they're not so different from us: spend their lives in pursuit of the three great imperatives – food, shelter, and sex – but never guess that Nemesis is waiting just round the corner. A soaring flight, a bang, and their posturing and parading ends in a heap of crumpled feathers. Still, infinitely better than being a battery hen.

Jericho's thoughts were elsewhere. 'Talking of getting ahead, I must send my shooting invitations out early this year,' he mused, and she looked at him in surprise. When it came to invitations, he was usually a last-minute man.

'Why? What's the hurry?'

'Well, you see I'm thinking of asking those boys – Team Owen – back for a return match. After all, Hartzog good as promised them one and as it turned out, they had a pretty raw deal. Enough to put anyone off shooting for good. I'd like them to have a day they can really enjoy – none of that Highflyers' nonsense – and if I invite them early I'll be less likely to find any of them tied up elsewhere in December.'

Marina said faintly, 'You mean to invite them all?'

'That's right. The whole shooting-match!'

'Even the uncle? The old man with the dog?'

Jericho's smile faded. He said seriously, 'Good point. We wouldn't want things going wrong again, so I might draw the line at Uncle Thomas. If he comes, it can be as an observer.'

Things going wrong again... She thought of Hansi's shattered face and shuddered. If Uncle Thomas hadn't wandered off his peg, hadn't broken his leg, hadn't disrupted the Highflyers' schedule – would Hansi have checked his barrels before the evening flight? Would Luz still be alive? Would Max and Pavel still trust that if they told the truth it would be believed?

Jericho put his warm arm round her. 'Penny for them, darling?' he said and she gave herself a mental shake.

'They're not worth that much. Hey, look at the time. I must get back. Come on, I'll race you to the bottom of the hill.'

'No chance. You'll win. You always do.' But he smiled, and as she ran off, slipping and sliding on the thawing turf, the strong tuneless voice that he only liberated when he was happy came floating down to her. '*Va, pensiero...*' he bellowed, and she knew that, for the moment at least, all was well in his world.

The End

Also by D.P. Hart–Davis

THE STALKING PARTY
a fieldsports thriller

£14.99 Hardback 256pp

ISBN 9781910723043

Beneath the smoothly civilised surface of the wealthy stalking party assembled for sport amid the wild grandeur of a Scottish deer forest, tensions are steadily ratcheting upwards.

Though the fishing and stalking are all they could wish, a lethal cocktail of sexual, social, and inheritance conflicts has combined to produce a highly dangerous situation in this untamed landscape where natural hazards threaten the unwary as much as man-made ones – and accidents don't always happen by chance.

D.P. Hart-Davis' chilling and labyrinthine mystery is handled with aplomb by this experienced sporting author.

An engaging and entertaining read. Her attention to detail in the spell-binding passages on stalking gives this thriller real gravitas among the genuine shooting community. And the author's characterisation of the main players will ring true with anyone who has spent any time in this sort of environment. But this crime thriller is not just for the green jacket brigade – it's an enjoyable read from any perspective. While you are waiting for that next shooting trip, it certainly makes for an entertaining way to fill a few hours.
– Shooting Gazette

Unusual but gripping whodunnit…. A thoroughly entertaining read. Having picked it up, you will not be able to put it down until all is at last revealed. Just the thing to take with you to a Scottish sporting house party.
– British Deer Society

A fast-moving and sinister thriller revolving around a wealthy stalking party assembled for sport amidst the grandeur of a Scottish deer forest.
– Fieldsports magazine

From all good bookshops or www.merlinunwin.co.uk